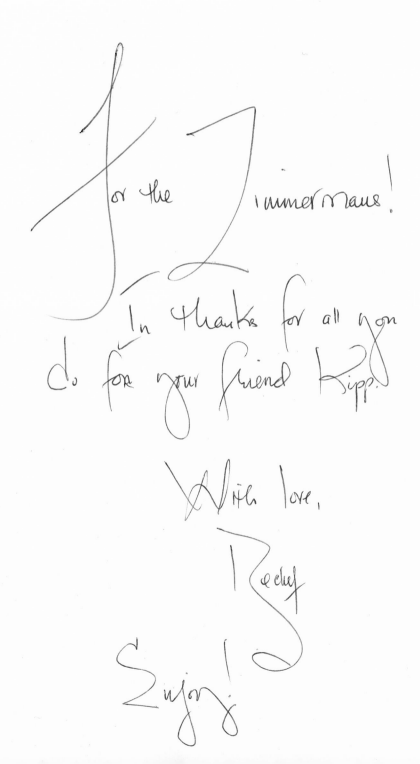

For the Zimmermans!

In thanks for all you
do for your friend Kipp.

With love,

Rachel

Enjoy!

AI!
PEDRITO!
—When Intelligence Goes Wrong

Other Selected Works by the Authors

L. RON HUBBARD

KEVIN J. ANDERSON

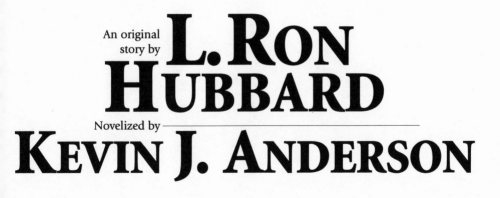

An original story by **L. RON HUBBARD**

Novelized by

KEVIN J. ANDERSON

AI!
PEDRITO!
—When Intelligence Goes Wrong

Bridge Publications, Inc.

Foreword

"Just as Ian Fleming drew from his real experience in British Intelligence to create James Bond, Ai! Pedrito! *is based on a true story, but in this case it was comedy."*

L. Ron Hubbard

To which we might add: that true story is just as enthralling as the fictional, and tells volumes about the life of an author who knew of what he wrote. All begins in 1932 when, among other adventures later to figure in his celebrated stories, a twenty-one-year-old (and significantly red-haired) L. Ron Hubbard set out for a then still remote Puerto Rico to conduct that island's first complete mineralogical expedition under United States' protectorship. There, in the literal "wake of conquistadors," and on the "hunting ground of pirates," he sluiced many an inland river for traces of alluvial gold. He also scaled many a cliff with a sample pick, probed many a tunnel at the end of an improvised harness and left many "bits of khaki which have probably blown away from the thorn bushes long ago."

But quite in addition to expected adventures—the near fatal collapse of a San German mine, for example, or a raging bout with malaria—there was that curious business of Señor Pedrito.

As a first and seemingly innocuous brush with the man, Ron writes of exiting a Cuban embassy in early October 1932 to hear a Spanish gentleman cry: "*Ai! Pedrito! Cómo está?*" When he reasonably pleaded mistaken identity, the accosting Spaniard offered only a savvy "Oh, that's all right, Pedrito. I won't tell anybody you're here."

Next, and rather more significantly, he writes of three engineers on a Puerto Rican mining trail, and their similarly exuberant "*Ai! Pedrito! Cómo está?*" While in reply to his plea of mistaken identity: "You can tell us. We won't write anybody. We won't let anybody know we saw you."

Then came the proverbial stranger in a bar with a pistol in his pocket—"and if I hadn't kicked him in the shins, I would have been a dead man"—and the equally unfamiliar Panamanian woman, who caught one glimpse of the red-haired profile and indignantly crossed the street. By which point, he could only conclude "Pedro's been here."

Thereafter, and particularly through the opening months of the Second World War when a then Lieutenant L. Ron Hubbard served United States Naval Intelligence in the South Pacific and elsewhere, this Pedrito remained a peripheral phantom. Most intriguingly, Ron speaks of encountering reports on his own supposed activities in places he had never even visited—specifically, running with Nazi spies in Brazil. Eventually, however, and like a figure first glimpsed from the corner of the eye and only gradually assuming shape, this Pedrito grew fairly definite as the prodigal son of a wealthy Brazilian clan. The man was also apparently on the lam from authorities in half a dozen nations, and further fleeing the fathers/brothers of at least a dozen jilted ladies.

Now, while we may find many an adventure from L. Ron Hubbard's fabulous years of exploration woven into earlier works for which he is now famous—*Fear,* for example, was partially crafted from tales heard within that Puerto Rican hinterland—Pedrito continued to simmer. By the early 1980s, however, and the author's much applauded return to popular fiction with the internationally best-selling *Battlefield Earth,* that curious case of mistaken identity began to plot itself into a story. As originally conceived, the story became a full-length L. Ron Hubbard screenplay, complete with detailed notes on direction, characterization, sets and sound. In accordance with his life-long commitment to younger authors, however, and fully appreciating just how difficult it is to break into the world of writing, he granted the novelization to another in what amounted to a golden opportunity.

In either case, the underlying theme of the story has since proven fully on the mark: the dark reality of a United States Central Intelligence Agency as anything but a slick and sophisticated stable of spies. To underscore the point, L. Ron Hubbard story notes reference an original agency failure to impede a flow of arms to Castro prior to the fall of Batista; while we might further reference all the agency has finally come to represent in terms of myopic bureaucracy or—as underscored by later revelations from an Iran-Contra affair—sheer buffoonery. As the reader will soon also discover, however, the L. Ron Hubbard view of an equally myopic and overbearing Soviet intelligence machine is hardly more flattering.

Yet *Ai! Pedrito!* is a story of far more than two dimensions, i.e., far more than the tale of two look-alike spies in the midst of a looking-glass war. Rather, here is the world in which those spies dwell, replete with muddled politics, convoluted schemes and highly ephemeral loyalties. Needless to say, this world of Pedrito is not only a place of devilishly clever gadgets, highly seductive women and wholly unpredictable situations; it is also a place that is real—where the wine is not always vintage and cigars are not always Cuban. By the same token, however, here is a world where action never flags, deception never ends and anything can follow from such seemingly innocuous questions as, *Ai! Pedrito! Cómo está?*

—Dan Sherman

Dan Sherman is the author of several highly acclaimed works on Cold War espionage. Mr. Sherman is presently engaged in the definitive biography of L. Ron Hubbard.

—The Publisher

Chapter 1

IN THE JUNGLES outside of Havana, Cuba, a squadron of black ducks crossed the sky at dusk, like bats. According to the tourist guidebooks it was considered a very bad omen. The ducks arrowed together, seeking evening prey among the numerous gnats and insects rising from the island's steaming jungles.

Then, as one, the flock of black ducks veered, quacking in instinctive fear as they skirted the imposing edifice of a grim fortress perched atop sheer, rugged cliffs high above the sea. Curling ocean waves crashed against the rocks below with a roar like a lion, guarding the citadel.

The treacherous road that led up to the spiked front gate of Morro Castle stopped in an ancient courtyard. Knotted vines protruded from the ground, buckling the flagstones. No welcome mat lay at the foot of the barred wooden doors; the daily newspapers had not been delivered in some time. An ominous sign announced in Spanish *No Soliciting*.

Over the years, the dark fortress had been used by an endless stream of torturers, mad scientists, and megalomaniacs with their tiresome schemes of taking over the world. By now, the locals had stopped paying much attention to Morro Castle, tending instead to their cane or tobacco fields, knowing that in an emergency some hero would eventually rectify the situation and all would go back to normal again.

As the sun set across the Caribbean, and soupy clouds gathered for an evening squall, Morro Castle's new inhabitants were up to the usual hi-jinks. . . .

◆◆◆

"Asombroso!" cried the Cuban intelligence colonel, astounded as he sat back in a creaking wooden chair, clapping a hand to his head to hold his beret in place.

His hair was black and thick, his bloodshot eyes dark and flashing. He wore a rumpled khaki uniform, adorned with numerous stars and medals he had pinned on himself. Some of them hung crookedly from his uniform, because when in front of a mirror, the Cuban colonel spent more time admiring his huge black beard than studying the neatness of his dress.

Across the stone-walled tower room, the Russian colonel said placidly, "Da, Comrade Enrique." Unlike his companion's, his own olive uniform was immaculate and well pressed. He used a ruler and a level every morning to make sure *his* medals hung straight. "Here, see for yourself."

The Russian stood up to place a SECRET folder on the rugged wooden table in the center of the chamber. Rusty manacles dangled from the edges of the table, and faded reddish stains adorned the hewn boards. Other torture instruments hung from hooks on the walls, available for the use of any of the castle's tenants; all of the equipment had been left behind as a courtesy by the castle's former inhabitants, before the revolution.

The Russian colonel knocked a jingling manacle out of the way, more interested in the photographs he removed from the folder. He held them up to the flickering light. The Cuban colonel hurried over to see the photo of the redheaded man—a face he had observed many times on WANTED posters, arrest warrants, propaganda leaflets. "Ai! It is him!" Astonished, he said, "Sacred mother of a dog, Ivan! This is incredible!"

"Our peerless KGB has verified it utterly," Ivan said with a sniff.

"I thought the KGB was disbanded with the fall of the Soviet Union," Enrique said.

The Russian shrugged. "It is now part of the Ministry of Mapmaking. New department, same job." He held a second photograph up to the flickering light. "See for yourself, Comrade."

As he looked more closely, Enrique saw that it couldn't be the same man, not in the same place, not with the same clothes. Could it be some hoax . . . or was it exactly what they had been hoping for?

"Come," said Ivan, gathering his photos and clapping a hand on the Cuban's shoulder, "this is our chance. They say that Communism is dead, just because it is in a coma. But you and I know better: There are millions of loyalists toiling around the world, ashamed to admit their true feelings, their longings for the glory days of the Soviet Empire, their innermost hopes for a glorious future. All they need is a little victory to make them feel better, just one small country to topple in a revolution—like in the old days, when everyone was eager to embrace the loving principles of Stalinism—"

Ivan had a faraway look in his eyes, and he stared off at the wall, as if gazing at some glorious, distant sunrise. Enrique was lighting a cigar. Ivan's voice then took on a hard, intense quality as he continued: "Once we bring one country down, my friend, the loyalists of the world will rise up with their hammers and their pitchforks and their Molotov cocktails and their nerve gas and their intercontinental ballistic missiles, and they will throw off the intolerable shackles of their horrible capitalist tormentors!"

Enrique shook his head in wonder. He was frankly baffled by capitalists and their strange way of life. The only time he'd ever seen a real, horrible capitalist tormentor was when he'd once been assigned to a firing squad detail, and he hadn't really gotten a good look at the man through the gunsights.

"Sacred nostril of a yak!" Enrique said, puffing his cigar smoke into Ivan's face. Ivan coughed. "Are you sure this will work? Pedrito Miraflores is a madman"—he decided he'd better quickly cover himself—"a loyal Communist madman, but a madman nonetheless. If we put your plan into effect, we could get into more trouble than we bargain for."

The Russian shook his head with a smile. "Or it might be an opportunity we cannot afford to pass up."

Just then, the single bulb that lit the dim room buzzed and died with a pop. The only light came from Enrique's cigar.

"Come," Ivan said. "Let us go down to the Operations Office, where there is better light."

◆◆◆

Deeper inside Morro Castle, switchboards and radar receivers were strung along a fortified outside wall that opened to the churning sea. Uniformed operators moved about. Everyone paused to look up as the two colonels entered, then they briskly went back to work with redoubled efforts. (Rumors of impending layoffs had rippled through the staff of the evil fortress.)

A reedy, nervous-looking aide hustled over to hover beside Colonel Enrique, awaiting his orders. Enrique ignored him.

"I have more evidence that Miraflores has a double," Colonel Ivan said. "We have an espionage photographer in New York. He operates as an undercover mime near the Office of Naval Intelligence. He took these photographs." The Russian snapped his fingers, indicating an attaché case on a console.

The reedy aide dashed over to the case, rummaging through papers and folders and antacid wrappers until he dragged out a sheaf of photographic enlargements, labeled *Other Evidence.*

"There, Comrade, is the proof!" the Russian colonel said. "Is it not wonderful?"

The aide handed the photos to Colonel Enrique, who fanned them out, staring at the top image. The curious aide crept close enough to peer over the Cuban colonel's shoulder, but Enrique elbowed him sharply in the ribs; the aide scuttled away, holding his side.

The color portrait showed a roguish man in stained jungle combat clothes and a big red star upon his cap. The cap covered shaggy red hair, as if he had sawed it to the proper length with a serrated knife. Two guns hung at his hips, a bandolier of bullets crisscrossed his chest, and several grenades had been clipped to his belt.

"I am already quite familiar with our man Pedrito Miraflores," Colonel Enrique growled.

Colonel Ivan said smugly, "Now look at the other one closely."

It was a formal studio portrait of what appeared to be the same person, the same red hair and blue eyes, but some sort of alter ego—this young man was an American naval officer holding his cap under his arm and staring with wide, bewildered eyes toward the camera. His red hair had been neatly cut and combed.

"Tom Smith," Enrique read the label below the portrait. "Lieutenant junior grade." He looked up in astonishment. "Holy brother of a lemur! They *do* look just alike, even side by side. That is too much to wish for. Don't tell me they're both the same height and weight!"

"They are," said the Russian colonel. "They also both speak Spanish and English perfectly. It would be ideal for us to make a switch."

Enrique shuffled up two more snapshots, one of each: Pedrito Miraflores swinging into a sports car on a Havana street, grinning hugely as if he knew he was posing for a spy camera. In the other photo, his spitting image, Lieutenant Tom Smith, stood looking somewhat mystified as he received an engineering award amongst top Navy brass.

"Sacred tailbone of a mollusk," Enrique said, scratching his huge beard and shaking his head in disbelief. His dark eyes shone with the possibilities. "The good God bless the KGB, or the Ministry of Mapmaking, or whatever they're called these days! This could be the greatest intelligence coup of all time! What if we could make a switch? By putting Pedrito in his place, we could infiltrate the United States intelligence service, while using Smith as a scapegoat down here. That Navy buffoon could take the fall for all of Pedrito's crimes."

"I thought you'd like my idea," the Russian colonel said. "We will get our best man, Bolo, to oversee all the details." He raised his bushy eyebrows over watery gray eyes, then lowered his voice. "Now how about another case of those cigars, Enrique? Monte Cristo No. 2. My, uh, wife likes them very much."

Ignoring the request, the Cuban colonel whirled to snap at his aide, who still stood nursing his sore ribs. "Quick, quick—get Maria! We must begin immediately. This is a marvelous plan for us to set in motion."

The aide dashed off, returning a moment later with a straggly haired brunette woman, whose face wore the hardened, deadly look of a dedicated revolutionary. Her mouth was an angry line. "Sí, Colonel?"

"Fast, fast, Maria!" Enrique said. He fumbled in the photos and eventually found a phone slip, peeling it from the back of one of the enlargements. "Get this number. Plan G goes into operation at once, at once!"

"Sí, Colonel! At once!" Maria seized the slip of paper, scanned the numbers, then stuffed the paper in her mouth, chewing it to bits before the colonel could stop her. He admired her dedication.

She grabbed the phone as if she were trying to subdue it, then dialed the number. "Operator," she said, her mouth still stuffed with wet paper. Her inflection remained deadly. "Operator—get me the New York Office of Naval Intelligence. I must speak with Lieutenant Tom Smith."

Chapter 2

THE STENCILED LETTERS on the translucent glass door read *Lieut. (jg) Tom Smith, USN, Missile Security Section.* Then, in larger letters, it proudly stated *Office of Naval Intelligence.*

"I just don't get it," Lieutenant Smith said. He sat at his desk in full uniform, scratching his bright red hair.

The phone rang beside him, but he ignored it. He couldn't afford to be distracted at this crucial moment as he studied the missile plans, trying to fathom how this design was different from the thousand similar plans he had approved for massive funding requests.

Two well-dressed civilian contractors fidgeted in front of him, looking at each other through narrowed eyes, as if afraid Smith might catch them at a prank. Both contractors carried other blueprints tucked under their arms.

"It's perfectly simple, Lieutenant Smith," one contractor said, seemingly perplexed that Smith did not grab the phone as it rang a second time. "The design is exactly the same as all the other ones you approved, only different."

"Then why do we have to fund new development, if this one's exactly the same?" Smith asked in confusion.

"It's substantially modified," the second contractor answered smugly.

"I don't know, gentlemen," Smith told the contractors, smoothing the curled edges of the blueprints spread out on his neat, military-issue gray desk. A *List of Things to Do Today* sat next to the IN box; very few of the items on the list had been checked off.

As if miffed at being summarily ignored, the phone rang a third time.

"There are so many new developments that I can't keep them straight." He gestured toward the corner of his office, where a drawing board groaned under the strain of heaped plans for new missile systems. The blueprints awaited his approvals, or revisions, or signatures, before they could be filed.

The first contractor reached forward to point at intricate lines scrawled on the blueprint. "Lieutenant Smith, you must admit this missile system is secure."

The second contractor exulted with an eager grin, "This modified design is so complex, it takes twelve years of college for anyone to operate it! The new concept is a testament to how much respect we hold for the education and intelligence of our proud men in uniform."

Smith shook his head and looked up at them, bewildered. "But *I* can't make head nor tail of it."

"Exactly, that's the point!" the first contractor said. "Completely secure. You're one of our most capable men, and if this system baffles you, imagine how it will confound our enemies! No enemy agent will ever be able to thwart this system, and our nation will be safe."

Smith continued to look up at the first contractor. "Then how can *we* use it, if nobody can understand it?"

The first contractor said patiently, tucking additional rolled blueprints under his arm, "You just push this red button, and the system handles the rest! Look, Lieutenant Smith, nobody is asking you to *understand* it. As a Naval Intelligence officer, all you have to do is stamp it approved!"

Smith frowned down at the plan, shaking his head. "If only the instructors at the Naval Academy had talked about these missiles a little more . . ."

He sighed deeply and picked up a rubber stamp, flipping it over to read APPROVED in reverse letters. Then he rummaged in his desk drawer for an inking pad, before finally banging the stamp haphazardly on the blueprint.

Jubilant, the two contractors whisked away the plan. Without bothering to roll the blueprint they rushed out the door, heading down the hall to the next office, where they would go through the same process with another set of plans and another Naval Intelligence officer with another rubber stamp.

Smith stared after the contractors, sighed deeply again, then finally noticed the incessantly ringing phone. He snatched up the handset, pressing it to his ear. "Yes? How may I help you?"

"Is this Lieutenant Smith?" a woman's voice asked. He thought he heard a crisp Cuban accent in her words.

"Yes," Smith answered.

"Lieutenant *Tom* Smith?" she continued. "Junior grade?"

"Yes."

"Office of Naval Intelligence?"

"Yes."

"Missile Security Section?"

"Yes, yes. Is this a sales call?" He looked forlornly down at his *List of Things to Do Today.*

"We just wanted to be absolutely certain, Lieutenant Smith. This is your lucky day—we have some exciting news for you, señor."

Brightening, Smith pulled himself closer to his desk. "What is it? Who's calling?"

"This is Maria calling from, uh, Pan-Latin Airways. Congratulations! You have just won our contest." Despite her attempts to sound like an American professional public relations specialist, the singsong quality of her voice carried an underlying coldness.

"I have?" Smith asked. "But I don't even enter contests. I never gamble."

"This is a contest you don't have to enter," Maria said. "You were the millionth person to enter the World Trade Center this month."

"There must be some mistake," Smith said, flipping back through the calendar on his desk. "I've never even been to the World Trade Center."

"Oh, I'm sorry. You should go there—I hear it's a wonderful place." He heard Maria shuffling papers. "Ah, sorry, you were the millionth person to enter the Cathedral of Saint John the Divine."

"I've never been there either. What city is that in?"

Maria's voice became deeper, colder, very deadly. "You were the millionth person to pass Forty-Second and Broadway."

"Look, I—"

"Señor, you *won*, do you hear? You won!" Her voice began to rise and become more frantic: "I don't know how you won, I'm just trying to do my job. Why are you giving me such a hard time? Do you want me to cry or something?" She sounded close to hysterics. "Oh, my God, now my supervisor is looking at me! Are you trying to get me fired?"

"Oh," Smith said, finally coming to his senses. "I didn't mean to get you in trouble. I'm so sorry."

"Look, Mr. Smith, just be happy. You're name is at the top of the list. You won a trip, and everyone else won little marshmallow candies shaped like skulls to help them celebrate the day of the dead. You're the big lucky winner, okay? The big man. Everybody is going to envy you!"

Smith seemed taken aback. "Uh, okay, what did I win? I've never won anything before."

Maria's voice became bright and happy again. "You have won an all-expense-paid three-day tour to the beautiful country of Colodor in South America. The finest hotels, the best cuisine. Three marvelous days in the beautiful capital city of Santa Isabel! You lucky, lucky boy! So just pick up your tickets at Pan-Latin Airways and away you go!"

Smith looked at the phone, excited but then curious. "Colodor? Santa Isabel? I've never heard of it."

"Ah, señor, Colodor is the pearl of South America! Lovely, lush, full of scenery and culture. And Santa Isabel has much history and interesting architecture."

"If you say so, but it still doesn't even sound like a real country. In fact, it sounds like something made up for a pulp-fiction adventure story."

"Now, now, don't be ridiculous," Maria said, her voice soothing. "How could you win a trip to a country that doesn't exist? It is a very important country in South America. I should know: My brother runs the Department of Education there— and also the Department of Plumbing and Insect Control!"

He swiveled in his chair and squinted closely at the large map of the world on his wall. Smith had joined the Navy to be more like his hero, Admiral Nelson, exploring the vast world on majestic sailing ships, defending the British Empire. Smith hadn't really anticipated sitting at a desk and stamping blueprints for his entire career.

"I'm looking at my map right now, miss, and I don't see Colodor anywhere in South America." He was more perplexed than suspicious.

"It is near Colombia and Ecuador," Maria answered smoothly, "but unfortunately the mapmakers' union has been on strike. You won't find Colodor shown on many charts. A very messy situation with the Ministry of Mapmaking. My family has nothing to do with that, I swear!"

"Oh, that explains it," Smith said, relieved. He jotted down the information he needed to pick up his prize tickets, thanked Maria politely, and then hung up the phone.

In a blessed moment of silence, Smith stared over at the stack of incomprehensible blueprints on his drawing board. Then, with a wistful glance over his shoulder, he focused on the map of South America again, imagining where the mysterious Colodor might be located.

He threw the whole pile of blueprints off his drawing board, stood up, and straightened his uniform jacket before walking out the door. He would just have to see the place for himself!

• • •

Back in the Operations Office deep in Morro Castle, Maria narrowed her dark eyes and gave a deadly nod to the Russian and Cuban colonels. "Lieutenant Tom Smith has fallen right into our clutches."

Colonel Enrique let out a whoop. "Ai! Plan G is at last underway!" He clapped a congratulatory hand on his bearlike comrade's broad shoulder. "Make sure Bolo is ready to do his part."

Colonel Ivan beamed, raising his bushy eyebrows. "Da, the switch will be a success." He snapped shut his briefcase. "Now, about those cigars, Comrade Enrique?"

Chapter 3

ADMIRAL TURNER, New York's director of Naval Intelligence, sat at his desk holding a dice cup in his hand. The portable radio on the windowsill was tuned to the "All Lawrence Welk" station, and soothing popular favorites tinkled in the air like floating soap bubbles.

The old admiral slammed the cup down to roll the six poker dice again and stared at the results. "Oh, blast and damn!"

As he moved, his gold braid, campaign ribbons and polished medals jingled above his stiff uniform. His steel-gray hair poked up, close cropped and bristly; his skin had the worn, old-leather look of a man who had spent his life facing the salt air of the sea . . . or just from using too harsh a brand of after-shave.

After knocking briskly, Tom Smith marched in and stood at the side of the desk, waiting until his superior officer granted him a moment of attention. The Lawrence Welk music on the radio made Smith drowsy, but he shook his head, rehearsing what he meant to say.

Admiral Turner did not glance up at Smith. "I just can't seem to beat myself today." He stared at the dice scattered across the paper clips and telephone message slips on his desk. With a rattle, he swept the dice back into the cup and thrust it across the desk toward Smith, knocking a few TOP SECRET memos aside. "Here, boy, you try your hand."

Smith looked at the cup, plucking out one of the dice critically. He understood what the dice were for, though he had never played, never tried to fathom the rules. Even if he had wanted to, though, he spotted no place to roll the dice on the cluttered desk. "But, sir, I'm afraid I—"

"Oh, I forgot," the admiral said with a sigh. He snatched back the dice cup. "You don't gamble, you don't drink. In every other way, you're a very promising officer—tops in your class. But you lack . . . I don't know—vision or Navy spirit or . . . whatever. We've got to do something about you, Smith." He opened his lower desk drawer and dropped the dice cup beside a silver whiskey flask, a stack of poker chips and two decks of playing cards. Then he folded his big-knuckled hands as he hunched across the desk. "Didn't they teach you *anything* at the academy? The Navy is going to hell these days, ever since we banned all the hazing rituals. You've got to keep up the tradition, young man— the burden rests on your shoulders."

Shaking his head, Admiral Turner heaved himself out of his creaking chair and walked over to the grime-streaked window. He looked past the pigeons to the bustling New York street. He clasped his hands behind his back as if he were on the bridge of a great sailing ship, gazing across the waves in search of an island.

Smith just stood there, a little crestfallen. The admiral often got into one of these moods.

"Sometimes I wonder what the world is coming to," the old man continued in a soft voice, self-absorbed. He rapped his knuckles against the window, startling the pigeons, and turned to look at Smith, his hands on his hips. "I try to be a father figure to my junior officers. I care about each and every one. But, Smith, I've almost given up on you."

He strode over to the clean-cut young lieutenant. "You just don't seem to care about your image, about the Navy's reputation. When you first came aboard, I had hope. I thought you were a man who was going to get on in the world, make his mark! Why, I was certain you'd even make *admiral* someday. But you're so fastidious you don't make a mark on *anything.*"

The old man slumped in disappointment. The Lawrence Welk station played a particularly maudlin song. Admiral Turner stood by the wall adorned with framed photographs of his former crewmates. Model ships of Navy destroyers, aircraft carriers and submarines sat on display atop his credenza, his bookshelves, his coffee maker.

Smith shuffled his feet in embarrassment. "I'm sorry, sir. I have tried my best."

"Your best? When was the last time you went into a bar and knocked the stuffing out of a few Marines? In my day, I had a girl in every port! But I'm beginning to think you'll die a virgin. What kind of sailor is that? You're getting to be the joke of this whole office!" The admiral raised his voice, as if he were giving his pep talk to a new group of cadets.

He stood directly in front of Smith, who remained at attention, wishing he had not come into the office to make his request after all. From the faint sweet smell that clung to the admiral's uniform, Smith thought the old man had been drinking more than coffee that morning.

"All I'm asking you to do is be a little *human*. Get drunk once in a while. Find some nice girl from a good family, someone who'll make a good hostess." The old man's eyebrows shot up. "You know . . ." he said coyly, as if the idea had just occurred to him, "why not marry somebody like . . . like my daughter, Joan? She just wants to marry some nice fellow and settle down, have babies, work in the kitchen. Isn't that what all women want? I've been reading those stories to Joan since she was a little girl. You could be that special fellow, Smith—if you'd just *reform!*"

Smith stammered, "But, but—I don't know *how*, sir."

The admiral's expression became severe. "Go out and live a little, expand your horizons!"

"Well, sir," Smith seized upon his opening at last, "that's what I'm here about. Sort of. I mean, I'd like to request some time off." He brushed down his uniform, fidgeting. "I just won a contest, sir."

"You?" the admiral said, startled. "Why, that's wonderful! Won a contest, eh?" He added hopefully, "Did you cheat?"

"Well, no, sir," Smith admitted. "I don't even remember entering. I just won, kind of." He shrugged. "But I do need three days off."

"To do what? Read some more books?"

"Oh, no, sir. I'll need to travel. It's an all-expense-paid stay in a luxury hotel. A vacation to some country called Colodor. I can't find it on my charts, though."

"Colodor? That little third-world hellhole? Ah yes, I've heard about their mapmakers' strike. Terrible situation." Then the admiral brightened, clapping a paternal hand on Smith's shoulder. "Wonderful! It'll do you a world of good, Smith. Oh, man, I can see you now! Dancing to soft lights and sexy music, climbing aboard a nice blonde and . . . relaxing! My boy, there's hope for you yet!"

"Does that mean I can have the time off, sir? I'll need to leave right away, if I'm to accept my prize. I've got tickets to fly into Santa Isabel—"

"Go! Go! By all means *go!*" The admiral practically shoved him toward the door, then jabbed a finger at him. "And try to get yourself in a little trouble for once, Smith. That's an order!"

"I, uh—yes, sir," he said, then fled into the hall.

Chapter 4

COLONEL ENRIQUE hid between two palm trees near the Santa Isabel International Airport, and watched the jet cruising down through the blue equatorial sky. "Here comes Lieutenant Smith, exactly on time!"

He adjusted his sunglasses, then tugged down his floppy golf hat, secure in his tourist disguise. He wore pants made of material most often seen on sofas and a windbreaker with the name of a bowling league silk-screened on the back.

Enrique turned to his burly companion who wore plaid shorts, black socks and penny-loafers in which he had discreetly tucked copper ruble coins.

Ivan said, "I'm sure he suspects nothing—Americans are used to winning prizes and getting free luxuries. It is all a daily part of their decadent, dying civilization. Make no mistake,

Enrique: once, religion was the opiate of the people. Now, it is prize shows and lotteries and the Publisher's Cleaning House Sweepstakes. That is how the bourgeoisie keeps the American pigs feeding at their troughs."

"Ah, you make me feel sorry for them," Enrique said. "Tell me, Ivan, what happens if Smith gets killed during this little escapade?" The Cuban colonel watched the plane come in for a landing.

"I'm counting on it, Enrique," the Russian colonel said with a shrug. He squirted a dab of suntan lotion on the palm of his hand and rubbed it on the tip of his sunburn-red nose. "Our impostor 'Pedrito' will become a martyr to the cause—he'll no doubt be much more manageable that way—and the real Pedrito will be our double agent in the United States. No one will know they have switched places. Long live the people's revolution!"

"Good," Enrique said, "now let's hurry before we get a parking ticket. This isn't peaceful Cuba, you know."

◆◆◆

A queue of passengers straggled past the customs counters, lugging suitcases and duffels, tucking passports and papers into their pockets. A brass band struck up a loud, off-key welcoming tune, which Tom Smith suspected must be the national anthem of Colodor, though it sounded strikingly similar to an old Frank Sinatra song. The band members, all mustached, all portly, all wearing colorful sombreros, didn't have quite enough enthusiasm to make up for their lack of musical talent. No one else seemed to mind.

Due in part to the mapmakers' strike, as well as Colodor's usual political turmoils, few jets landed in Santa Isabel. However, kiosks packed with entire families of smiling souvenir vendors, tour providers and T-shirt sellers lined the bright open-air receiving area beyond the customs counter. A newsstand sold Santa Isabel's official national newspaper, as well as postcards and place mats showing beautiful scenic photographs. *Santa Isabel—Pearl of South America, So Beautiful, We've Kept Our Entire Country a Secret!* and *Don't Let the Maps Fool You! We DO Exist!*

"Passengers for Santa Isabel from New York now debarking at Gate 7," the PA announced.

A man dressed as a taxi driver stood outside the terminal, watching every person who emerged from the customs counter. He was plump and moonfaced, sweating in the South American heat. His features had an exotic Turkish cast, a distinctive mix neither Eastern nor Western. He most certainly did not belong in the cabby's uniform, and none of the other drivers had ever seen him before.

The man tried to remain unobtrusive, but ready to spring into action as he scanned the passengers for a particular red-headed American, ignoring all other potential customers.

He had a mission to accomplish.

He removed his name tag—HI, MY NAME IS BOLO! Lieutenant Smith had no need to know his name. The American would be seeing enough of him as it was.

"Flight 731 for Rio de Janeiro now loading at Gate 5," the PA announced, echoing in the empty terminal and crackling with static. "*Vuelo sieteciento . . .*"

Blinking in the sunshine and looking lost, Tom Smith came through the gate as other passengers swirled around him. He wore a sport coat, trim and professional, and he carried a single black suitcase. His red-gold hair was quite distinctive. Bolo spotted him instantly.

Vendors thrust brochures and coupons in Smith's hand, and he thanked them obliviously until he could hold nothing more. Finally, the young lieutenant took the entire stack and politely handed it to another vendor, who proceeded to distribute the coupons to new potential marks. Street urchins dashed up to sell unauthorized maps of the country, before they were chased away by officials in dark uniforms. All along the streets, groups of out-of-work mapmakers walked picket lines.

Bolo snapped to attention beside his small yellow cab, then made his move. He hurried forward like a real taxi driver, intent on getting his customer and providing the best service possible. He had his orders from Colonels Ivan and Enrique—which he followed whenever it was convenient. Bolo had even greater plans up his sleeve. . . .

But then a portly, well-dressed man also rushed toward Smith, overjoyed and waving urgently for attention. Despite his fine clothes, the portly man carried a battered cardboard suitcase held together with gray duct tape. Puffing as he ran, he skidded to a halt before Smith, dropped his suitcase and spread his arms wide.

"Ai! Pedrito!" The portly man wrapped his arms around Smith, hugging him in greeting.

Bolo paused, not knowing what to do. He had expected nothing like this. Could there be another agent on the case?

Unable to move, Smith spluttered, "Um, excuse me, sir, I—"

The portly man pulled Smith toward the cantina a few steps down the walkway from the vendors and taxis. Umbrellas and awnings provided welcome shade over wicker chairs and rickety tables. The airport lounge was deserted in the bright afternoon sunshine. Big, languid ceiling fans stirred the humid air, occasionally whacking stunned tropical insects that flew too close to the blades.

"Ai, Pedrito, how glad I am to see you," the stranger said, pounding Smith so hard on his back that the young lieutenant stumbled forward, almost dropping his black suitcase. "We've just got time before my flight so I can buy you a drink! As I promised last time we met, eh? Do you still remember those wild women? And they said they were nuns! Ha-ha!"

Bolo thought fast, and decided to wait coolly outside. This encounter could prove interesting.

The portly man pushed Smith into a creaking wicker seat beneath a *Modelo Especial* umbrella. With a chubby hand studded with gold rings, the man swept cockroaches and a small lizard aside and grabbed for a bowl of fried plantain chips. He demanded the attention of the bartender. "Quickly! My friend Pedrito here is an impatient—and *important*—man! And I have a plane to catch in a few minutes."

"Please, please," Smith said, still trying to be polite. "There must be some mistake. My name isn't Pedrito."

As the portly man slumped into his own seat across the table, he grinned, as if understanding an inside joke. "Ah, now, Pedrito, you can trust *me!* After all we've been through together." He placed a chubby finger across his lips and lowered his voice. "Just like old times, eh? Bartender! Two margaritas, fast! Use your best tequila for my friend here!"

"But, but—I don't drink tequila," Smith protested.

The fat man slapped him on the back, guffawing loudly. "You don't drink tequila! Hah, my friend, that is a good joke! No tequila. Agave worms tremble in fear when Pedrito Miraflores walks near."

Outside the cantina, Bolo continued his wait. The two colonels had given him explicit instructions, but Bolo had more important plans of his own. Calm and patient, he knew he could make everything work out.

". . . and I always wondered if your horse really made it through the Orchid Jungle of Death!" the portly man continued, not letting Smith get in a word edgewise. "And how did you survive the stampede of poison tree frogs? Ai!"

The bartender came with the margaritas, two glasses of questionable cleanliness crusted with salt and filled with lime and tequila.

"But I'm trying to tell you," Smith said, blinking across at his unexpected companion, "I don't know anyone named Pedrito." The bartender set the salt-rimmed glass before him, but Smith nudged it aside. "Excuse me, perhaps a glass of milk? *Leche, por favor?*"

"*No leche, señor,*" the bartender said with a sneer. "In this heat, it curdles too quickly."

The portly man cracked up with a belly laugh. "Milk!" He recovered a bit, still chuckling, and swiped the back of his hand across his glistening forehead. "Pedrito, you'll be the death of me yet! Tell me the one about the scorpion wranglers in the underground city—"

"*Rio. Rio. Abordo!*" the PA announced.

"Rio? Ah, that's my plane." The stranger gulped his entire margarita, threw a bill onto the table and patted Smith's hand. "I wish we could talk more, but I've got to run. Someday you'll have to tell me how you survived the raid on the valley of the cactus poachers. You are a legend in Colodor, *mi amigo!*" He leaned forward, speaking in a stage whisper, "But I see you must be on another mission now. Never mind, Pedrito, your secret is safe with me!"

The portly man rushed off, heading for his plane. Smith stared after him. "What an odd man."

He pushed away his untouched margarita, picked up his black suitcase and rose from the wicker chair. He brushed tiny splinters from the seat of his pants. As he left, the bartender came to clean up the table, eyed Smith's pristine drink and slurped it down himself. . . .

Outside the terminal, Bolo stood by the fender of his taxicab, still waiting. As his second opportunity arose, he remained studiously calm, the model of bored confidence as he watched Smith approach, looking for a cab.

Another taxi driver bustled forward, eager to snag a well-paying American tourist. Barely moving, Bolo's foot expertly tripped the other driver and made him sprawl flat on his face on the cobblestoned street. Bolo stepped on the prostrate driver's back, walked over him and moved up toward Smith, completely professional and businesslike.

"Cab, sir?" Bolo said in a flat, unemotional voice as he courteously opened the door for Smith. "I am the finest driver in all Santa Isabel."

Still distracted by his odd experience with the portly stranger, Smith climbed into the back of the cramped yellow cab. Propping his suitcase beside him on the seat, Smith rummaged in the pockets of his sport jacket until he found the crumpled itinerary paper. Maria, the contest administrator, had faxed it to him, describing his luxury accommodations and the schedule for his once-in-a-lifetime vacation in exotic Colodor. He scanned the blurry handwriting, then handed the paper forward to Bolo. "It says here 'Hotel Grande de Lujo,' biggest hotel in Santa Isabel. Think you can find it?"

Bolo read the slip cursorily, then gave it back. "Oh, you're in good hands, sir." Without looking or signaling, he jerked the cab away from the curb and out into traffic. A bus honked and swerved, driving a skinny bicyclist up on the curb. Bolo didn't even glance back. "Leave it to me, sir."

Chapter 5

BOLO DROVE ALONG a broad cobblestoned avenue with stately hotels, marble columns, lush fountains and ornate statues. Wrestling with the wheel, he seesawed around pedestrians on bicycles, old men pushing carts, Volkswagen vans and tourist-packed buses belching greasy exhaust smoke.

Reassured by the sight of all the luxury resorts in Santa Isabel, Smith fished out his well-read paperback, *Famous Naval Battles*. He began to reread the chapter about his hero, Horatio Nelson, and his seven years at war in the Mediterranean. Sighing, Smith read on, admiring Nelson's battles, his snap decisions with the fates of mighty nations depending on his success.

Then he thought instead of Admiral Turner back in New York, as well as his own tedious job approving blueprints for new missile systems. He wished he could have lived back in the days when joining the Navy actually meant a lifetime of excitement. . . .

The engine roared as Bolo accelerated, threading the cab through a narrow alley. Sudden chicken squawks and a flash of white feathers past the car's rear window caused Smith to look up from his paperback. The street was flanked by whitewashed buildings with blue-painted doors, topped by crumbling tile roofs and sagging electrical wires used as clotheslines. Tar-paper strips patched crumbling stucco. Feral chickens flew out from their path, dive-bombing the windshield. Dogs barked and chased the cab, but fled in fear from the vicious chickens.

"Almost to your hotel, sir," Bolo said, turning to look at his passenger without watching the road. "Just a few more minutes." The cab bounced and thumped as he ran over something large and moving. A blizzard of white feathers flew into the air as the cab screeched down another alley.

Finally the taxi came to a halt before a broken-down edifice that might have been a moderately nice hotel if it were torn down and rebuilt entirely from the original plans. No sign adorned the hulking building, but Bolo gestured proudly to a front door that hung off-kilter on bent hinges.

"Here you are, sir. The Hotel Grande de Lujo." He beamed.

Around the cab, the street was deserted. Everyone had fled, even the angry chickens. Smith stared out the back-seat window in surprise.

"Is this the best hotel in Santa Isabel?" he asked, incredulous. He rubbed his eyes.

"That's what they say," Bolo said, his voice proud. "Highly recommended."

"But . . . there must be some mistake," Smith said, swallowing hard. "I won the grand prize."

"And it's the *Grande* hotel."

"Well, but we passed plenty of nicer hotels back there in the resort district." Smith turned around in his seat, trying to see the end of the long alley behind the taxi.

Bolo waved his hand in dismissal and made a raspberry sound. "Ah, those are mere tourist traps, no character, no substance. Certainly not a place for a man of your caliber, sir. A distinctive hotel like *this* is where the locals stay. It'll be a true experience for you, a genuine taste of Colodor. You can see what our country is most famous for."

◆◆◆

Inside the hotel's foyer, two tough Colodoran gangsters hid behind the sagging door. Each in his own shadowy corner, they pressed against the crumbling whitewashed walls, keeping an eye to the cracks.

"It figures he would show up *now*," said the first one. "I was just going to take a break."

The other snorted. "A break? What do you need a break for? We've just been standing here all morning long."

"I need to go to the bathroom," the first gangster said.

"Well, you should have planned ahead," his partner answered. "This is the most important part of the plan, where we make the switch. Now be quiet. He's getting out of the cab."

◆◆◆

When Smith remained unconvinced about the suitability of the hotel, Bolo finally said, "Well, if you don't like it, you can always go in and complain to the management. Maybe they'll clean the place up a bit."

"In fact, I will talk to the management," Smith said. "I don't like to complain, since this was a free trip, but I'm sure Maria, the contest administrator, would like to know about this."

Smith stuffed his paperback into the pocket of his sport coat and climbed out of the taxi. He fumbled for money to pay the driver, but Bolo just waved and puttered on down the alley. "My congratulations on winning the contest," he called. "No charge."

Smith gripped his black suitcase and trudged up the sidewalk, but the hotel didn't look any better when he got closer. As he watched, one of the terra-cotta roof tiles, apparently dislodged by an extremely large tarantula, tumbled down the side of the building to smash on the street.

"They ought to be ashamed of themselves." Smith frowned, craning his neck to look up at the windows of the other rooms. He set the suitcase down at his feet.

Knocking at the front door but hearing no answer, Smith pushed open the creaking door. He walked in, blinking to adjust his focus in the sudden interior shadows. He glanced around, but could see nothing but a narrow landing and coat hooks nailed to old wooden paneling. Bright smudges of sunlight splashed through the windows in a steep stairwell in front of him. All the rooms seemed to be upstairs.

"Hello?" he said. His voice echoed back at him. Anxious to get on with his prize vacation, he marched up the groaning stairs, making no attempt to be quiet. "Anybody here?" He heard skittering bugs, but no other sound.

Behind him, on tiptoe, the two hoods emerged from their respective hiding places and stalked after him. They adjusted sturdy ropes looped around clips at their waists; in each hand they carried strips of rags, convenient for gags or blindfolds. The first man walked in a strange scissorlike fashion, trying to keep his legs crossed and his full bladder under control. The second man hovered close to him, hiding in his partner's shadow.

"Is this the Hotel Grande de Lujo?" Smith shouted again. "Where's the lobby?" He stopped at a landing next to a grime-streaked window. The view looked out onto an alley piled with rusted automobiles stripped of parts—nothing scenic at all.

As Smith stood at a loss, one hood crept up behind him and looped his ragged strip of cloth around Smith's face in an attempt to jam it into his mouth.

Smith grabbed the cloth and yanked it out of the hood's hand. "Hey!" In a brief struggle, the first hood scrabbled to snatch the cloth back.

Smith's naval commando training—honed and refined by living and working for years in the mugger-rich suburbs of New York—suddenly came into play.

He expertly grasped the hood's wrist, hunched and elbowed him in the stomach. A sudden dark wet spot blossomed at the man's crotch. Smith turned backward, spun around and hurled him through the window.

The second thug charged up the steps to join the fray.

As he sailed through the shattering glass, the first hood's heels struck the second thug in the chin and knocked him back down the stairs. The second hood thumped and rolled and bounced down from landing to landing, picking up speed.

Smith watched him, arms crossed over his chest. He sniffed in annoyance. "I could tell this wasn't a first-class hotel."

•••

Outside, Bolo sat behind the wheel of his stolen cab. He had parked half a block away, and now the skittish, predatory chickens had begun to return, creeping out of their hiding places and looking for unsuspecting food.

Hearing the glass crash from above, he looked up to see one hood sail through the splintering window and fall into the alleyway below. The thug thumped with a metallic clang onto the rusted hood of an ancient Mercedes. The cautious chickens perked up, looking from side to side, then raced clucking toward the helpless man in the alley.

After another sound, Bolo looked to see the second thug tumble down the last few stairs and out through the half-open front door to sprawl in a heap on the porch.

Bolo raised his eyebrows in admiration at Smith's handiwork. Perhaps the naval officer would be salvageable for his purposes after all. "Two down, one to go."

•••

On an upper balcony above the stairs, Smith looked all around him, still clutching his black suitcase. "I sure don't like the service in this hotel." He glanced back down the stairwell, scowling. "I hope they don't plan on charging me for that window glass."

A third man crept into sight at the balcony rail, carrying a stained bedsheet like a safari net. Smith saw him and waved. "Are you the manager?" he asked. "I've been looking for—"

The thug threw the sheet, and the tattered and fouled cloth descended on Smith, enveloping him. "Hey, no fair!" He flailed his hands and kicked at the edge of the cloth, but his expert kicks missed their mark as the thug dodged aside.

Before the lieutenant could fight his way out, the thug rushed forward and swung a club down on Smith's sheet-wrapped head.

Though he had not even finished his complaint, Smith stopped grumbling in mid-sentence. He saw only stars and then blackness.

Chapter 6

NEXT MORNING AT DAWN the band of chickens set up a loud crowing among the junked cars in the alleyway, announcing their claim on the territory. From one high window, a severe-looking old matron threw an empty tin can at them. Another woman diligently took down the previous day's laundry hung from a clothesline that connected the two buildings, then hung a new dripping batch.

In a dim, shabby room in the Hotel Grande de Lujo, slanted sunlight trickled through holes in a tattered window shade to illuminate a narrow bed and a wardrobe that tilted awkwardly on one broken leg. The bathroom walls were so blotched with mildew and water spots that it was impossible to tell where the stains ended and the tile began.

A tan suitcase leaned against the tilted wardrobe. The book *Famous Naval Battles* lay discarded against the wall; the bookmark had fallen out in the scuffle.

Lieutenant Tom Smith lay in the middle of the floor on his face, stripped down to his skivvies, with silver duct tape across his mouth. A braided cotton rope bound his ankles together and tied his wrists behind his back. The position wasn't very comfortable at all, as Smith discovered as soon as he returned to consciousness.

Groggily, Smith twisted on his side and gave a muffled groan through the tape covering his mouth. His head hurt as if a rambunctious child with his first toy drum set had taken up residence inside his skull. He fell back on his face in the middle of the filthy floor, where he blinked repeatedly, trying to remember where he was and how he had gotten there.

He rolled his eyes upon hearing a clatter of buckets in the hall outside, the thunk of a mop handle striking the wall. A key clicked in the lock, and the splintered wooden door opened on its ancient hinges with a truly amazing squeak.

A bland-faced maid entered the room, looking tired and not the least startled by seeing Smith's prone form on the floor. She was dressed in colorful clothes, her glossy dark hair braided neatly. She was hard-working and intent on her job—but she apparently hadn't been hired to get hapless tourists out of trouble.

He squirmed and made a muffled sound through the duct tape, begging her to help him, though the efforts only made his head pound harder. She paid him no mind at all.

Carrying a mop, a ring of keys and a feather duster, the maid went right to work. She propped her equipment in the doorway, then began to hum as she dragged in a sloshing bucket filled with soapy water.

Nonchalantly, the maid used her feather duster lightly on Smith's back, then tucked it under her arm. Seeing the dirt on the floor in front of his face, Smith couldn't imagine why she was being so meticulous now. Maybe she is a new employee, he thought.

Still humming, the maid dallied in the bathroom, splashing chlorine-smelling water on some of the worst stains, emptying the chamber pots, then came into the main room to smooth the bed coverings. Finished, she grabbed her bucket and mop, and turned for the door.

Smith struggled and squirmed in the center of the room, trying to get her to help him. He groaned and mumbled, then waggled his eyebrows.

Finally, the maid paused and stopped humming. Her forehead furrowed. She looked on the bed and on an ancient dresser, as if she'd forgotten something. After an interminable moment, she glanced down at the bound man on the floor.

"*Wrrr umph*," Smith said behind his gag, his eyes flashing.

The maid hummed again as she bent over to untie the knots around Smith's ankles and wrists, not hurrying, as if this was just another part of her job. No doubt she routinely found men tied up on the floors of various rooms—especially in a place like this. When she finished, she held out her hand and waited for a tip.

Smith struggled with the remaining ropes around his wrists and at last pulled his hands free. He sat up, rubbing his throbbing hands, then bent to wrestle with the ankle cords and slid them off.

He patted his boxer shorts, as if to apologize for not having any change. Through a sealed mouth, he grunted an apology.

The cleaning woman eyed him with a bland look, then grabbed the duct tape around his mouth. She gave the tape a ferocious yank. Smith gasped with a shock of pain.

"I'm sorry, but someone has taken my clothes," he apologized.

"Lying pervert," she muttered in Spanish. "I see your kind all the time." She wearily picked up her bucket and exited, closing the door behind her and clicking the key in the lock.

Smith put both hands against his stinging mouth and cheek, then tore open the tan suitcase, looking for the bottle of soothing lotion he had carefully packed. It worked on sunburns, and he hoped it would work on his face. He found a pint bottle of clear liquid, and splashed the lotion onto his face.

It burned the raw skin like acid.

Gasping, Smith fanned his hand rapidly to cool his face. He looked at the bottle in his hand and finally registered what the label said. "*Rum!* But I never drink rum—in fact I never drink alcohol. How did that get in my luggage?"

Still smarting, he pawed through the contents of the open suitcase, perplexed. "No wonder—this isn't my suitcase."

He stared at the unfamiliar objects. He pulled out a straight-edged razor. After looking at the long and wicked blade, he snapped it shut again. "That's definitely not my razor. It doesn't even look safe." Then he rubbed his raw cheeks and reconsidered, frowning at the rough stubble he had grown. "Well, I'll just have to make do for now. I need to make myself presentable before I give the management of this hotel a piece of my mind." As he considered the situation, he pursed his lips. "Besides, I'll bet Admiral Horatio Nelson used a straight razor, even on choppy seas."

A while later, Smith stood in his skivvies before the cracked bathroom mirror, trying to shave with the primitive tool. He had tried to smooth his unkempt hair back into place as he attempted to figure out what had gone wrong. This was supposed to be his perfect vacation! He should have stayed in New York looking at missile plans.

He went on shaving, but the straight razor was very unkind.

◆◆◆

The strange suitcase lay open on the bed, its contents ready for inspection. Smith, damp from a sponge bath and feeling somewhat better at last, stood with a towel wrapped about his middle. Bloodstained flecks of tissue paper clung to the numerous nicks and cuts from his shaving adventure.

Rummaging through the strange suitcase, Smith lifted out a khaki safari suit and pants. He held them against him. "Well, at least they look like they'll fit." He patted the pockets, feeling perplexed.

Why would someone mug me, he wondered, and then leave me in a room with the wrong suitcase? Maybe this guy mugged lots of people, and just happened to mix up the suitcases.

"Hey, I wonder if he left my wallet?" That wallet had more than his money in it; it had credit cards and ID. Smith searched through the strange suitcase, frantic, then he rushed across the room to open the leaning wardrobe. But he found it empty except for a few mouse droppings and a dead spider in the corner.

Dropping to his knees beside the narrow bed, he lifted the mattress, peering under it for any scrap of his own belongings, but found only a discarded sock with holes in the toe.

His only belonging in the room was the paperback history book he had been reading in the taxi. Seeking comfort in his historical hero, he picked up *Famous Naval Battles*, sat down in his underwear on the end of the bed and looked sadly around.

"No money, no papers, no passport." He looked down at the book, which apparently the thieves hadn't considered worth stealing. He was certainly in a fix, and he had no idea how to solve it. "I wonder what Nelson would have done in a case like this?"

Chapter 7

IN FRONT OF THE ANCIENT HOTEL, Bolo's taxi nosed in and stopped. The puttering sound of the engine echoed off the close walls of the alley. Behind the wheel, he yawned elaborately and stretched, blinking his eyes. He had shaved less than an hour ago, and his square chin felt smooth and clean.

Ah, nothing like a fresh morning in the slums of Santa Isabel, he thought. He settled back behind the wheel, just waiting, biding his time. When plans were afoot, Bolo could have all the patience in the world. He figured Smith would be just about ready for the next stage of the process by now.

The tall door of the Hotel Grande de Lujo swung open, dangling on its broken hinges, and Smith exited, looking wide awake. He wore a new khaki safari suit that fit him well, and he carried the tan suitcase that Bolo had provided, as the two colonels had ordered.

45

Bolo marveled at the redhead's appearance. Exactly like the renegade Pedrito Miraflores. Exactly as planned.

As Smith stopped on the porch, dazzled by the morning sunlight, the hotel's heavy door snapped free of its remaining hinge and crashed backward into the foyer. From above, chunks of stucco pattered down like shrapnel. Small lizards scrambled for cover into the nearby alley, and the wild chickens fell upon them with hungry glee.

Ducking from the falling tiles, Smith ran down the steps to the sidewalk, but he didn't seem to know where to go. He looked around and finally spotted the waiting taxicab. Bolo raised a hand in salute.

With a visible sigh of relief, Smith called, "Taxi! Taxi!" He ran down the street as if he wanted to get as far away from the hotel as he could.

Bolo leaned across the seat and opened the door without getting out. Smith tossed the mysterious tan suitcase inside, then dove into the cab, plopping down beside the driver in the front. "Whew! Something terrible has happened. Take me to the American Embassy. I'll pay you when we get there." Smith brushed a hand across his forehead, wiping his hair back into place. "What sort of currency does this country use, anyway?"

"Your credit is good in Santa Isabel, sir," Bolo said mildly. Smith didn't seem to recognize him at all. "You are an American, and that is good enough for me." Wrestling the vehicle into gear, he drove away with a lurch that threw Smith back against the seat. Bolo turned a corner, then accelerated, his gaze fixed ahead through the windshield. He smiled happily, content with the situation.

In less than a mile, Bolo had taken them into a lovely quarter along a boulevard lined with splashing marble fountains and lush parks filled with hibiscus flowers and flamingos. Rose vendors sold gorgeous bouquets; women sold fried bananas from big black pans.

"You look very fine in those new clothes," Bolo said. "By the way, didn't you have a *black* suitcase when you arrived yesterday?"

"Don't remind me," Smith groaned, rubbing his still-sore head. "Do you have a high crime rate here in Colodor?"

"Nothing to worry about," Bolo said. "Every country has a few bad apples." As he spoke, the taxi passed a knot of sign-carrying protesters insisting on equality for mapmakers everywhere.

"You ought to do something about it," Smith said, closing his eyes. "You might get more tourists. Your economy could probably use it."

"Oh, we try, we try. We keep deporting the criminals, but then they just sneak back over the border." Bolo turned away from the wide thoroughfares, down another two alleys, until he came to a sleepy street. He checked the addresses, locating the exact spot where he intended to abandon Smith.

In a place not at all close to anything important whatsoever, he coasted to a stop against the curb. He shifted into park.

"Why are we stopped?" Smith said, sitting up. He looked behind them, then out the side window. He saw only whitewashed apartments and houses with wrought-iron bars on the windows. Laundry hung on lines across the rooftops.

"We are very close to the American Embassy, if you would like to walk the rest of the way." He grinned sincerely, flashing white teeth. "They have traffic restrictions in front of the main building. No taxis allowed."

Smith rolled down the grimy passenger-side window and poked his head out. He looked up and down the quiet street. "I don't see any embassy."

Bolo pointed calmly toward a side alley. "Turn left. It's up there about three blocks. You'll see it. It's got a chicken over the door."

"A chicken? For an American embassy? Don't you mean an eagle?"

"My mistake, sir. Here in Colodor, the chickens are fearsome birds, and one does not trifle with them."

"Just like the United States," Smith said proudly. He climbed out of the cab, retrieved the tan suitcase from the back and stood looking lost.

Bolo leaned across the seat to smile reassuringly out the passenger window. "I'll wait right here for you, sir."

"How can I be certain of that?" Smith asked.

"For one thing, sir, you haven't paid me yet," Bolo said, deadpan. "Why would I leave now, when such a generous tip hinges upon me waiting here for you?"

Smith saw the logic and nodded. "I'll have to see if I can get my ID and credit cards replaced at the embassy. My wallet was stolen yesterday."

"Whatever you say, sir."

Smith walked up the street, whistling a tune that Bolo recognized as "Anchors Aweigh," in search of the promised embassy. . . .

As soon as the lieutenant turned the corner out of sight, Bolo leaped from the cab like a shot, and raced in the opposite direction down the sidewalk, his feet slapping on the concrete. It was time to put Smith through a few more ordeals so that Bolo could test the man's mettle. The two colonels were just trying to kill Smith, but Bolo had so much more in mind. . . .

He dodged fire hydrants, an old man on a bicycle, and a knot of giggling children tying strings around the pincers of a deadly black scorpion they had caught.

Once he reached the corner to the main street, Bolo knocked aside one of the protesters, tossing her hand-lettered sign—NO MORE UNOFFICIAL MAPS!—into a gutter. The stringy-haired woman hurled imaginative multilingual insults at him, but Bolo had eyes only for a brightly painted phone kiosk under a cast-iron street light.

Bolo dug his fingers into his pocket, snatched out a few oddly shaped coins and jammed them into the slot. He picked up the receiver and dialed a number he had memorized.

A woman answered at once. "United States Embassy," she said in a drawling Alabama accent, as if reading from a cue card. "This line is for official business only. Would you care to be added to our mailing list?"

"Never mind that—give me your CIA man. Quick!" Bolo said. "This is a national emergency."

♦♦♦

In the embassy's CIA office (which was located next to the kitchenette and the soda-pop machines), gleaming automatic rifles filled cherrywood racks that covered two entire walls. A sprawling chart marked potential covert assault plans, satellite photos showed close-up views of suspicious military bases and shopping malls throughout South America. A map of the world hung behind a large desk, studded with tiny flag pins. The location of Colodor and Santa Isabel had been crudely drawn in by hand.

A radio man hunched over his equipment in the far corner, nearest to the candy machine. His large padded headphones hid the fact that he was actually listening to a portable cassette player; the rock music blared loudly enough that the drumbeat trickled through the headphones.

The large desk dominating the room bore a meticulously painted CIA crest. A hulking brute of a man sat behind an engraved name plaque that said HI! MY NAME IS O'HALLORAN! A yellow smiley-face sticker grinned idiotically beside the nameplate.

O'Halloran read from a book, *How to Come in from the Cold, and Still Feel Good about Yourself.* His face was wide and rough, his eyes close set, his mouse-brown hair parted nearly down to his earlobe so that he could comb long strands up over his gleaming bald spot.

The phone rang loudly, drowning out the muffled beat of the radio man's rock music. Growling at the interruption, O'Halloran folded the corner of a page to mark his place in the book. He reached over to grab the ringing phone as if it were a bug to be squashed. "Passport Control Officer O'Halloran—it's my pleasure to serve you. What the hell do you want?"

He listened to Bolo's reply, and his expression changed as if he had been struck with a thunderbolt. "Pedrito Miraflores? You must be joking! For six months now we've had orders to bring him in dead or alive!"

O'Halloran slammed down the phone and raced to the door. "This is our lucky day," he called to the radio man, who simply drummed his fingers on the communications set to the beat of the music. . . .

In the U.S. Embassy foyer a tough Marine sergeant sat at the front reception desk, where a paperweight that promised "Service with a Smile" held down a stack of *Wanted* sheets and *Shoot on Sight* orders.

O'Halloran rushed up to him, and the sergeant snapped to attention. O'Halloran whispered frantically into the Marine's ear, pointed toward the street, pointed at himself and gestured to a small observation closet near the reception area. He raced to the closet and dove inside, cramming himself in among the brooms, mops and cleaning chemicals. He slammed the door.

The Marine sergeant looked grimly out at the street, putting his hand on the pistol butt, out of view from the door. O'Halloran tensely stared out through a small peephole in the spy closet.

The vile revolutionary leader Pedrito Miraflores was headed this way.

Chapter 8

SMITH STROLLED UP THE STREET, anxious to get his ID straightened out and his credit cards replaced so he could enjoy the rest of his prize trip. His vacation in Colodor had gotten off to a bad start, but he didn't want to let that ruin the rest of his time here. Trying to be a good American, welcoming to all the world's people, he smiled at passersby and wished them good day.

Just where the cabdriver had told him it would be, he found the big white building, the stenciled U.S. Embassy sign and a flapping flag. Smith sighed in relief. "Ah, here we are. A place where I can always feel welcome."

♦♦♦

After making his treacherous phone call, Bolo eased up in his taxi to where he could watch Smith approach the embassy. He sat behind the wheel and held a portable walkie-talkie close to his face, waiting, waiting. He pushed the transmit button and spoke into the radio. "I will give you the countdown, *amigos.*"

Right on schedule, Smith strolled up the street.

Nearby, in a rented room above a florist shop, two Colodoran hoods looked out onto the street from a high window. One held a walkie-talkie, the counterpart to Bolo's. The other thug squatted beside the remote controls of a set of planted explosives, gripping the plunger of a radio detonator switch. He wore dark glasses, and he held the detonator the way that another man might hold his lover. "Now?" he pleaded, as if anticipating the thrill. "Can I blow them up now?"

"I see him. He's just going inside," the hood with the walkie-talkie answered. "Twenty . . . nineteen . . . eighteen . . ."

The second thug fidgeted, looked away, clearly distraught. "Can't you count any faster?"

"No. Now wait for it. Seventeen . . . sixteen . . ."

♦♦♦

As Smith entered the embassy, he walked up to the receptionist—a tense-looking bear of a Marine sergeant. The Marine watched him, hand gripping the butt of his pistol.

"Hello, gyrene," Smith said brightly. "I've got to report—"

From the peephole in the spy closet, O'Halloran squinted, ready to explode forward. He forced himself to take half a second to be sure and another half second to enjoy the flush of triumph. "That's *him!*" he bellowed, yelling through the flimsy closet door.

Hearing the CIA chief's muffled cry, the sergeant drew his pistol and said, "Excuse me, sir: kindly put your hands on your head!"

Smith's words faltered to a halt in mid-sentence as he stared down the barrel of the drawn weapon. "I've lost my passport . . ."

O'Halloran aimed his revolver through the tiny spy port in the wall. He fired.

The echo of the gunshot inside the cramped closet nearly deafened him. He shook his head, trying to clear the dazzle from his eyes and the ringing from his ears.

Smith's commando instincts, well honed from years of dodging gunfire in the streets of New York, took over.

He turned tail and jogged frantically from left to right. The Marine sergeant opened fire with his own revolver, blasting again and again as Smith scrambled for the door. The glass blew out, hammered by whining bullets.

Smith felt sure that Admiral Horatio Nelson never had to contend with such outrageous circumstances.

From the outside he heard the roar of an approaching taxi, the familiar putter of a poorly tuned engine. He charged for it, running pell-mell.

The cab swerved to a screeching halt in front of the embassy, its door already open. "Here, sir," Bolo said. "Perhaps I could be of assistance?"

Smith dove into the back seat, sprawling across the upholstery. Gunshots bored holes into the right rear quarter-panel of the vehicle. The cab raced off.

◆◆◆

Meanwhile, the hood at the window above the florist shop stared out onto the frantic street activity as he counted down. "Five . . . four . . ."

"Now? Can I do it now?" the second man said at the detonator.

"Hold on to your britches, Boom Boom," the first thug scolded. "Three . . . two . . ."

The Marine sergeant and O'Halloran burst from the embassy's shattered glass entry and stampeded down the marble stairs. "There! Shoot, shoot!" O'Halloran ordered the sergeant. "Don't let Pedrito get away!"

Both men stood on the sidewalk and fired after the departing taxi, but they succeeded only in gunning down a few pedestrians, mapmaker protesters, souvenir vendors and wild chickens.

"One!" the hood at the window shouted triumphantly.

The whole front of the embassy blew out in gouts of orange flame. O'Halloran and the sergeant were knocked into the street.

"I hope you enjoyed yourself," the first thug said, looking over his shoulder at his partner with the detonator.

"Oh yeah, that was good," said the man with the detonator, his voice husky with ecstasy. "Almost as good as that airport in Panama in '87." He hugged the detonator close. "Can we do it again?"

◆◆◆

Bolo drove at breakneck speed. Smith climbed to his elbows on the back seat, then scrambled to a sitting position. He glanced through the rear window, yanked the rattling door the rest of the way shut, then popped his head up alongside the driver. "Jiminy Christmas, what was that all about? I just wanted to report my stolen wallet."

"It's a national holiday today," Bolo said. "Many unexpected things happen this time of year. All in good fun."

"Does it usually involve shooting unsuspecting tourists?" Smith said, still trying to catch his breath.

"Sometimes," Bolo nodded. "You have seen few people with red hair here in Colodor. Perhaps now you know why."

The cab raced up the street, careening around other vehicles. Bolo continued to accelerate, though his face remained bland and unemotional. The cab skidded around a corner, leaving black tire smears on the pavement, then straightened out to speed along a wide expanse as pedestrians and street vendors leaped out of the way. Smith searched for a seat belt in the old cab, but found only loosely connected strands of baling twine, which didn't seem to help.

Sirens shrieking, a police car turned the same corner after them, roaring in their wake.

"We're being followed," Smith said.

Bolo tilted the rearview mirror. "Don't worry, sir. I'm sure they're after someone else. After all, what have we done wrong?"

♦♦♦

A banged-up O'Halloran sat beside a uniformed driver in the police car. Plaster dust and tiny cuts from the embassy explosion covered the CIA man. His hair hung in disarray, the overlong strands flopping down his cheek and leaving his bald spot uncovered.

57

O'Halloran gesticulated madly ahead and pounded the dashboard. "After him! After him!"

The driver hunched over the steering wheel and continued to race along, not daring to argue with his boss.

The streets became narrower, the houses more ramshackle in a poorer neighborhood. Graffiti covered much of the white-washed stucco. Ahead, the road ended in a line of telephone poles covered with garish posters for political parties and fruit-based soft drinks. Beyond the telephone poles, the road veered in a steep slope off into a garbage dump, where small, smoky fires were burning.

Far ahead, the fleeing cab careened up the street, but the police car narrowed the distance with every block. Still hammering the dashboard, O'Halloran turned livid, as if he could physically urge the car forward through the sheer force of his high blood pressure.

"Oh, that dirty son of a bitch! I'll get him if it's the last thing—"

Bolo's cab yanked sideways and slid like a thrown dart into a labyrinthine alley, scattering more chickens.

Unable to make such an unexpected turn, the police car continued straight ahead as the driver wrestled with the steering wheel. A spray of white feathers flew in front of his windshield, blocking his view.

"—I ever do!" O'Halloran said. "Faster!"

The driver stomped down on the accelerator—and rammed full speed into the nearest telephone pole.

After the hissing steam from the radiator cleared, O'Halloran wedged his shoulders out of the window, looking down at the buckled door of the police car. He shook his fist in the direction where the cab had vanished.

"I'll get you," O'Halloran vowed, because he could think of nothing more creative to say. With his other hand, he dragged his hair back into place over his bald spot. "I'll get you, Pedrito Miraflores!"

Chapter 9

THE CANTINA DE ESPEJOS—the cantina of mirrors—was two stories high, though the foundation didn't look sturdy enough to support both levels. The crumbling adobe facade was held together by moss clumps and pigeon droppings. Painted campaign slogans and portraits of political candidates flaked away to reveal similar paintings but for the opposite parties in previous elections. Mildew stained the small patches of clean whitewash below the arched entrance.

Attached to the back of the cantina, down a flanking alley, stood three low outbuildings with flat roofs of corrugated sheet metal. A wrought-iron balcony at a second-floor window marked the closest thing to a penthouse the building had to offer.

Despite the cantina's garishly painted sign that welcomed new customers, the area was quiet in the morning air. Muffled music and the background sounds of yelling throbbed through cracks in the walls. Other households went about the day's business—women hung the laundry, fruit vendors set up their stands and cooks fried bananas or Inca corn. They waited for customers to come.

Bolo's cab sped into view, swerving on the slick cobblestones as it turned into the side street. In a cloud of dust and street debris, Bolo braked to a halt against the rear wall of the cantina just under the second-floor balcony. An iguana sat on the corrugated metal rooftop of the nearest outbuilding, blinking down at the newcomers, but otherwise unmoving.

The cab's engine coughed, shuddered and died with a loud backfire. Bolo stepped out, holding the driver's-side door as he scanned the side street toward the front of the Cantina de Espejos, then back the way they had come. With a relieved sigh, he gazed up at the second-floor window. Smiling broadly, he nodded. "Yes, that will do nicely."

"Where are we?" Smith asked.

"A new hotel for you, sir," Bolo answered. "I know you were not happy with your previous accommodations. Perhaps this one will be more to your liking."

Smith's head popped out of the car window, his red-gold hair disheveled from the frantic chase. "I hope you're keeping track of the fare," he said. "I'm afraid my embassy wasn't much help to me."

"We'll settle the bill later. You're an American—we trust you." Bolo yanked open the cab's back door.

"Is there going to be more of that fiesta?" Smith said. "Maybe I should see some of it, as part of my Santa Isabel vacation experience. Though it did seem dangerous."

Grabbing Smith's safari jacket, Bolo hauled him from the cab. "Sorry, sir, but this is a No Parking zone. You must hurry and get to your room." Bolo pointed to the second-floor window.

More powerful than he looked, he picked up the lieutenant by the collar of his jacket and pushed him onto the hood of the cab. "Here, climb up." Smith tried to go through the motions, though he didn't understand why he was climbing on top of a car.

Bolo leaped onto the hood himself. "Here, sir, let me help you." He kneed Smith in the seat of his pants, boosting the young lieutenant onto the roof of the taxi. "There you go—a much better scenic view."

"But, what am I doing up here?" Smith said, turning around slowly with his hands on his hips. "I don't see any scenic view." In fact, all he could spot were the low outbuildings, the corrugated roof and the cramped alley.

On the step of a barricaded door in the rear of the alley, a scrawny dog perked up its ears and watched the performance.

"This is a cantina room, sir," Bolo said, as if that explained everything.

"Oh, good," Smith said. "Thanks for taking care of that for me. But where's the entrance?"

"That window. The assistant manager is a friend of mine, and he has guaranteed your room. But the head manager is very mean and will demand cash in advance. So the assistant manager insisted that you must slip in the back way."

"Very unorthodox," Smith said.

"This happens all the time. I assure you it'll all work out in the end."

Smith looked up at the window on the second floor, then looked at his empty hands. "Where's my suitcase? Well, it's not really *my* suitcase, but it's the only one I've got. I need to find its rightful owner."

Bolo bounced to the ground in exasperation. "I'll get it from the cab and throw it up to you. You just go inside your room."

Smith stood on tiptoe on the cab roof, and stretched his arms, but the bottom of the windowsill was still several feet above him.

From below, Bolo tossed the tan suitcase up. The case struck Smith off-balance and knocked him backward from the roof of the cab. Smith windmilled his arms, to no avail. He landed on his back, and the suitcase dropped on top of him. The latches sprung, spilling clothes in the alley. Now the scrawny dog began yapping.

Sprawled on the cobblestones between the taxi and the rough wall of the cantina, Smith tried to get up. Covering his impatience, Bolo helped him stuff the scattered clothing back into the case, brushing off dust and street grime. Bolo clicked the suitcase shut, then boosted Smith and the case back onto the roof of the cab.

"Now let us do it once more, sir. The first time was just for practice."

Smith tried again to stretch for the balcony window, but couldn't. He walked very softly, trying not to dent the metal on the cab's roof. "Hey, even if I could reach the window, I can't get inside. The window's closed."

"Throw the suitcase through it," Bolo said matter-of-factly. "Then you can get inside."

"But that'll damage private property."

"It's okay. Remember, I know the assistant manager. Besides, Americans are always up to such antics here in Colodor. It is expected. We forgive your eccentricities."

With a shrug, Smith gripped the handle and swung the suitcase up. The tan case that had somehow gotten switched for his own sailed up and hit the lower pane, shattering the glass and going on through.

"I hope nobody was sleeping under the curtains."

Broken fragments of the window tinkled around him on top of the cab and to the cobblestones. Smith brushed glass shards off himself.

"Now just go inside and wait," Bolo called from below. "You'll be safe, and you can get a good night's sleep."

"After what happened yesterday, I could use a good night's sleep," Smith said, looking up in dismay. "But I still can't reach it."

"Then jump!"

Smith sprang as high as he could go, missed with his fingers and crashed back to the roof of the cab, leaving enormous dents. "Uh-oh," Smith said, looking at the dents.

The model of forced patience, Bolo rolled his eyes, then climbed up to help the young lieutenant.

"Are you sure this is the only way in?" Smith asked, shaking his head. "Isn't there a back entrance? You must have fire doors, in case of emergencies."

"Colodor is a very relaxed place. We do not worry about emergencies." Bolo tried to get Smith to stand on his shoulders. Like inebriated acrobats, they managed to keep their balance for just a few minutes, Smith tottering on the cabdriver's shoulders.

Although he couldn't help but be wobbly, Bolo boosted Smith toward the window. Smith finally managed to grab hold of the lower window ledge with his outstretched fingers.

"Got it?" Bolo said.

"I got it," Smith said. "This certainly isn't very easy."

"The good things in life seldom come easily, sir. That's part of the adventure."

Bolo moved out from under him, peeling Smith's gangly legs from his shoulders. Smith swung forward to hug the white-washed wall, hanging by his fingers from the second-story window ledge.

Bolo dropped down beside the cab and climbed back into the driver's seat, gripping the wheel. He started the engine with a coughing roar.

"You'll be fine now," he called up to Smith, leaning out the driver's window. "Get inside before anybody finds you out here, sir. Part of the festivities for the national holiday involves target practice, so you don't want to be left hanging in a vulnerable position."

"But, I—uh . . ." Smith said, his voice strained, but the cab drove off beneath him, leaving him dangling. He stared after the taxi's red taillights as it departed.

Sweating, he looked down the long two-story drop to the hard ground. If he fell, he would never make his way up here again. He squinted back up at the window above and flinched. It was jagged with broken glass. His fingers gripped the outer edge of the sill.

With a sudden jerk he let go with his right hand. Then, hanging by one hand above the alley, Smith struggled to get out of his safari jacket. When he managed to tug his arm out of his right sleeve, he recaptured the ledge with his right hand, then let go with his left. "Okay, this seems to be a good plan," he muttered to himself. "Good plan."

Sweat dripped from his hair into his eyes, but he eventually managed to pull the jacket from that arm. Then, with a desperate effort, he threw the jacket up and over the sharp glass edges. "It sure would help if I just had a credit card."

His heart pounded as he boosted himself up and catapulted through the window, into the room. He crashed to the floor, safe at last. He kissed the floorboards.

Smith untangled himself and stood up, shaking. He brushed his shirt and pants off as he surveyed the room. Suddenly, he sneezed violently, encountering enough perfume to poison a skunk. He wondered who the previous guest was.

Around him, flickering candles lit the ornate cantina room. A brass double bed took up most of one wall beneath numerous knickknack shelves that displayed ornamental crockery and plates. The bedspread and curtains were scarlet trimmed with gold edges and small tassels. Feathered fans had been spread and fastened to the stucco wall. One shelf, higher than the top of the bed, held a huge beaten brass pitcher. On the ceiling directly above the bed hung a large bullfighting poster. Smith wondered at the decor. It was certainly a much nicer room than the previous hotel, and it had all of the old-world charm he'd expected to find in Colodor.

Smith opened the frame of the shattered window, then fanned in some fresh air to dilute the perfume. He self-consciously looked at all the broken glass on the floor. He picked up the largest shards and dropped them in the wastebasket. He hated to leave a mess.

When he had cleaned up some of the damage, Smith set his tan suitcase on a pink velvet footstool. He shook out the battered safari jacket and glanced around the room, searching for a closet in which to hang it. It was, after all, his only set of clothes.

Billowing drapes covered an alcove, and Smith swept the curtains back. He extended his hand for a hanger, but halted in mid-reach.

The closet was full of a woman's flamenco clothes and mantillas. The floor was an archipelago of fancy shoes with high heels, a hundred pairs. More perfume smell clung to everything. Smith picked up a red satin shoe, looked around the otherwise empty room.

Did somebody live here? Perhaps the taxi driver had showed him the wrong room. Or maybe the last tenant had accidentally left her clothes. Smith shrugged and put the shoe back. On the inner wall of the closet hung a braided bullwhip.

Well, he could talk it over with the manager, he supposed. Eventually.

For now, though, he needed just a few minutes of rest. He pulled the paperback of *Famous Naval Battles* from his pocket, then threw the jacket across the pink stool.

Aching and weary, he collapsed on the bed, his back against the brass headboard. Smith put his feet on the scarlet spread, and with a luxurious sigh began to read about the exploits of Admiral Nelson.

"Ah," he said, "This is more like the vacation I was hoping for."

Chapter 10

BOLO DECIDED IT WAS TIME for a quick change and slight alteration of his appearance. He tossed aside his taxi-driver's cap and pulled on a leather aviator's jacket, becoming a different person entirely. Bolo walked up to the front entrance of the Cantina de Espejos in broad daylight. He was expected here, in this alter ego.

Standing under the painted *Bienvenidos* welcome sign, he looked up and down the morning street with exaggerated caution, like a juvenile delinquent about to launch into an elaborate prank. Then he squared his shoulders and walked through the front door. His dark hair hung loose and flowing.

Inside, the side walls of the main room were covered with mirrors that jutted out in Vs, multiplying every image, no doubt to increase drunken confusion. At night, when the disco lights flashed, the scene became dazzling and dizzying; the manager's thinking, apparently, was that many patrons, unable to find their way outside, would simply stay behind and order another drink.

The cantina had few customers this early in the morning—few conscious ones, anyway—and no bartender. One groggy man at a tilted table snapped fully awake for a moment and threw his long knife to impale a black scorpion on the back wall. Then he slumped back across the table, snoring again.

At the rear of the cantina, a curving metal staircase wound up to a second-floor balcony, where a single door marked the room Smith had stumbled into. At the moment, Bolo heard no sound from upstairs, so he assumed the redheaded lieutenant had gone to sleep, as he had expected. Still, he had no time to lose.

Bolo headed toward a curving, knife-scarred bar next to a raised stage; fishnets and chicken wire offered meager protection for the musical act. Under a single white spotlight, the band members fumbled through their morning rehearsal with trumpets, horns, drums and guitars. They wore shabby rhinestone-studded clothes that might have looked fine if the bar's interior lighting remained dim enough and the customers remained drunk enough. The musicians were out of tune and out of enthusiasm.

A fiery-eyed, dark-haired beauty paced around the stage like a crouching lioness. She was barelegged, her black tight pants cut off high on the thigh above black boots. A broad black belt with a huge silver buckle held a bolero jacket together just barely enough to cover her breasts. She rapped a baton wickedly against the palm of her hand with a painful slapping sound as she glared at the band members.

They played a few more bars, hitting a bad discord. Her temper snapped, and she stamped her foot in rage. "No, no, no! One more wrong note out of you and I'll have your stinking heads!" she fumed. "Or some other body part."

The musicians flinched in shock. "*Por favor,* Yaquita!" the trumpet player said. "We are trying our best—but we learned to play *disco,* not this kind of music!"

"*Disco!* You ungrateful dogs—I cannot sing disco!" Yaquita shrieked. "Have you no sense of tradition?"

Bolo stood patiently in the shadows just inside the bar, waiting for Yaquita's typical outburst to fade. He had expected nothing else from her, and it was good for his plan that her temper was already stoked for the day.

"I want a sad love song, you swine!" Yaquita snapped at the band. "A passionate ballad of a beautiful young woman with a great future, betrayed by the redheaded man to whom she gave her heart. All she wanted in her whole life was to get married, and now she is brokenhearted." Her face grew stormy. "We'll now practice my first number. Don't you *dare* hit any wrong notes. One, two, three, four!"

Yaquita turned around and closed her eyes. Bolo winced in coiled anticipation as the band began the intro, which was so dolorous it became a parody of the too-too sad, too-too tragic Spanish love ballads he had heard many times during his long task of infiltrating the South American operation of Colonel Enrique and Colonel Ivan.

On stage, Yaquita began to assume the pathos of the song, her gestures utterly extravagant. Her ebony hair whipped about like lashes.

I'll cut my throat for love of you,
I'll stab my heart if your love's not true.
I'll strangle—

Coming into the lighted area near the stage, Bolo tried to snag her attention. Yaquita broke off and glared down at him. "What the hell do you want, Bolo?"

His face remained bland, unemotional. "An agent has arrived." He pointed at the balcony room. "Sent by the two colonels."

Yaquita nodded to Bolo, then turned to snap at the band. "That's all for me this morning. But you keep practicing so that you aren't such a miserable disappointment to my singing voice!"

Moving like a cat, Yaquita stalked offstage. She trotted up the curving steps and entered the single upstairs room without knocking. Business was business.

◆◆◆

Still in the khaki safari outfit he had taken from the tan suitcase, Smith lay back on the bed, once again marveling at Nelson's victory at Trafalgar, the greatest naval battle in history. It was a peaceful moment, resting and reading, just the sort of vacation he liked.

He looked up as the door opened, startled. A beautiful woman slipped inside and closed the door, her back to him so that he could see only her shapely waist and bottom, her long black hair. He raised a finger, embarrassed, just about to excuse himself, when she turned.

The moment she saw Smith, her dark eyes flared with shock. She went rigid for a moment, then exploded in fury. "Ai! Pedrito!" she spat, full of venomous rage. She extended her fingers with long red nails like claws to gouge his eyes out.

Though he didn't understand her sudden anger, Smith recognized danger when he saw it. His eyes flew wide, and he held up his hands. "But I'm not Pedrito," he said hastily. That was the same name the portly man at the airport lounge had called him. "You've made a mistake."

As Smith scrambled off the bed, rolling in the opposite direction and thumping on the floor, Yaquita grew more furious. "*Dog!* Oh, how you lie!" She grabbed a small souvenir plate from the nearest knickknack shelf. "You always lie, Pedrito! Snake!"

"Uh, please don't—" Smith said.

She hurled the plate at him with the skill of a circus knife thrower. He ducked as the object shattered against the brass bedstead. Stinging shrapnel struck his cheek. She grabbed a jug from the shelf and threw it as well.

"Ape! You said you were going to marry me, just like in a storybook!" She threw another ornamental plate. "And all you do is run around with other women!" She threw a cluster of castanets that flew at him like chattery teeth. "Armadillo! Llama dung! Wart-hog spittle!"

Smith hunched low, slinking away from the bed, his arms up to defend himself. This vacation was getting worse and worse. "Wait, wait—can't we talk about this? Can I buy you a drink or something?"

"Drink? Goat—all you ever do is drink!" Yaquita said. Her lips curled away from fine white teeth. A brightly painted porcelain bell shattered on the wall beside Smith. He could see no place to run.

Yaquita grabbed a china doll off the shelf. "Pig! Aardvark! You borrow money you don't pay back! Cockroach!" Smith ducked as she hurled the doll; broken ceramic arms and legs and little black shoes showered around him.

"Hamster!" Yaquita said. "Sewer rat! You gamble everything away!"

She yanked down a cluster of gourds and they rattled as they sailed through the air. Smith couldn't squeeze a single word into the conversation. He didn't drink, didn't gamble . . . she certainly had him confused with someone else.

"Jackass! Wildebeest! I wouldn't take care of you if you were the last man on the earth!" She grabbed up a big vase. "Or even on the moon!"

Smith backed up to the wall, just under the shelf that held the beaten brass pitcher. Yaquita hurled the vase.

"Monster! Jellyfish! Verminous worm!"

The vase shattered against the brass pitcher, knocking it sideways. Smith just had time to look up and see the brass object falling, then it struck him hard on the head. The befuddled lieutenant slid down the debris-spattered wall. His head lolled sideways.

Yaquita truculently advanced two steps to glare down at him, hands on her rounded hips. She marched into the bathroom, grabbed the wicked-looking straight razor and came back, holding it out as she contemplated his crotch, weighing her options. Finally, she snorted at Smith's prone form. *"Humph!"*

Satisfied that he would be unconscious for some time, Yaquita grabbed a trench coat from the closet, *her* closet. How dare he sneak into her room, sleep on her bed! She would have plenty of time to deal with him later.

"Somebody in authority is going to hear about *this!*" And she decided to go straight to the top.

Chapter 11

BOLO WAS NOWHERE IN SIGHT when Yaquita burst downstairs into the cantina. She paused only a moment to preen in front of the numerous mirrors on the wall while the practicing musicians hid from her, then she raced into the alley. Her eyes blazed, her coppery skin flushed with simmering anger. Even the feral chickens squawked and scuttled out of her way, ducking to safety under rusty gutters.

By one of the outbuildings with the corrugated metal roofs, Yaquita tore away a stained tarpaulin to reveal a beat-up black Volkswagen beetle. She tossed the tarp into the gutter, adding more stains, then leaped into the car. Even before she managed to swing the door shut, she twisted the key as if wringing the neck of one of the chickens.

Yaquita sped away at a suicidal pace. Leaving Santa Isabel behind, the VW scrambled up a steep Andes mountain road, careening over potholes, grinding gears and belching blue-white exhaust. She did not look over the crumbling edge to where a graveyard of crashed vehicles lay far below, glinting in the sun.

The black VW hurtled toward a shallow stream in a gorge. Gritting her teeth and clenching the steering wheel, Yaquita plunged the puttering car into the water. She managed to roll up her window an instant before a fury of spray and mud made a rooster tail on either side of her car, but she drove straight across. No mountain and no river was going to slow *her* down, not today. If Pedrito was back, and if Colonel Enrique and Colonel Ivan expected her to cooperate with their schemes, she would give them a piece of her mind . . . or preferably a piece of her fists. She could always make it back in time to castrate Pedrito, if she still felt like it.

Finally reaching a grassy plateau, Yaquita saw several military vehicles hidden under nets and pyramidal tents painted in camouflage colors. Brightly dressed Indian farmers tended their sheep and cows, completely oblivious to the military presence.

The mud-covered Volkswagen streaked up and braked in a cloud of dust thirty feet from the central headquarters tent. Guerrilla soldiers took one look at Yaquita's eyes, then rushed from her path. She marched toward the open tent flap with murder in her eyes.

Inside the main structure two cluttered cots sat against the near canvas wall, stacked with odds and ends of military equipment. Across from the entrance flap a field desk supported a crude radio setup.

The Russian and Cuban colonels reclined on frayed camp chairs, their backs foolishly turned toward the tent opening. Ivan puffed on a huge, fragrant Cuban cigar. Casually, he tilted the bottle of vodka in his hand to pour into a pair of glasses on a tray between them.

"What a day," Colonel Ivan said, exhaling a long curl of thick cigar smoke. "What a glorious day!"

Enrique slouched in his chair, decidedly drunk. "Tell me what you said before, Ivan," the Cuban said, his eyes fixed on the vodka bottle, as if he wanted another drink but was too tired to pick it up. "You know, about the revolution . . . and the rabbits."

"You want to hear it again?" Ivan asked. "But I've told you, so many times before."

"Again," Enrique demanded. "And don't forget the rabbits."

"Ah, you tell it," Ivan said. "You've heard it so often, you know how it goes."

"No, I want to hear it from you, Ivan," Enrique begged.

Ivan took a puff from his cigar, and after a long, satisfied sigh, he said, "Men like you and me, Enrique, we are not like other men."

"That's how it goes," Enrique said. "Don't forget the rabbits. . . ."

Ivan grinned patiently. "Of course I won't forget, Comrade. . . ." Ivan said. "You see, other men are lonely creatures, men who toil from day to day, seeking lowly creature comforts, ground beneath the thumbs of tyrants and capitalist oppressors. But we aren't like that, are we?"

"No," Enrique said. "We aren't like that . . ."

"Because?" Ivan prodded.

"Because we have each other!" Enrique shouted triumphantly.

"That's right, we have each other. We are *comrades*, yes?"

"Yes," Enrique said.

"That means I take care of you, and you take care of me. And while other men toil for worldly gain, struggling just to keep their heads above the ever-rising deluge of greed and degradation that their taskmasters heap upon them, you and I do not do that, eh, Comrade. We do not do that. Instead of toiling for money, we toil for what?"

"For the revolution!" Enrique shouted triumphantly.

"That's right, for the revolution. We toil for revolution." They lifted their glasses for a toast. Ivan tossed the vodka into his mouth, sloshing it around his cheeks.

"Don't forget the part about the rabbits!" Enrique said and gulped his own vodka.

Yaquita appeared in the tent door, smoldering and speechless. "You droppings of a syphilitic vulture!" she shouted with venom. "How dare you do this to me?"

The colonels sprayed out their vodka, then both fell out of their camp chairs.

Yaquita advanced two steps into the tent, pausing beside the cots loaded with surplus equipment. "You did not say *Pedrito* was the agent I was supposed to meet!" She seized upon the nearest throwing-size object, a leather case that contained a pair of field glasses.

The colonels wheeled away from their fallen chairs; Ivan dropped the bottle of vodka. The field-glass case swooshed between them and struck the billowing tent wall even as they ducked.

Next Yaquita threw a military compass. "You hoodwinked me!"

The Russian ducked the compass and turned to the Cuban. "Why does she always *throw* things, Comrade?"

A metal first-aid box hit Enrique in the chest just below his billowing beard and knocked him back down. "*Ouch!* I've tried to get her to put down her feelings in a letter, express herself in prose. I think it would be safer for all of us—but she won't listen!"

"You betrayed me," Yaquita said, "both of you! You know how I despise Pedrito!"

A canteen hit Ivan in the head and knocked him down as well.

"You tried to con me!" She swung a glittering ammunition belt around her head like a heavy sling, then she let it fly.

Enrique's reedy Cuban aide scuttled up behind her with a drawn pistol. He ducked beneath the swinging bandolier and jammed the pistol into her back.

Yaquita dodged sideways like a cobra on a hot rock just as she threw the belt. She grabbed the reedy man's wrist and hurled him across the tent at the colonels, just another object to throw. He struck the center pole, which buckled under his weight. The entire headquarters tent collapsed, dumping folds of canvas on all the occupants.

Outside, as bored guerrillas stood around, lumpy forms moved about under the collapsed canvas, searching for a way out.

"Yaquita! Be sensible!" Colonel Enrique said, muffled under the tent.

"Da! The pay is good," Colonel Ivan said.

"Yaquita," Enrique said, "you do not realize how important this is."

"Your mission will deliver all of South America into our hands!" Ivan said. "And when South America rises up—the whole world will follow! We must be successful. You are not cleared for all the details, of course, but believe me—Pedrito Miraflores is the only man who can accomplish this."

Yaquita lifted the corner of the tent and emerged unruffled, like a princess. She paced back and forth, her face stormy but contemplative. The guerrillas took one look at her and immediately found other important duties.

"Yaquita," Enrique wailed from under the canvas, "think of the *cause!* Remember . . . remember the part about the rabbits!"

She stopped in her tracks as a hurricane of emotions passed across her face. Finally she tossed her flowing black hair over her shoulder, set her jaw, then raised her fist in a stern revolutionary salute. "All right, then. Long live the revolution!" She muttered under her breath, "Even if it means I have to kiss and make up with Pedrito for now! But I warn you: when the revolution comes, he will be *first* against the wall!"

As the two colonels clawed free of the collapsed tent, Yaquita strode back to the battered black beetle, still dissatisfied, but resigned to do what was necessary.

The Volkswagen tore back through the rocky stream, where splashed water washed off the first coating of mud. She streaked back down the steep mountain road, whipping around hairpin curves and dodging packed buses. Yaquita managed to keep the majority of wheels on the road at any one time.

She drove so well that her tire tracks lined up with her previous marks on the dirt road, but all the time she was preoccupied with extravagant visions of everything she would do to Pedrito when all this was over.

She had quite a vivid imagination.

Chapter 12

THOUGH AN HOUR HAD PASSED, the Cantina de Espejos was still without customers, and the band still hadn't managed to get in tune.

The haphazard musicians saw Yaquita reenter and began to play with terrified enthusiasm. They didn't sound any better after all their practicing, but Yaquita ignored them as she marched past the mirrors and up the curving stairs. She strode through the balcony door into the bedroom.

Smith lay where he had fallen unconscious on the floor, in exactly the same position. Yaquita closed the door, locked it and stared with lip-curled disdain at him.

"Pedrito!" She spat in his direction, but decided not to throw anything else, for now. She glared for another moment, filled with repugnance which turned to resignation. She was a passionate woman, but she wondered how she could ever have been passionate with Pedrito. Still, those had been some fun times. . . .

She shucked off her trench coat, then tossed it into the closet alcove on top of her hundred pairs of shoes.

"I do my duty for the revolution," she sighed, "even if it is with *him*."

◆◆◆

Working with brisk movements, all business, Yaquita set an enamel coffeepot on the small bedside table. Her own special brew, the coffee steamed a pungent aroma that should have been enough to wake a man from the deepest coma. She splashed a big white china cup halfway full of the inky black liquid and added hot foamy milk from another pitcher.

Smith still sprawled on the floor, snoring. A swollen egg on his forehead marked where the brass pitcher had smashed him. Yaquita knelt beside him, adjusting her boots and tight black pants, then tilted the cup to dribble some of the potent coffee into his mouth. Groaning, Smith swallowed—but even the coffee didn't wake him up.

Yaquita looked at the red-haired man intently and shook her head. All right, she would have to try more desperate measures. She stood, straightening her pants, then looked with narrowed eyes around her room. Luckily, she had many contingency plans.

Reaching under her pillow behind the enamel coffeepot, Yaquita drew forth a fifth of black rum, glanced at the label and pulled the cork out of the bottle with her teeth. She poured half of the contents into the coffeepot and sloshed it around.

"Try this, Pedrito. I guarantee it'll have some effect."

Yaquita took Smith by a handful of his hair and tipped his head back. His mouth fell open in a faint moan, and she mercilessly dumped the hot, rum-drenched coffee down his throat.

That worked.

Smith surged forward, his eyes bugged wide open. He gasped, trying to get his breath, coughing coffee. He grabbed at his head with both hands, pressing against the big lump.

"I'm glad you like it." With a satisfied smile, Yaquita poured the rest of the rum into the pot and stirred it with the bottle neck. She filled the cup again. "Have some more."

Still trying to shake off the disorientation, Smith staggered around the room, holding his pounding head. "This is the second time in two days I've woken up on the floor of a hotel room. Who are you, anyway, and why did you attack me?"

Forcing a smile, Yaquita gave him a push. He stumbled backward onto the bed and sat down heavily.

Yaquita thrust the refilled coffee cup into his hands. He drank it down reflexively. Bleary-eyed, Smith lowered the cup and peered into it. "Hey, that's good coffee," he said. "Mellowed with chicory?"

"It is a local blend grown in the Andes," Yaquita answered, taking the empty cup and handing him a new one. He drank it down.

Now even more disoriented because of the effects of the rum, Smith reeled as he sat on the bed. "Funny, coffee usually wakes me up. But now I just feel . . . strange."

Yaquita sniffed at the comment. "Pedrito, you act as if you've never been drunk before."

He blinked at her innocently, working his lips until the slurred words finally came out. "Drunk? Drunk?" He closed his eyes, but the room still spun. "This is embarrassing. I don't drink."

Yaquita leaned against the side of the wardrobe with her arms folded. She looked at him in a deadly way, then steeled herself and made up her mind. "For the revolution . . . and for old times' sake." She ran her fingers along the edges of the black bolero jacket that barely covered her breasts.

"Pedrito, the only thing you were ever good for was bed," she said loud enough for him to hear. She slid off the skimpy jacket. In keeping with her habit of throwing things, Yaquita even hurled her clothes across the room, one item at a time. "So get in bed."

Smith stared at her aghast as she pushed him backward onto the mattress. "But, miss, I'm not—" Then he forgot the rest of his sentence. He couldn't control his blinking eyes, nor could he focus on the multiple images of the devastatingly lovely naked woman who climbed onto the bedspread with him. . . .

◆◆◆

Yaquita's clothes and boots lay strewn across the floor. So did Smith's khaki safari clothes, shoes and skivvies. The headboard of the brass bed shook, then went still. It shook again. And went still again.

Yaquita sat up, raising her head and bare breasts, glistening with perspiration. She gripped the brass headboard with a wide-eyed expression on her face. "Ai! This isn't the same Pedrito

I remember!" Her long black hair was mussed and her lipstick was smeared.

Beneath her, Smith still tried to say something, but Yaquita wouldn't let him get a word out. "Oh! Ai, Pedrito!"

The headboard began to shake once more, briskly enough that another few knickknacks fell from shelves to floor. Neither Smith nor Yaquita paid any attention.

Chapter 13

MEANWHILE, BACK IN NEW YORK CITY, an endless string of yellow taxis honked at each other in a bizarre cab-driver's Morse code. Old Admiral Turner sat at his desk, writing out a check. He scratched his bristly gray hair as he tried to add numbers in his head.

As a full admiral and director of the New York Office of Naval Intelligence, he could have commanded any underling do the work for him. In matters of his own heart, though, his brash daughter, Joan, outranked him, and the admiral had no choice but to follow her orders.

Joan sat across from her father, wearing an unbuttoned street coat and a stylish hat into which she had neatly tucked her strawberry-blond hair. Her loveliness was like a statue's, serene and stony. She crossed her legs in her tight lavender wool skirt, showing off plenty of calf, knee and even a bit of thigh. She rested a sequin-studded purse in her lap.

At times, the old admiral had trouble remembering that his little girl, Joan, was now in her mid-twenties and her own woman. Most definitely her own woman.

"Five hundred bucks will be fine for this afternoon, Daddy," she said indifferently, gazing past his checkbook to the window behind him, where pigeons flew about. "Or more. Whatever you feel is best."

An intent expression creased his weather-beaten face, and the admiral scribbled a larger number in the amount line.

After a brisk knock, the office door swung all the way open. A redheaded lieutenant, junior grade, marched into the office, his white cap tucked under his left arm. The redhead caught himself beginning to swagger, then wiped a confident grin off his face in an attempt to look meek. He had to work hard not to ogle the strawberry blonde at the admiral's desk.

"Lieutenant, uh, Smith reporting for duty, sir," he said, pronouncing his words carefully to squelch any lingering trace of a Spanish accent.

Joan wrinkled her nose in distaste at the young lieutenant, giving him the brushoff with her blue eyes. She uncrossed her legs and straightened her lavender skirt to hide as much knee as she could.

Pedrito Miraflores walked briskly up to the desk with military precision, stopped with a click of heels and gave a snappy salute. He stared straight ahead, awaiting Admiral Turner's pleasure. With a sinking feeling Pedrito realized he had already slipped up, since members of the U.S. Navy did not salute when not wearing a formal cap, and most especially did not salute under a roof.

But the admiral didn't notice. He leaned back, giving Pedrito a friendly smile. "Oh, Tom, relax! I'm glad to see you back from your trip already, boy." He tore the check from his pad and tucked the checkbook into the pocket of his uniform. "Did you have a wild time on your vacation down in Colodor? How goes their mapmakers' strike?"

Pedrito smiled his most charming smile. "It's been quiet down there lately. Santa Isabel is a fine city, though I'm sad to say that the mapmakers have still not been able to hurl off their foul oppressors' yoke." His eyes twinkled as he tried to work his charms on Joan. "The lovely lady might enjoy a vacation there sometime. I would be happy to show her around."

Joan raised her eyes to the ceiling with a clearly exasperated sigh. She knew Lieutenant Tom Smith and didn't think much of him.

Pedrito sensed her mystifying disdain—women weren't supposed to treat him like this—and shifted his attention back to the old man. "To answer your question, Admiral, I got plenty of rest and relaxation. I even finished reading my book of naval battles."

"Sorry to hear it," the admiral said with a frown, "but still there's hope for you, Smith." He made a point of glancing at his watch and pretending to be surprised. "Well, well, look at the time. Eleven o'clock." He handed the seven-hundred-dollar check to Joan, and she tucked it into her sequined purse. "Tom, why don't you take my daughter, Joan, here out to lunch and recover from your trip?"

Joan winced visibly at the suggestion. "Oh, Daddy!"

Pedrito smiled like a wolf at the admiral's gorgeous daughter. "It would be my pleasure, sir!" he said, sensing the challenge. But she refused to look at him. She stalked toward the door, displeased, her high heels clicking on the floor. He promptly about-faced and followed Joan out, reaching for her arm to escort her. "How about it, Joan? Admiral's orders."

Joan jerked her arm away and turned on him with scathing contempt. "Go piss up a tree. I wouldn't marry you if you were the last man on earth!"

"I thought we were talking about *lunch*, not marriage—"

"One thing leads to the other, you oaf. Now go away. I've got higher standards than a loser like you."

Her vehemence surprised Pedrito, but he was used to dealing with opposition. "Why, what's the matter with *me*? I'm, uh, a clean-cut, nice young man."

"What's the matter with *you*?" Joan repeated with a snort. "Does the word *boring* mean anything to you? How about *dull*? How about, I'd rather listen to radio coverage of an amateur golf tournament? I'll bet you've never told a lie in your life!"

Pedrito stared, surprised, unable even to respond to such a preposterous accusation.

"You don't even gamble at bridge!" Joan continued. "Some party animal—you wouldn't have the slightest idea how to show a girl a good time."

Pedrito grew even more surprised, but he tried to remember to maintain his act. He didn't even know how to play bridge. "But I—"

Joan flicked her hand at him as though to brush away a fly. "And to top it all off, you won't touch liquor either. What the hell do you think you are, you strait-laced jerk? A saint? I have no interest in marrying a saint."

Pedrito flushed as he tried to contain his anger. This Tom Smith character sounded like a real prize. "But who said anything about marrying—"

Joan gave a snort of contempt and stalked off. Pedrito thought better of following, so instead he stared after her tight lavender skirt as she strutted down the hall in high heels, showing off her lean and muscular legs.

"A saint?" he muttered to himself, incredulous. "Nobody's ever called me that before." He scratched his head. "*Caramba!* The things they don't tell you in a pre-mission briefing!"

Chapter 14

THE STREET LIGHT in front of the cantina flickered, then burned out as night fell. Finally, customers began to arrive from the grocery markets, from the fields, from their fried banana kiosks and souvenir stands. Outside, an old woman had set up a roast pig over a barbecue drum. She used an acetylene blow-torch to scorch off the pig's bristles.

Inside the cantina, rowdy patrons filled the tables, seemingly lost in the mirror maze of the walls. On stage, protected behind the chicken-wire barricade, the band played out of tune, to no one's surprise.

The drunken knife-throwing man still sat at his small round table, somewhat conscious now. During the afternoon he had finished skewering all the black scorpions in the place and had eliminated most of the cockroaches as well. Now he held his knife in one hand, impatiently looking for a new target. He eyed the band members, considering.

"Where's Yaquita?" the knife man demanded, then skewered an ant on the tabletop with the tip of his blade. The other customers glared at the stage and echoed the question. The band kept playing, somewhat skittish.

The fat manager waddled out from behind the bar and climbed onto the stage, working his way through the protective fishnets and chicken wire. He mopped sweat off his brow and held out his hands, sputtering excuses and trying to quiet the audience.

The crowd started throwing margarita glasses and brown *cerveza* bottles at the band. Patrons banged their glasses and rum bottles on the tables in rhythm to their chant. "We want Yaquita! We want Yaquita!" The angled mirrors on the walls multiplied their images infinitely.

The manager gave up and raced away from the stage. Puffing for breath, he headed across the floor as bottles and glasses smashed against the mirrored walls, following him in his flight. A large knife thunked into the narrow gap between mirrors, quivering near the manager's ear. He gawked at the deadly blade, then scuttled along faster, rushing for the stairs.

The music stopped as the band members surrendered. The chant continued.

Red-faced from climbing up to the balcony room, the manager stopped outside Yaquita's door. He wrung his hands, glanced down at the crowd below, as if weighing the two types of danger. Someone hurled a beer bottle that arced up, then crashed down at his feet.

The manager timidly opened the door, swallowing hard. "Yaquita? Please, señorita?" The room was dark inside. "Yaquita?"

"Out! We're busy in here. Out!" The brass headboard rattled against the wall again.

A huge white *olla* flew out of the dark, and sailed past the balcony rail to drop down into the crowded cantina. The wide pot bombed the knife thrower's table in an explosion of fragments and water. The knife thrower stood up, blinking and confused, then went to retrieve his knife from where it still quivered in the wall.

"Sí, Yaquita." Obsequiously, the manager shut her door, backing away before she could throw anything else at him. "Whenever you are ready, señorita."

From the balcony rail he looked down at the crowd and spread his hands in resignation. "There is nothing I can do, my friends," he said. "She is . . . Yaquita."

The crowd, still seated, spread their hands just as expressively in resignation, all in unison. They were also familiar with Yaquita's unpredictable behavior.

"Perhaps if you would just listen to the band?" the manager suggested.

But when the musicians started playing again, striking up a disco tune this time, they were forced to flee the stage under a storm of smashed bottles.

Chapter 15

YAQUITA NEVER MANAGED to sing that evening for anyone but Smith.

The next morning, sunlight streamed through the window Smith had smashed with his suitcase the day before. The gold-tasseled curtains hung open, ruffled by a breeze. The big brass bed had been knocked askew; the rumpled scarlet bedspread looked as if a herd of llamas had stampeded across it.

Smith lay on the mattress, dead to the world, or at least wishing he was. One arm dangled off the bed to the pile of his discarded safari outfit. The buttons were loose, threads frayed from when Yaquita had torn off his clothes.

The aftereffects of the rum made his head pound, and Yaquita had ridden him hard. Smith cradled his head in his hands; he had already learned not to sit up. "Oh, my skull!"

Yaquita stood on the other side of the bed wearing only a thin cotton robe untied in front. She wrung her hands with worry. "I've never seen you like this, Pedrito! I'll get a doctor. Maybe you have the Black Death, or the Scarlet Fever, or the Green Gout!" She grabbed her trench coat and rushed from the room.

To the barely conscious Smith, the door slam sounded like cannon fire on one of Admiral Nelson's ships during the Trafalgar battle.

♦♦♦

The wild chickens outside crowed every hour on the hour, like feathered alarm clocks.

A Santa Isabel doctor with a gray suit and a white goatee examined Smith's head, measuring it, pressing against it. Throughout the examination, the doctor thrust out his lower lip and muttered incomprehensible sounds. Yaquita paced back and forth like a caged lioness, concerned for Smith's health.

The young lieutenant's eyes were bleary. The doctor pried up the lids with his thumb and shone a light into the pupils. He picked up his bag and beckoned for Yaquita to follow him for a grim consultation. They went out onto the balcony, where they could talk in private above the empty cantina. Down below, the knife-throwing man snored across his usual table, his image reflected in the numerous mirrors.

The doctor shook his head solemnly. "I examined him very thoroughly, señorita. There's not the slightest sign of concussion."

Yaquita sagged with relief. "Good! I didn't hurt him by throwing all those things, or by . . . by working him too hard last night. Any signs of the plague?"

. "No symptoms of fever or brain swelling. I performed a complete phrenology exam, and all the lumps on his head are completely normal," the doctor continued. "He does seem to have a hangover, however."

"A hangover!" Yaquita said. "That's all?"

"I'm amazed that the infamous Pedrito Miraflores is not familiar with the symptoms of too much drink—but he's perfectly all right. He could get up right now, if his head could take it."

Yaquita smiled, exuberant with relief. Bag in hand, the doctor clomped down the curving staircase. Upon reaching the cantina floor, he wove his way around the toppled tables, kicking discarded beer and rum bottles. Out of professional courtesy, the doctor inspected the few unconscious patrons sprawled on chairs or on the floor, verified that they all still breathed, then departed through the front door.

Yaquita returned to her room where Smith still lay groaning on the bed. She touched his head tenderly, brushing his red hair aside. Something was very different about this man, but she couldn't quite figure it out. Then her face grew sad, much in contrast to the expression of relief she had shown the doctor. This was definitely not the Pedrito she knew—perhaps he had amnesia, or brain damage of some kind.

If so, then she had plans of her own. . . .

Blinking with the pain of his splitting headache, Smith looked up at Yaquita in alarm. He raised an arm to fend off any other objects she might throw at him. But she kissed his hand instead.

"Oh, you poor boy," Yaquita said with sympathy. "The doctor says you are very, very ill. *Shhh!* You must not get up or go out, even for a minute. Just stay here with me, dear."

With her back turned, Yaquita dribbled another fifth of dark rum into the enamel coffeepot. "He did say, however, that you ought to drink more of my special coffee. Plenty more."

Yaquita sat on the side of the bed with the steaming cup. She lifted his head gently and put the cup to his lips. "There you go, take a big sip." He gulped trustingly. She took the cup away, setting it on the bedside table, then bent over him. A breast escaped from her flimsy robe. She leaned closer to kiss him.

"In fact," she said as she lifted one of Smith's arms to wrap it around her neck, "the doctor told me to use whatever means possible to *keep you in bed*." She ran her hands over his chest and kissed him again, until Smith groggily responded.

She fell onto the sheets beside him. "And I intend to follow doctor's orders."

Chapter 16

ON THE SECOND FLOOR of the Cantina de Espejos, the late morning air carried the smell of hot cooking oil, bananas and boiled Inca corn from the doorsteps below. Roosters crowed and dogs barked.

Smith stood in the open bathroom dressed only in his skivvies. He rinsed the dangerous straight-edged razor in the sink, then inspected his shaving job in the chipped mirror. Better than yesterday, at least; he'd kept the injuries to a minimum. Satisfied, he patted his face with a damp towel.

The jackhammer pounding in his head was better as well, especially now that Yaquita had stopped throwing things at him. She had dressed in a bright red skirt and frilly white blouse with intricate embroidery, then left him early in the morning. She had promised to bring him fresh roses from the flower market as soon as it opened. He tried to tell her he was allergic to pollen, but she just laughed and trotted out the door with a swirl of her skirt and a flash of her bronze calves.

Refreshed for the first time in days, the redheaded lieutenant sang out loud as he went to the tan suitcase on the footstool. "'What you gonna do with a drunken sailor? What you gonna do with a drunken sailor?'"

Of course, his big question was what was *he* going to do, now that his vacation was ruined, his passport and luggage stolen, and the Marines at the American Embassy were shooting at him. . . . Stupid Marines . . . you could never trust them. He decided not to worry about that, at least not until he was dressed.

With one hand he fumbled to open the tan suitcase, but the damp towel slipped from his shoulder. He grabbed it, losing his grip on the suitcase so that it tumbled off the footstool, striking the floor.

Unperturbed, Smith lifted the case onto the footstool—but something odd happened. Its back opened, a crack widening from a false panel he had not noticed before. Curious, he bent to inspect the case, wondering if it had been damaged by the same baggage handlers who had mixed up his luggage with this stranger's. He hoped the case could be repaired without too much cost. Its actual owner would likely be upset.

He tried to get the back panel open further; his cheery sailing tune faltered, then stopped altogether as he became distracted with the problem. Smith flopped the suitcase one way, and the secret back compartment opened. He flopped it the other way, and the innocent front opened. "Something suspicious here."

He thought of all the stories he had heard about South American drug smugglers, and he grew suddenly concerned. What if the authorities mistakenly went after him? What if they confused Lieutenant Tom Smith with a bad man, with a . . . *lawbreaker!*

He removed the contents of the suitcase's hidden compartment one at a time, holding each up to the light and setting it aside on the bed.

A broad, wicked-looking commando knife.

A camouflaged, waterproof jungle suit.

Two alien-looking holstered weapons on a web belt.

He pulled out one of the pistols, curious. He had never seen such a sleek, high-tech weapon before, like something from a science fiction movie. Laser pistols? He had heard the Navy was developing firearms like those. In fact, he thought he might have signed off on the blueprints himself.

Next, Smith popped open a black case to reveal a suicide kit containing needles and poison capsules (marked as "grape flavored"). From the bottom of the secret compartment, he removed a fancy military digital wristwatch that sported more incomprehensible buttons than even his VCR at home. A military chronograph.

Smith peered at it, reading the maker's label. "Made in Russia? Uh-oh." He snapped his head up with the belated realization. These weren't the possessions of a drug smuggler—this was intelligence stuff! How could he possibly be mixed up with spies?

Then his eyes flared wide in greater astonishment as he saw the date displayed on the fancy watch. "Oh, my God, it's the *eleventh*." He looked up in horror. "I'm AWOL! They'll send the Marines after me!" All of Naval Intelligence would fall apart without him—who would stamp all their blueprints now that he was missing?

A loud knock on the door startled him. He whipped his head around, then he tossed the damp shaving towel over the scattered weapons and illegal espionage equipment on the bed. What if this was the Colodoran police?

An oddly familiar dark-haired man with exotic Turkish features walked in, dressed as a waiter. Bolo carried a tray that held a breakfast roll and a pot of strong coffee with hot milk. He gave no sign of recognition or friendliness on his calm, bland face. "Breakfast, sir? Compliments of the establishment."

Smith stared at Bolo, who looked very different from his previous guise as a scruffy taxi driver. "Hey, haven't I seen you someplace before?"

"Oh, no, sir," Bolo said. "I've never been here before."

Smith's thoughts were on other things, particularly being AWOL, and he didn't pursue the matter. He went to the broken window, as if pondering the best escape route.

Smith glanced again at the complex Russian military watch, double-checking the date. He winced, then turned to the waiter, worried. "Excuse me, but can you fetch me a telephone, quick? *Teléfono?* I've got to call the United States."

"Sí, señor." The waiter casually set the breakfast tray on top of the towel that covered the scattered weaponry on the bed, not noticing the lumps. He closed the door behind him as he left Smith to ponder what he was going to do next.

Chapter 17

THE MOMENT HE STEPPED onto the balcony, Bolo immediately clicked into motion, smooth and professional. He trotted down the staircase without so much as breaking into a sweat or wrinkling his formal waiter's uniform.

Down in the cantina the ill-experienced band had gathered on the stage for another morning of discordant practice. The music squawked like the wild chickens outside; the brass and drums and guitars sounded like a car accident. Luckily, Yaquita was not in sight to snarl at every mistake, nor were there any (conscious) customers to hear.

The chubby manager sat behind the bar doing accounts; both of his buttocks sagged off the sides of a small metal stool. The earplugs he had taken to wearing during the band's practice sessions worked wonders for his concentration. He bit his lip as he scribbled figures with a stubby pencil. When Yaquita refused to sing, his daily sales suffered significantly.

The musicians didn't pause as Bolo dodged overturned chairs on the cantina floor. He glided into the back room where the manager took his siestas, picked up the phone and dialed the memorized number. Time to see if Smith was ready to roll with more punches.

Bolo knew he could pull off this entire mission, if everyone cooperated. It all depended on timing. He waited for his duped contact to answer.

♦♦♦

At the CIA office in the U.S. Embassy, O'Halloran sat at his desk meticulously cleaning another Thompson submachine gun, his third of the morning. Cleaning automatic weapons always gave him a sense of calm.

He scratched the white gauze bandage taped diagonally across his forehead, near his right temple. He tried to cover the wound with the long strands of hair that failed to hide his bald spot.

The Marine sergeant who had messed things up the previous day paused in the hall, hiding from yet another upbraiding by the CIA man. He swallowed, uncertain whether to risk passing the open doorway where the chief might see him.

Then O'Halloran's phone rang. The chief dropped the machine gun, tossed aside his oil rag and picked up the phone. His head hurt, and he was even crankier than usual. "American Embassy, Passport Control Officer O'Halloran speaking. What the hell do *you* want?"

Seeing the chief distracted, the Marine sergeant tiptoed past the door to the kitchenette, where he snagged a bottle of pineapple soda, then dashed back to his duty station near the front entrance. Carpenters were busily replastering the bullet holes in the wall and fixing the damage caused by the explosion.

As he listened to the voice on the phone, O'Halloran's eyes sprang wide. *"Who?"* Then he went into a fury. "You saw him *where?"*

The CIA man scribbled frantically on a notepad, then leaped to his feet, howling for the Marine sergeant. "Fetch me another car—the armored assault cars this time, the ones with the big guns! And bring weapons, lots of weapons!" O'Halloran grabbed the submachine gun he had just cleaned, attempting to tuck it into his belt.

He yelled across the room at the radio operator who sat with heavy-lidded eyes at his equipment station, listening to *ABBA's Greatest Hits, Volume 7.* "You! Sound the alarm! We've located Pedrito again." O'Halloran stormed off down the hall.

Lost in his own world behind his headphones, drumming his fingers in time to the music on his cassette player, the radio man did not react at all.

◆ ◆ ◆

Back at the Cantina de Espejos, Bolo hung up the phone with a secretive smile. Then he crept outside to watch the fireworks start. . . .

Chapter 18

STILL IN HIS UNDERPANTS, freshly shaved and show-ered, Smith paced back and forth in Yaquita's room, crunching on the broken shards of knickknacks she had hurled at him the first night. He remained intent on the date displayed on the complex watch. The last couple of days had been a blur, and his head was still aching. He felt confused. He wondered if his brain was going mushy. What was he going to do now? How was he going to get out of this?

"Where is room service with my telephone?" he grumbled. He had to get to Santa Isabel's airport and take the first flight to the United States. But first he'd have to get a new passport and get his credit cards straightened out, then try to get his plane tickets replaced.

He couldn't believe he had bungled his trip so badly. He had never done anything like this before—he was normally such a responsible person. Everything had been so confusing since he arrived here, though, he had paid no attention to the schedule. This was supposed to be a prize vacation, but now he might well have ruined his Navy career. Old Admiral Turner was probably furious with him for abandoning all those vital blueprints.

He imagined how bad it would sound if he told the truth: "As soon as I got to Colodor I was mugged and tied up in a hotel. When I got out, I went to the embassy and they shot at me, so I went to another hotel, and a beautiful woman beat me up and then made passionate love to me. I got sick for days on end, and everything about my vacation was a blur. I'm sorry I came back late."

The admiral would never buy it. He'd heard similar stories far too many times before. Though he might have a soft spot in his heart for drunken sailors, Turner still demanded that his men be disciplined. Smith could be court-martialed for this!

In stark contrast to his gloom, humming happily to herself, Yaquita danced through the door into the room. She smiled brightly, and her fresh layer of lipstick gleamed in the sunshine. She was gorgeously turned out in a floppy straw hat, white summer frock, high-heeled shoes.

She tossed an armful of shopping bundles on the bed along with a bouquet of fresh roses, and pirouetted, displaying her new clothes. "Well, how do you like it?" Yaquita halted before him, arching her eyebrows.

"Just fine." Smith nodded distractedly, but returned to fiddling with the military watch. He tried to use the watch to figure out the day of the week. If it was the weekend, maybe no one would notice he had been gone for an extra day or so.

"This dress is just like the one Margarita de Sanchez was married in." Yaquita plucked at her frock. "Do you think it'll be suitable in the best church? Only a fine historic cathedral will do for you and me."

Smith didn't know what she meant. His brain felt so mushy after the past few days. "A church? Is it Sunday?" He hoped it was Sunday. If he got back to New York today, maybe no one would notice he'd been AWOL. But then, if it really was Sunday, how would he get his whole ID mess straightened out? The embassy wouldn't be open on Sunday, would it? "Tell you what, I'll buy you some lunch in the airport restaurant," he said hopefully. He noticed he wore only his skivvies. "Oh, I'd better get dressed."

Yaquita was suddenly reminded of her duty for the revolution. "Oh, no, no—you're much too ill to go out. Much too ill. Where are my priorities?" She wrapped her arms around Smith's bare chest. "We'll bring the priest in here. No need for you to put clothes on at all, my darling. Let me take care of everything."

Smith looked at the door, then at the breakfast tray on the bed. He had eaten only half of one of the rolls, and by now the coffee was cold. "Where's that guy with the telephone? I asked room service to bring me a phone an hour ago."

He started for the door, but Yaquita stopped him. "I'll get him. I need to find our priest anyway. Luckily, in Colodor, we don't need a license." She turned happily, then called back over her shoulder. "All right, I suppose you could get some clothes on. It's a matter of formality, and I want to remember this day as just perfect."

Smith looked for his clothes, shaking his head in confusion. What kind of license was she talking about, and why would

Yaquita need a priest to help him get to the airport? Maybe it was just to pray that his AWOL charges would be dropped.

◆◆◆

Outside the cantina, two unmarked CIA commando cars skidded to a stop on the slick cobblestones. The second car bumped into the rear fender of the first, jostling the passengers. The windows on both cars rolled down, bristling with guns. The most recent stitching of bullet holes on the cantina's facade looked at least several weeks old, patched with new adobe and whitewash.

O'Halloran leaped from the lead car, but lost his balance in the gutter. He grabbed the car's side mirror to keep from falling on his backside, then attempted to regain his dignity. He pressed a bullhorn to his lips with a sneer. "Pedrito Miraflores! Come out of there, you goddamned Communist spy!"

Inside, Yaquita had skipped halfway down the stairs when she heard the bellowed announcement. Below, the unconscious knife thrower groaned drunkenly, eased to one side and tumbled to the floor. His big blade remained stuck in the table.

"Come out or we blow the place apart!" O'Halloran's voice echoed through the crumbling adobe walls.

Cockroaches fled for cover. In the street, chickens squawked and ran about in a flurry of white feathers.

"I'll give you a countdown, Pedrito! Say your prayers!"

Yaquita raced back up the steps, pressing a hand to her head to keep the straw hat in place on her lush black hair. Time for a change of plans. She had so wanted her wedding day to be memorable—but not with a CIA shootout.

While Smith blinked in confusion, still looking for his socks, Yaquita flew into the bedroom, locked the door and began to tear off her clothes, ripping the delicate fabric of her brand-new white lacy frock. "Hurry," she said. "Hurry!"

"When I'm done with you," O'Halloran went on outside, "we'll hang your corpse . . . twice, maybe! This is your last chance, Pedrito!"

Smith scratched his red hair. "Just who is this Pedrito, anyway? He seems to be quite a troublemaker. I wouldn't want to be in his shoes."

Yaquita peeled off her dress and kicked off her pumps. Wearing only her satin bra and panties, she threw the curtain aside from the closet alcove and hauled clothes down from her shelves and hangers. She dragged out an empty plaid suitcase and tossed it open on the bed. Piles of clothes and pairs of shoes sailed into the open luggage.

Smith just stood, staring. He'd never seen anybody pack so fast. "I thought you were just going along with me to the airport. Hey, and I still need to make a phone call. Where is room service?"

"Get dressed!" Yaquita said.

"Five!" O'Halloran bellowed.

"Get packed!" Yaquita said.

"Four!" O'Halloran's voice grew more eager.

"But there's something going on out there." Frowning, Smith stepped toward the broken window, nudging the curtain aside to look down into the narrow alley. "Maybe we should just stay here. It might be dangerous."

"Don't go near the window!" Yaquita screamed.

"Three!" O'Halloran said.

Down below in the cantina, the band members, some still holding their instruments, cowered together behind the cover of the raised stage. The drummer separated from them and crawled toward the front door. He squirmed under the shelter of tables, trying to fit his huge sombrero between the tumbled chairs.

The cantina's manager had ducked behind the bar, holding the narrow metal stool over his head, though it offered scant protection.

"Two!" The bullhorn distorted O'Halloran's voice.

The drummer reached the front door and frantically tied a white handkerchief on his drumstick. He yanked the knot a final time to be sure it was tight.

"One!" O'Halloran howled.

The drummer thrust the white flag around the edge of the door, flapping it back and forth.

O'Halloran whirled upon seeing the white flag. He grinned with triumph. "There's the son of a bitch! He's trying to surrender. *Fire!*"

A resounding storm of bullets tore the white flag to singed scraps that blew away in the smoke of gunpowder.

The rest of the band crouched out of sight by the stage. A string of machine-gun bullets knocked a bass drum and metal music stands off the stage on top of them. When they cried out in terror, for once their voices worked in unison.

In the alleyway, with a flurry of white feathers, the feral chickens expertly dodged the bullets.

At the door, the drummer stared stupidly at the splintered remains of his drumstick. Then with a yelp he scrambled back into the dim shelter of the cantina.

In his room above, Smith hopped about, trying to pull up his safari pants, but the fabric caught around his knees. He tried to fish his left shoe out from under Yaquita's bed. This mysterious unprovoked attack was bad enough, but the fact of being so *disorganized* unsettled him even more.

Yaquita slithered into her own tight-fitting jumpsuit, still only half zipped up. She jumped up and down to cram shut her plaid suitcase stuffed with shoes and changes of clothes, everything from evening wear to coordinated outfits of casual dress.

Outside, the guns of the armored car pounded round after round of automatic fire into the cantina building, shattering every mirror in turn.

"Look at all those broken mirrors," the guitar player moaned, tilting his sombrero to keep the spraying glass fragments from hitting him in the eyes. "As if we didn't have enough bad luck!"

"Now they'll have to change the name of the cantina," the trumpet player said.

Hammered by bullet impacts, tables tilted and toppled, spinning across the floor. The unconscious knife thrower rolled over, oblivious to the bullet impacts that hammered the spot where he had just been.

On the cobblestoned street beside the lead-armored car, O'Halloran danced about, egging the gunners on. "Kill 'em! Kill 'em! How dare he try to surrender. Slaughter everybody!"

Colodoran soldiers piled from the two armored cars, fixing bayonets to their rifles. They lined up, falling rapidly into ranks, making ready for charge. The machine guns continued firing, which forced the foot soldiers to step back out of the way, unwilling to move forward until the gunfire paused.

The band members, including the drummer who had retreated back to his companions, cowered under the protection of the bandstand lip. Plaster and broken glass showered down on them.

Behind O'Halloran, the line of haphazard troops was finally ready, and the frenzied gunfire had stopped. The CIA commander gesticulated wildly toward the cantina. "Charge!"

Eager soldiers howled a loud yell, "For Colodor!"

Inside the cantina, the manager cowered back under the bar, making himself as small as possible in a corner. He propped the bullet-dented stool up to shield him. Taking a huge risk, he reached up to grab a bottle of rum, then brought it down into his hiding place.

The government troops charged through the door with fixed bayonets, shouting in triumph amid the sulfurous smoke and dust. The soldiers' booted feet crunched across the glass from broken mirrors.

Kicking chairs aside, they rushed toward the bar and began to loot the liquor supply.

◆◆◆

In the locked room upstairs, Yaquita hauled her overstuffed plaid suitcase in one hand; with the other she dragged Smith toward the tiny bathroom window. "Time to go, my love."

Smith finally managed to get himself dressed in the safari suit, though his buttons didn't match up with the proper buttonholes. He broke away from her and jumped back to grab his tan suitcase. "All this spy equipment might come in handy."

In the same instant, Yaquita returned to the closet to grab her guitar case, clutching it to her chest. "You and I might want some music during our romantic evenings." She scooped up the dark rum bottle from beside the white enamel coffeepot. A stray bullet hit the ceiling in a burst of plaster.

Worming through the opening, Smith slipped out the bathroom window. With a clang he dropped to the corrugated roof of the outbuilding below. Smith turned and reached up to help Yaquita as she leaned out the window. "Catch this first!" She dropped her battered guitar case down to him, then her heavy plaid suitcase, which nearly knocked him off the building. Carrying their precious baggage, Smith and Yaquita raced along the corrugated rooftops. Their footsteps banged like thunder.

Inside the cantina the Colodoran troops yanked the fat manager out from under the bar. The forlorn band members stood together, also prisoners. Some still held their instruments, but the soldiers eyed them suspiciously, as if the trumpets or guitars might be potential weapons. The intact drumsticks had already been confiscated.

The troops herded the manager and band out the front door and into the road. They stood blinking in front of the armored cars, surrendering repeatedly. O'Halloran looked at them, displeased and growling. None of these men was Pedrito Miraflores.

The band members held their hands up, helplessly gripping their instruments. All of them were terrified. The drummer begged, "I know we are bad musicians, but none of us sympathize with those pesky mapmakers." All of the band members shook their heads earnestly. "Please don't shoot us!"

Chapter 19

AS GUNFIRE BLAZED and the two fugitives staggered along at top speed across the rooftops with their baggage, Smith saw an opportunity: at the end of the last out-building, a ramshackle stake truck bulged with a cargo hidden by a lashed-down tarpaulin. Its Mercedes-Benz emblem gleamed from the hood, the only part of the truck that looked well maintained.

"Maybe we can borrow this vehicle," Smith said hopefully. "I'm an American, so they'll trust me."

"You? An American?" Yaquita laughed. "Then you really aren't the Pedrito I know." Smith didn't know what she found so funny.

He stepped down from the corrugated metal overhang to the top of the truck's cab. The roof of the vehicle was rough with rust and patched with primer-coat paint. Like a true gentleman, he reached up for Yaquita's bags. "Here, let me help you."

"What an awful thing! I deserve finer transportation," Yaquita said as she looked over the stake truck from front to back. "Well, I suppose they didn't have much time to provide a getaway vehicle for us."

◆ ◆ ◆

On the street outside the cantina, the Colodoran troops lined up the captive band members and the cantina manager. O'Halloran strode down the line, roughing up the prisoners. He waited for no answers as he slapped the first man, the trumpet player. "Where's Pedrito Miraflores? We were tipped off he's in this cantina."

"Pedrito?" the man asked. "Oh, he's—"

From somewhere down the line, the guitarist said, "If you tell him, Yaquita will kill us all. Who would you rather be killed by: the government, or *her?*"

The trumpet player suddenly froze, and the beads of sweat that formed on his brow spoke volumes. He'd rather be killed by a government agent ten times over than face this woman Yaquita.

O'Halloran cuffed the next prisoner. "Where's Pedrito?" The man turned red and shook his head vigorously.

He slapped the third one. "Where's Pedrito?"

Hearing the distant roar of a truck engine, O'Halloran stared down the alley. The overloaded stake truck, backfiring and smoking, jerkily moved across the end of the street, picking up speed like a charging rhinoceros.

Inside the truck was a man with red hair.

O'Halloran pointed frantically at the ramshackle truck. "That's Pedrito trying to escape! After him, *after him!*"

The soldiers piled into the armored cars with a clatter of automatic weapons banging against the sides of the vehicles. O'Halloran leaped onto the sideboard of the first armored car and shook his fist. As the car raced away, the long strand of hair dangled along his sweaty cheek.

The cantina manager and band members stared after the departing armored cars. The band members still held their instruments and kept their hands in the air, though no soldiers had been left behind to guard them. It seemed the safest course of action.

"Do you think we should go back in to practice?" the drummer asked.

"I suppose so," the guitar player said contemptuously. "Those guys were rough, but Yaquita will squash them like mice!"

•••

Yaquita knocked Smith over to the passenger side and slid behind the wheel. She hot-wired the engine and drove madly, wrestling with the gearshift as if it were a hungry python.

Smith looked behind, but couldn't see around the bulging tarp on the back of the overloaded truck. The engine backfired and jolted. Yaquita hammered the steering wheel with the heel of her hand as if she could somehow make the truck go faster.

"This Pedrito doesn't seem to be a very popular guy," Smith said.

"He isn't!" Yaquita said.

"I don't think I'd ever like to meet him," he muttered, blinking.

Yaquita just raised a dark eyebrow at him.

Armored cars skidded around the corner, appearing from the side street. The truck bucked along, wheezing and sputtering. Dogs barked at it, then fled from the wheels. Gunshots rang in the air.

The two-lane highway led into mountainous country outside the city limits. As the truck roared through traffic, three small cars provided a buffer from the armored vehicles in pursuit. Yaquita glanced in her side mirror at the civilian cars, but paid no attention to them.

"Who are those men, anyway?" Smith asked.

"CIA."

"Oh, then I don't have anything to worry about. The CIA is our friend."

Yaquita snorted, looking at him in disbelief. "Yes, but they're looking for *you*."

Smith swallowed hard. His thoughts had been clouded and muzzy all day. Now everything came clear—why they hunted him, why they'd tried to shoot him at the embassy. "They think I'm Pedrito? But then we just have to explain to them—"

"Shut up, Pedrito!" The knowing look in Yaquita's face pinned him like a wanted poster to the wall. Even *she* thought he was Pedrito.

O'Halloran's armored cars were a considerable distance behind and following. The soldiers shot their machine guns into the air, but the rest of the traffic reacted indifferently, as if the gunfire was no more significant than a honking horn. Colodoran drivers were probably used to the sound by now.

"Maybe I should go talk to them," Smith said, "and explain that I'm not Pedrito."

"They wouldn't let you get within a hundred yards before they'd shoot you dead!" Yaquita laughed.

"Sure they would," Smith said. "They can't shoot you just because they think you're a criminal. What about due process of law? What about 'innocent until proven guilty'?"

"That's just for rich white Americans living in their nice houses," Yaquita laughed. "Those rules don't apply to us here in Colodor. If they think you are a Communist, the CIA will shoot you."

Smith groaned. Obviously she was right. "I wonder what Nelson would do in a case like this."

"Who's Nelson?" Yaquita asked. "Some U.S. agent?"

"He was the greatest naval hero of all time."

"Look around, darling," Yaquita said. "We're on dry land. It doesn't make any difference what a naval hero would do."

"Wait!" Smith said. "Nelson would jettison his cargo to increase maneuverability."

It was time to take action—and he experienced the thrill of adventure. He opened the door of the moving truck, holding on to the frame and standing up. Wind blew in his face. Smith climbed back onto the truck bed. "Keep driving, Yaquita. Now we're going to pick up some knots!"

In hot pursuit, O'Halloran stood up in the armored car. Whipped by the wind, his hair flew aside. The CIA man had been chasing this hard-drinking, bloodthirsty, womanizing revolutionary for years. He could already have retired from the CIA, but he wouldn't rest until he saw the redhead's corpse on the ground, attracting flies.

Ahead, across the tops of the three civilian cars that separated the armored vehicle from the stake truck, he could see
Smith on top of the lumpy cargo, climbing around on the
tarpaulin and undoing the lashings.

O'Halloran peered through a pair of field glasses, focusing
on the lieutenant's shock of red hair. "Hah!" he shouted ecstati-
cally. "That's Pedrito, all right." He lowered the binoculars. "*Start
firing!* Get those commuters out of our way."

The leading car's guns blasted, ignoring the intervening
civilian traffic. Explosions kicked up on the right and ahead of
the fugitives. The top of a yellow taxicab just behind the fleeing
truck exploded. The hapless driver roared off the curve in the
road.

"Correct your targeting!" O'Halloran shouted angrily. "And
don't waste ammunition on civilians, unless it's absolutely
necessary."

On the tarpaulin, holding the ropes to keep his balance,
Smith stared, incredulous, at the careening wreck behind them.
"The CIA shouldn't be doing that—they're the good guys!" He
ducked out of sight from the pursuing armored cars, now separated by only two passenger cars. In a sweat, he worked on the
lashings. He had to put an end to this crisis right away.

"Shoot straighter!" O'Halloran shouted.

The leading armored car's guns fired, and the back of the
nearest civilian auto exploded. The vehicle vaulted over the
center divider into the opposite lane and blew up. Other cars
honked and swerved into crowded buses. The bus drivers just
continued to drive as haphazardly as usual.

"I didn't mean straighter at the car in front of us! Get
Pedrito!" O'Halloran pounded on the roof of the vehicle.

The driver of the remaining civilian car—a timid old man—wrestled with his steering wheel. He swerved madly off the road onto the steep shoulder. The car rolled over and wrecked itself without O'Halloran needing to fire a single shot.

"That's better. *Now* we'll get someplace." O'Halloran hung farther out of the top of the assault vehicle, enthusiastic. He looked at the final wreck as he went by, seeing the old man struggling to get free of his mangled car. Then he focused again on Pedrito's lumbering stake truck ahead. "The CIA always gets its man!"

On top of the truckload, Smith managed to unfasten the forward end of the tarpaulin. He lifted it and let the entire canvas fabric fly into the wind, draping onto the oncoming armored vehicle. The canvas struck O'Halloran in the face, knocking him against the back of the car. He thrashed madly to lift it off while trying not to fall off the vehicle.

With his windshield covered, the driver swerved from side to side, banging into other cars and buses as he continued at full speed, completely blind. Finally, O'Halloran managed to yank the tarpaulin aside and send it flying back into the second armored car close behind them.

The canvas blanketed the windshield of the second armored car, which swerved into a bus before running off the road and into an embankment. O'Halloran looked back. "Incompetents," he snorted.

◆◆◆

Now that he had finally removed the tarpaulin, Smith looked down at his feet. "Okay, now to jettison the cargo."

The truck carried a brimming load of huge green bananas, freshly cut and still on the stalk. Piles of oversized bananas, unfit for export, dotted the pastures in the country as feed for the livestock. Smith grabbed a heavy stalk, then tossed the bananas onto the road behind them.

The assault vehicle had to swerve to miss the bananas.

"*Fire!*" O'Halloran shouted. "We're under attack!"

The armored car's gun muzzles blazed. Bullets exploded into the bananas in the back of the stake truck, spraying yellow-green mush everywhere.

Smith lifted a second stalk high over his head and pitched it off the rear of the truck, then grabbed another. The bananas were heavy, and deadly. Stalks of green fruit landed on the road in front of O'Halloran's armored car. The driver veered to avoid them, but the speeding wheel hit a clump of bananas that squirted slime like ice on an oil-slick road. The vehicle spun sideways, struck the ditch and rolled to its side. Its guns continued to fire, punching holes into the roadside mud.

A few moments later, O'Halloran wrestled himself free of the smoking wreck and stood in front of the crashed vehicle. He shook his fist after the banana truck.

Down the road, meanwhile, the second armored car had managed to free itself from the embankment, pulled back onto the road and approached with great speed.

O'Halloran did a dance of rage aimed at Pedrito's truck now receding into the distance. He stomped forward as if he could catch the redheaded fugitive with his own fury.

On top of the fleeing banana truck, Smith cupped his hands to shout a warning back at O'Halloran: "Hey! Look out!"

Behind him, the second armored car skidded on the bananas and plowed into the first vehicle with a huge explosion. Both armored cars burst into flame. Leftover ammunition detonated, making white trails like fireworks in the sky.

O'Halloran looked down at himself in disgust, not even glancing at the exploding vehicles. He picked yellow mush off his uniform, tasted banana.

His superiors wouldn't want to hear that two million dollars' worth of armored assault vehicles had been destroyed because Pedrito Miraflores had lobbed a bunch of bananas at them.

Thinking quickly, he snarled, "I'll have to call them Soviet missiles in my report."

Chapter 20

IN NEW YORK CITY, meanwhile, the real Pedrito Miraflores sat behind Tom Smith's desk in the Office of Naval Intelligence, uncomfortable in the strange and formal uniform of a lieutenant junior grade. He flicked his gaze from side to side, always uneasy at being confined within walls for too long a time. At least he didn't have to sit with his back to the door.

In his time, Pedrito had spent many days in rundown and dirty prisons, held captive by competing guerrilla groups, terrorists, and South American police departments. He had survived by the skin of his teeth, clung to life by his fingernails, beaten impossible odds in dire situations.

But this—working eight hours a day in a bustling and clean government office—seemed the worst of all! He didn't know how much more of it he could stand.

He wanted excitement so badly that for the last two nights he had gone out and wandered in Central Park, beating up would-be muggers. Now the place was so safe that this morning the park was full of old ladies, walking their dogs.

Sprawled on the drafting table beside his desk lay stacks of meticulous blueprints for new missile systems. The U.S. Navy was constructing them in secret at remote industrial facilities that ostensibly manufactured exotic plumbing supplies. Though he had no engineering knowledge at all, Pedrito studied the plans, drooling over the information he could bring back to his superiors. He was the perfect spy here, and he could pass along incredibly useful intelligence information to Cuba and Russia.

Even uneducated, Pedrito was astonished to find so many fundamental design flaws. The weapons seemed to have been reverse-engineered by committees so that they could not possibly work, yet the blueprints were so complex that the designers must have hoped no one would notice.

Pedrito noticed, though. He smiled with great relish as he located Smith's red rubber stamp in the top desk drawer and happily stamped APPROVED on every single blueprint. Colonel Ivan and Colonel Enrique were going to love this!

Feeling restless, and knowing he had done a good day's work for the revolution, Pedrito glanced at the clock on the wall, donned his formal Navy cap—because he was supposed to wear it every time he went outside—and left the office building. He was sure he could find a good time somewhere in the city.

After all, late afternoon was called "happy hour" for good reason.

♦♦♦

Halfway down the block from Naval Intelligence headquarters he found a cozy-looking bar—exactly what he was looking for. Removing his cap to show off his head of red-gold hair, Pedrito strode into the dim pub, inhaling the smells of beer and cigarettes and pretzels. He heaved a sigh of relief. Finally, at last, someplace that seemed like home.

This wasn't exactly his old stomping grounds of the Cantina de Espejos—in fact, the place had only one mirror, behind the bar—but it would do for now. He was desperate for a stiff drink after tolerating office work all day long.

The ruddy-faced bartender waved at him, smiling broadly. "Lieutenant Tom Smith! Good to see you again."

Pedrito cringed, uncomfortable at being recognized, but he had to go through the motions, for the sake of the mission. He waved back. "Hello, sir."

"The usual, Lieutenant?" The bartender reached for a glass. "Coming right up."

Pedrito's eyes became adjusted to the comfortable dimness of the bar. He made out a pool table, a pinball machine, and several dark tables lined up against the wood-paneled walls. Neon beer signs shed colored light into the murk. In the back, a group of men laughed loudly as they played a low-stakes game of poker. Pedrito raised his eyebrows, his interest piqued. Poker!

"Here you go, Lieutenant," the bartender said. "I'll put it on your tab." He slid across a foaming glass of cold milk.

Pedrito looked at it with a strangled expression. "What is this?"

"Your milk, Lieutenant. Cold and foamy, just the way you like it. I made it a double, 'cause you looked like you needed it today."

Pedrito spluttered. This had gone far enough! He pounded his fist on the bar. "Forget the milk. Today, I want a tequila. In fact, make it *two* shots of tequila. Your finest gold."

"Tequila?" the bartender said, astonished. He looked at Pedrito for a moment, then burst out laughing. "That's a good one, Lieutenant." He turned around and began washing glasses, clearly with no intention of replacing Pedrito's drink.

"Bartender, I mean it. I want a tequila."

The bartender continued laughing so hard he nearly dropped one of the glasses. "Be careful with your joking, there, Lieutenant. I just may call your bluff."

"I'm not bluffing. I want a tequila! *Now!*" He slammed his fist down, but the bartender just gestured in dismissal, then wiped sweat off his brow.

"Tom Smith, I remember the last time you took the tiniest sip of hard liquor. You turned green and fell backward off the stool. We had to call an ambulance. Thought you'd have learned your lesson by now." He turned to the cash register and added up Smith's tab, ignoring Pedrito.

Fuming, Pedrito grabbed his glass of milk, took a sip and frowned in distaste—the stuff came from *cows!*—then decided to pursue other amusements. He stalked over to the card players in the back, watching eagerly. He recalled many nights in rebel encampments, huddling in tents in the Andes cloud forests, listening to the rain outside and playing just such a game until the others in the group realized how good a player Pedrito Miraflores really was. Then the others refused to bet against him anymore.

"What's the ante?" Pedrito said, pulling up a chair. "Can you deal me in?"

"Oh, hi, Tom," one of the men said, looking down at his hand and folding the cards in disgust. "We heard you joking with the bartender."

Pedrito withdrew his wallet, counting out how much American money he had. Given a half-hour of playing cards, he could triple his spending money and then buy his own tequila.

"Whatever it is, I'm in. Deal me for the next hand."

The men looked at him, then cracked up laughing. "Deal *you* in? We're not playing 'old maid,' Tom."

"I can see that," Pedrito snapped. "It's stud poker, and I want to play the next round."

The men at the table looked at him, then chuckled louder and louder, slapping their palms on the table. "Smith, you're a kick. I never knew you had a sense of humor." The men went back to playing.

Pedrito stood seething, clenching and unclenching his fists.

"Could you get us another bowl of pretzels, Tom?" one of the players said, glancing up.

Fuming, Pedrito turned about, gulped down half of his milk, then gagged as if he had swallowed a fistful of garden slugs. He stormed out of the bar.

He had been in many unpleasant situations before, even life-threatening circumstances—but living in the disguise of Lieutenant Tom Smith was turning out to be one of the most unpleasant assignments he had ever undertaken.

Chapter 21

STANDING AMONG THE VEHICLE wreckage on the winding road that led out of Santa Isabel, O'Halloran wiped smashed banana slime off his cheek. As he watched the now empty stake truck lumber away into the hills, he had a sudden realization, a sudden hope.

Perhaps there was a way he could get Pedrito after all—even in the wake of this disaster.

He stabbed a hand into his pocket and came up with a walkie-talkie, a compact new design that could also receive Top 40 radio stations.

"Cain-Idiot-Alpha One to Cain-Idiot-Alpha 465. Come in!" Instead, he heard only a peppy old tune from the Osmond Brothers revival tour. Snarling, he twisted the frequency knob and repeated his call until he received a response.

"Call the Colodoran Air Force and order out jets," he demanded. "Yes, jets! Their best jets—yes, *both* of them! Pedrito will try to get out of the country by air! It won't be as much fun to shoot him out of the skies, since I wanted to murder him with my bare hands—but the most important thing is that we *kill* the bastard before he causes more trouble."

The next most important thing, he decided as he smeared more banana mush on his trousers, was to change his clothes.

◆◆◆

Beyond the end of the paved road out of Santa Isabel, an old Stinson monoplane stood parked on a grassy plateau, its paint peeling. Brightly clad Indian shepherds shooed their dogs and sheep and children out of the way as the plane prepared for departure. The pilot sat in the enclosed cockpit, waiting for Yaquita and Smith.

As the rickety stake truck approached, the pilot tucked down the flaps of his aviator's cap to hide his swarthy Turkish features. The monoplane's engine sputtered to life, and the propeller reluctantly began turning.

The empty old truck rattled up to within twenty feet of the monoplane's wing. Eating a salvaged banana, Smith climbed out the passenger side, carrying his contraband tan suitcase. He needed to get back home any way he could, yet he didn't like the looks of this. "Are you sure this is an airport? This doesn't look like the gate for international departures."

Yaquita slid out the driver's side, dragging her overstuffed plaid suitcase and her precious guitar. "Hurry, before the pilot takes off!" she said, and Smith took that as his answer. "He's not wasting any time."

They sprinted for the old plane as the throbbing engine sound grew louder; the propeller spun in a faster blur. In the cabin, the pilot sat ready and eager at the controls. "Hurry, my friends. We have a departure schedule to keep."

Yaquita hustled to the back, lashing down her luggage and guitar case, then doing the same for Smith's. "I'll sit back here," she said. "You take the copilot's seat, just in case there's an emergency."

"Copilot's seat?" Smith asked. "What do you expect me to do in an emergency? I can't fly a plane."

The pilot smiled a secretive smile at him. His dark hair was tucked in his aviator's cap, but his exotic features seemed very familiar to Smith.

"Don't worry," Bolo said, "I don't know how to fly a plane either. But I'm sure it's simple enough. I just skimmed the instruction manual." He began to taxi along the short, bumpy runway, narrowing his dark eyes as he leaned forward to look through his bug-spattered window.

Into the engine roar, Smith yelled back to Yaquita, "Where are we going?"

"It's time that you went home!" Yaquita called.

"Home? Let's go!" Smith hollered back.

In the pilot's seat, Bolo smiled to himself as the plane took off.

◆◆◆

At the government airfield of the Republic of Colodor, two pilots rubbed their eyes, swallowed another gulp of Nescafé instant coffee and jumped into their F-14 jets, which had been purchased at a discount by piecing together parts from a U.S. military salvage yard.

In their spare time, the members of the Colodoran Air Force had applied decals to the wings and bodies of the jets, as if they were giant model airplanes. Unfortunately, several large wrinkles showed. The Colodoran Air Force had ordered replacement decals from a catalog, but had to wait several weeks for shipping and handling. If the pilots flew fast enough and shot straight enough, though, they could knock their enemies out of the skies before anyone noticed the botched insignia.

Afterburners roaring, the two jets took off, looped up into the skies, switched on their radars (which were inferior models that had been salvaged from police cars in Mexico City), then engaged in pursuit.

◆◆◆

The Stinson monoplane flew over low clouds and bumpy air in the Andes. Smith clutched the copilot's seat, trying to figure out where they were going. The mountains below looked very rugged, and very close. Since he had never seen an official map of the country, he could make no guesses as to the terrain below, or where the actual borders were. He only knew they were somewhere in the vicinity of Colombia, Ecuador or Peru.

Smith wondered how long it would take for them to reach the United States, especially in a tiny plane like this. Failing that, he wondered if a flight attendant would come by with peanuts and soda. He peered into the back of the plane. As far as he could tell, though, the only other person on the plane was Yaquita, and she didn't seem the least inclined to act as a stewardess.

"I've got a nervous stomach," Smith said. "I'm a sailor, not an aviator."

Yaquita came forward and handed Smith the bottle she had snatched from the table in her room. "Here, this always helps."

Smith glanced at the label. "What is this? Rum?"

"You ought to know," Yaquita said with a grin. "You've been drinking it for days."

"I have?" He took a swig straight from the bottle and tasted it carefully in his mouth. "So I have." He took another swig. "Funny, I never thought I could tolerate alcohol. Maybe it's just beer that makes me sick." He supposed he should be open to new experiences.

While Smith nursed the bottle and stared out the cockpit window, Yaquita unlashed her guitar case and removed the instrument before she sat back down and buckled herself in. With the guitar in her lap, she turned a tuning peg and whispered secretively into the hole. "Roger-Echo-Dog Eighteen to Roger-Echo-Dog One."

"Come in, Roger-Echo-Dog Eighteen," the Cuban-accented Colonel Enrique responded, his voice crackly with static.

"I've got baggage aboard and am heading for home," Yaquita said.

"Any trouble?" Enrique said.

"Everything's wonderful," Yaquita said, a dreamy smile on her face. "Just wonderful. He seems to have a bit of amnesia . . . but I don't mind."

"Good," Enrique said. Yaquita leaned closer to the hidden speaker. "To you, Ivan sends his love. Roger-Echo-Dog One—out."

Smith was puzzled at the muffled sounds coming from behind him. He had never heard of a talking guitar before, but it seemed that telephones were hidden in all kinds of things these days. Maybe this was the next trend—cellular phones hidden in guitars. He knew he would get even queasier if he turned around to look. "Who are you talking to?"

Yaquita strummed a chord on the guitar, smiling. "Oh, it's just a song. I wanted to listen to the words before I played it for you." She began to play a simple melody, a forcibly rhymed ode to her future husband. She kept her big dark eyes on him through every stanza.

Now that they'd gained a bit of altitude, Smith's ears felt as if they were going to pop. He wondered if that had caused him to hear funny noises, imagine that her voice was coming from a guitar.

Listening to her sing, Smith smiled. "You're going to get married?" he asked idly. "Congratulations."

"You just wait!" Yaquita said. "It will be exactly like in a storybook."

As the Stinson droned along above a level of thick cloud, a fighter jet screamed by, jostling the windows in the cockpit. Smith held on for dear life as a second jet whooshed past even closer. Their monoplane bucked, nearly out of control.

"Hey, those are F-14s!" Smith said. "I thought we sold all those to military surplus dealers."

"Look at the decals," Bolo said through gritted teeth. "Those aren't U.S. planes. They're from the Colodoran Air Force. They're after you!"

Bolo released the controls and grabbed a submachine gun from under his seat. He elbowed open the window, aimed the submachine gun, and fired as the first F-14 made another pass. The gunfire made a deafening roar in the enclosed cockpit, and wind roared into the old plane. Below, clouds scudded along the tree-covered peaks of the mountains.

With no one at the cockpit controls, the Stinson tilted and began to descend recklessly toward the jagged Andes. Smith grabbed the copilot stick.

"I thought you said you couldn't fly," Yaquita said.

"I can't, but it looks like a good time to learn."

Somehow, he managed to keep the plane level, but as he jerked on the stick he overcorrected and tipped the craft violently the other way. The Stinson slid sideways down toward the clouds just below and the tall, spindly trees of the lush cloud forest. Bolo fired the machine gun again, but his strafing bullets went wide.

The two fighter jets circled back for another pass. They rushed by the Stinson just as it sliced into the cloud cover. Smith covered his eyes, but even blind he did no worse keeping the plane on a level course.

• • •

In the ground control tower, O'Halloran yelled into a microphone. "Goddamn it, shoot them down! Use missiles, use rockets, use bullets!" He wiped a spray of spittle from the microphone, then shouted again. "Use *stones* for all I care—just shoot them down!"

In a jet cockpit, one of the two Colodoran pilots spoke through his in-helmet microphone. "That old Stinson is so slow we keep missing!" He knocked his radar. According to the old police radar unit, the Stinson had been traveling sixty miles per hour. He couldn't slow the F-14 that much, or he'd stall and crash.

The pilot felt terrible. All of his previous flight experience had been gained by crop-dusting for a local guava plantation owner. He'd thought that shooting a gun would be very much like dropping a load of pesticides, but he'd never flown a plane that was so fast, and he'd never had to drop pesticides on a moving spider—except for that one time, when millions of banana spiders were migrating from Colombia. He wasn't at all prepared for this!

He looked below, trying to see through the narrow cockpit windows. The sharp, folded mountains were so close they skimmed just below the fighter jets. "Yes, sir. Well, they've gone into cloud cover now. They seem to be safe."

"Safe!" O'Halloran screamed. "Well, make them un-safe!"

"But, sir," the pilot whined, "there might be mountains down there, and how would we know, with the mapmakers all on strike!"

"You go into those clouds after them," O'Halloran shouted, "or I'll come up there and kill you myself."

"*Madre de Dios!*" the pilot muttered, crossing himself.

The two jet pilots opened their throttles wider, then dove into the fog and low clouds after the monoplane.

The Stinson plowed through thick mist, with Smith at the copilot's controls. He could barely tell they were flying upside down. "Hey, maybe I can pilot this thing after all."

"Something doesn't quite feel right," Bolo said. "I better take over. Can't see anything to shoot anyway."

"No need," Smith said, "I'm a sailor at heart. You can't see through fog like I can."

Dark treetops appeared through the mist just above the top wing, flashing past. Leaves and twigs scraped against the Stinson's fuselage. A gargantuan vertical cliff came up at them like a hammer. Calmly, Bolo pushed the stick into the panel and hit the throttle full open. The Stinson put its nose straight up in a swoop, standing on its tail.

"Then again, maybe I'd better stick with books about Nelson," Smith said, chagrined. "You can pilot us the rest of the way, sir."

Behind them, lost in the mist, came the rumbling boom as two F-14 jets—the entire Colodoran Air Force—slammed into the cliff face.

Continuing to cruise low, Bolo took them out of the clouds until the mist drifted away in tatters, allowing them to see ahead. Smith spotted a rudimentary landing field on a rugged grassy plain beyond the heavy mountains. They had passed the main Andean ridge.

"That doesn't look like any airport I'm familiar with," Smith said. "I take it we're not flying directly to New York? Are we changing planes here?"

On the ground, a group of vaqueros waited beside an ancient coach drawn by four horses. They waved colorful ribbons in the air, signaling the plane.

"What happened to those jets chasing us?" Smith asked.

"We're over the border by now," Yaquita said. "They can't follow."

"How can they tell where the border is, if nobody has any maps of Colodor?" Smith asked.

Bolo shrugged. "Instinct."

After circling the field, Bolo came in for an easy landing, touching down in the smooth, flat grass. The horsemen yipped and galloped along, pacing the Stinson. The horse-drawn coach rolled forward to meet the passengers.

"You're home now, my darling," Yaquita said, leaning forward to kiss Smith on the cheek. "We're safe."

"Home?" Smith said. "This isn't the United States!" He looked from her to Bolo, but neither seemed perturbed. "I need to report to my superior officer. I need to call the office—and I need to do my laundry. This isn't where I want to be."

"You're home just the same," she said. "You'll see."

Bolo remained in his pilot seat as Yaquita and Smith climbed down the plane's folding stairs to the ground, then walked toward the horsemen, carrying their suitcases. Yaquita also brought her spy-radio/guitar.

"Do we have to go through customs?" Smith asked.

The vaqueros stood in their stirrups, waving their ribbons and roaring a greeting, "Ai! Pedrito!" He saw broad grins and many gold teeth.

Yaquita waved back at them, clutching Smith's arm possessively. Smith shook his head as he stared at the horsemen welcoming him.

"You see, Pedrito?" Yaquita said, smiling. "This is your home, whether you like it or not."

Chapter 22

LEAVING THE DISTANT, misty mountains behind, the ancient Spanish coach rolled across the vast grassy highland plains. The horses galloped down a rutted and puddled road.

Before slamming the door of the plush coach, Yaquita had kissed Smith goodbye, then ran back to the plane with the pilot, claiming other "important business" she had to attend to. She'd warned the coachmen sternly before she left, "I think Pedrito hurt his head or something. He is acting just a little loco. Take good care of him, and get him to the hacienda safely, or I'll rip out your eyes and feed them to the crows. Understand?"

Smith had no idea what he was supposed to do now, or how he would make his way with these strangers. They wouldn't believe that he wasn't Pedrito.

Perhaps, at least, they would have a telephone wherever he was going, and he could call Admiral Turner. Maybe then he could get this whole mess straightened out.

Smith sat on the coach's narrow padded wooden bench across from an enormous major-domo. Straining brass buttons barely held his black vest together across his gut.

The major-domo gazed fondly at his redheaded passenger and patted Smith on the knee. "Ai, Pedrito, how glad I am to see you again!" He swept his chubby hand out the window to indicate the plain. "You'll be glad to hear that everything on Rancho Miraflores is just fine, the whole five thousand square kilometers. We're taking very good care of it for you, awaiting your return."

"But I've never been here before," Smith said, and then the number registered in his mind. He looked at the major-domo. "Five thousand square *kilometers?*"

The enormous man put his head close to Smith, conspiratorially. He smelled of bacon grease. "Thanks to you, sly Pedrito, I think we'll add a little more territory to the rancho soon. After the wedding. Ha-ha-ha."

◆ ◆ ◆

Compared to Yaquita's tiny balcony room in the Cantina de Espejos, the bedroom of the villa was the size of a baronial hall. Colorful Indian blankets woven from alpaca wool hung on the whitewashed walls, displayed diagonally alongside quirts, spurs, riatas. A carved mahogany wardrobe held twenty-five outfits, all exactly in Smith's size.

The out-of-place lieutenant walked through the arched doorway, gawking in astonishment, sure that he had gone into the wrong bedchamber. Before he could ask any questions, an ancient, gray-haired servitor rushed to him on wobbling legs. The old man threw his arms about Smith. "Ai! Pedrito! *Cómo estás?*"

The servitor held him off to look at him, paternally smoothing down Smith's mussed hair. Veins stood out on the old man's sinewy, big-knuckled hands. "How *glad* I am to see you!"

Smith decided it wasn't worth arguing with the man about his identity. At least Pedrito was *liked* around here, for a change.

The servitor led Smith off toward a side room with a tiled bath raised up on marble slabs. Freshly cut roses and carnations in crystal vases scented the room. "Come, Pedrito! Have a bath and get into some of your *decent* clothes! You can't present yourself to your father looking that way!"

Smith stopped in amazement. "My father?" He knew he would never get past a father's scrutiny, and these people might actually get mad if they thought he was trying to deceive them. "I'm not Pedrito Miraflores. I'm an orphan!"

"Everything will be forgiven, I am sure, after all that you have accomplished for the people of our country. We're quite aware of your escapades, and your mother has convinced the don that your heart must have been in the right place. Passion runs high in your family!" The servitor laughed. "Your madcap pranks have outdone even the things your father did when he was younger." He lowered his voice, "I think the old man is secretly proud of you, eh?"

"Really, I'm not Pedrito! My name is Tom Smith. I'm from New York, and I work for the Navy. You're all making a huge mistake!"

The servant clucked his tongue sympathetically, "Ah, the bump on the head . . ." He smoothed back Smith's red hair, touched one of the bumps on his forehead—Smith couldn't recall whether he'd gotten it from Yaquita or the muggers in the Grande Hotel. "I heard about that. Well, of course you are Pedrito Miraflores. I changed your diapers when you were young. How could I not recognize you?"

Another servant stood in the bathroom door with plush towels and a robe draped over his arm. The old servitor swept his hand out expressively. "See how nice they've kept your room— and that says something, doesn't it?" Now he slid in a few words, as if hoping to jog Smith's memory of his childhood, "Considering how you always made such a mess when you were a rambunctious boy."

Smith stared at the trappings, the furniture, the spacious- ness. Now this *was* a lot better than being chased and shot at. His vacation had been a disaster, and, so far, he hadn't really been able to enjoy himself. Any time soon, these people would realize their mistake, and Smith felt sure they would be properly embar- rassed and help him straighten this whole mess out. But for the moment, he decided he'd simply relax and enjoy.

The old man beamed to the servant standing in the door. "Paco, draw Pedrito's bath! Can't you see he's in need of some relaxation? I think he's going to raise a little hell while he is with us, so let him rest and get his strength for now."

Smith stood speechless. No one had ever expected him to raise hell in his life.

◆◆◆

Later, he tugged his fancy new clothes into shape, though they were already in perfect order. He wasn't used to being dressed like a Spanish grandee: gray bolero jacket, lace-front shirt, tight gray pants and cummerbund. It made his formal Navy uniform seem like casual clothes. He wondered if he was going to some sort of costume ball or a fiesta.

More than that, he felt bothered by something else. He'd begun to wonder about things. Everyone here thought he was Pedrito Miraflores, and treated him accordingly. Yaquita, the police, servants and strangers on the street. Even these clothes fit him as if they'd been tailored to his body.

And it caused him to wonder, Is it possible that I *am* Pedrito Miraflores? Could I have really bumped my head and be suffering from amnesia or some kind of delusions?

He'd always thought that alcohol made him sick, yet now he found that he loved the taste of rum. And everyone here thought he was Pedrito.

What if I go back to New York and find that I don't really have a job in the Navy? he wondered. What if I went home and the apartment I think I live in is locked, or what if the whole neighborhood never existed?

Is it possible that I could be Pedrito?

As strange as the thought had seemed at first, Smith began to wonder, and the more he considered, the more frightened he became. It all sort of made sense. Pedrito Miraflores was apparently a bad man, a murdering revolutionary who had no love for Americans.

But if I felt guilty for my deeds, Smith thought, and if I were hit on the head and were suffering from amnesia, so that I constructed a new identity for myself—wouldn't it be possible

151

that I just might take on the identity of an alter ego, the man I wish I were, rather than who I am?

The idea seemed baffling, terrifying. But it also seemed plausible. Smith was an orphan, a man who had no wife or girl-friend or even close drinking buddies at home. Such an empty life in so many ways—as if his mind, unable to concoct a suitable fiction, had simply left the whole field of human relationships blank. Even his name, Tom Smith, seemed a handy fiction.

Smith had been worried that he would get home and find that his life had been shattered, that because he'd gone AWOL, everything would fall apart. Now he began to wonder. What life? What if I lost my apartment, and my phone bill went unpaid? When was the last time anyone of import called me? Do I even have a life?

It was with such thoughts that the old servitor led him to an immense library in the villa. Red Moroccan leather chairs and sofas with brass studs were spaced on terra-cotta tiles around a big fireplace. A wrought-iron chandelier hung from the arched ceiling. Standing lamps lit the bookshelves and a huge mahogany desk where an ancient Remington typewriter sat. An antelope head was mounted above the fireplace, and a large bull's head hung on the opposite wall. The far door of the study stood closed and imposing.

The heavy door opened, and Don Pedro, Pedrito's father, strode in dressed exactly like Smith. He was a very proud grandee, his pale hair turned an iron gray, as was his neatly clipped goatee.

"Ai, Pedrito," the elder man said, his expression severe. "So you have finally come home. I thought you'd forgotten who you are, what family blood flows through your veins."

Smith remained confused, but leaped at the chance to ask a question. "All right, sir—perhaps you can indeed explain it all to me. Who am I, really?"

The father clapped his hands briskly, his eyes flashing fire. "You are Pedrito Miraflores Santa Garcia de Consolvo Guzman y Hildago Clarida," his father said, "and *don't you forget it!* You are a descendant of the barons of Germany and the grandees of Spain."

"I am?" Smith said. The father seemed certain. This Pedrito fellow was getting more and more interesting all the time.

"Indeed you are!" The father paused and looked even more severe. "And you are also a reprobate, a turncoat to your class, a drunken sot, a despoiler of women and a complete disgrace!"

"Oh, no!" Smith said. "That couldn't be true."

"Yes, it is true!" the father said, emphatically. "And don't interrupt me! Now that you have come home to stay, I can begin to repair the damage you have done to the Miraflores reputation. I still have political influence. I can contact the President of the Republic of Colodor. By posting, shall we say, *a bond,* I can get you amnesty, remove the price from your head, and you can settle down like a good son. Get married, make me a grandfather."

Smith's head spun. Why was everyone talking about marriage all the time? He felt certain that he'd never wanted to be married. In fact, he felt certain that his whole uncertainty over the past few hours had just been a moment's irrational fear. "But sir—I'm sorry to contradict you, but—"

"No argument! Go see your mother! *Go!* Before I change my mind and banish you to work on the llama ranch for five years." He shooed Smith off, chasing him down the hall. "Oh, and welcome home, son!"

◆◆◆

Pedrito's mother was about fifty. Her hair was nearly the same shade as Smith's, but tinged with gray. She wore a black lace dress with a mantilla comb perched in the back of her hair. She sat in the drawing room in a brass-studded armchair and fanned herself with a black, folding Spanish fan.

Seeing Smith approach, she sprang out of her chair to throw her arms about him. "Ai! Pedrito!" she cried. "Oh, my darling son! At last you have come back to your *mamacita!*" She stepped back, holding his arms, staring at his clothes. She stroked his face, and tears streamed down her cheeks.

Her emotional reaction made Smith terribly embarrassed— so disconcerted, in fact, that he didn't dare even tell her he wasn't really her son. He had never been treated this way before.

Once the woman had mastered her display and sat back down in her chair, she looked up at him, censoriously. "I've prayed and prayed day and night for you to reform, Pedrito." She jabbed her closed fan in his direction. "Tell me, have you given up drink?"

He was about to answer emphatically that he never touched alcohol . . . and then recalled he had indeed been drinking lately, but it was only the small amount of Yaquita's rum. Well, a moderate amount. "Oh, yes! Well, I mean mostly."

The mother clearly tried to maintain a severe expression, but she could not stop her doting. "And gambling?"

"I never gamble," Smith said, shocked. "That's for sure." But then he remembered the contest he had won. But that didn't really count, did it?

"And loose women?" She raised her eyebrows.

"Oh, heavens no!" He blushed crimson as he remembered Yaquita. "Well, I mean, sort of." Smith couldn't keep up this act much longer. He needed to sit down. Even more so, he needed to fly back home to New York, and get his life back to normal.

The mother leaned back in her chair with a sigh of satisfaction. "You see, Pedrito? My prayers are answered." Smith thought she would have been happy with him, no matter what he said. "The good God reigns in Heaven, and all is well here on our Miraflores ranch."

She coyly reached forward and tapped him with her fan. "Now that you have been properly welcomed home and properly scolded by your mother and your father, I have a surprise for you!" Her dark eyes gleamed.

The mother raised her voice toward the lacy curtain that blocked a side room. "He's here! You can come in now, Bonita, my dear."

A gorgeous blonde swept aside the frilly curtain, flouncing in to greet him. Her gown was a descending poem of ruffles; she wore a white comb in her hair and a white mantilla. Her large catlike eyes were the color of gleaming Colodoran emeralds, her skin a dusky bronze.

In a theatrical gesture, Bonita stepped out and spread her arms wide. "Ai! Pedrito!"

She engulfed him in an embrace. Smith had no recourse but to return the hug. His face above her shoulder stared at Pedrito's mother. "Uh, who's this? Do I know you, miss?"

Bonita giggled and then hugged Smith again.

"This is your childhood sweetheart, of course!" the mother said. "See how little Bonita has grown!"

Bonita kissed him so avidly that Pedrito's mother covered her eyes with her black fan. When Smith did not respond to the blonde's passion, she pushed him back. "Why, Pedrito! Don't you know me? That little bump on the head may have made you forget everyone else, but certainly you wouldn't forget *me*."

"Well," Smith mumbled, "it's kind of sudden . . . uh, Bonita. Was that your name?"

Clucking like a hen, the mother stood up and waved her fan at them. "Why don't you children change your clothes and go for a lovely horseback ride? Enjoy yourselves while I discuss the marriage plans with your father."

"Marriage?" Smith said. "Again?"

The mother beamed at him. "Of course, you silly boy. Bonita's family owns half the next province. Once you are married, our ranch will double in size. You two have been betrothed since you were five."

"We have?" Smith said.

"Come along, you silly monkey." Bonita locked her arm in his. "You don't get out of it that easily. We've got a lot of plans to make." She whispered into his burning ear, "And a lot of . . . *practicing* to do!"

The mother waved happily as they went out into the hall.

Chapter 23

BACK IN LIEUTENANT Tom Smith's New York apartment, Pedrito Miraflores felt like a trapped animal. The place was offensively clean and neat. The air smelled of antiseptic fluids and air fresheners instead of sweat, liquor, bad food and cigarettes. How could Smith stand it?

Pedrito single-handedly engaged in a valiant attempt to make the place more livable.

First, he bought several rank cigars—not good Cuban cigars, unfortunately, and smoked them one after the other until the apartment air was laden with their stench. Though they were bad American cigars, it had been so long since he'd had a decent smoke, even these were tolerable.

Then Pedrito stalked about, tearing down the paintings of beautiful sunsets and big-eyed puppy dogs, leaving only crooked nails and dangling picture wires, which seemed to him more appropriate. He went into the bathroom and left the toilet seat up.

Now all the place needed were some cockroaches, a stray dog or two, some scorpions and a few chickens.

In the kitchen cupboards, Smith had neatly lined up all of the cans. The grocery list clipped to his freezer door had been *typed*. Pedrito didn't find a single item of spoiled food in the refrigerator.

Shaking his head sadly, Pedrito couldn't figure out how a man could live like this. It sickened him.

He flicked on the TV and saw that Smith had preset the cable box to the local public broadcasting station. Pedrito clicked from station to station until he finally settled on a series of bad movies, after which he watched an hour of all-star wrestling.

Finally, nursing his own bottle of tequila, he felt more relaxed.

He went into the bedroom, opened the closet and saw Smith's Navy uniforms all hanging neatly, their creases crisply ironed, top buttons buttoned. With a mischievous smile, he shook the hangers, ruffling the clothes. He jostled the shoes lined up in ranks on the floor until the pairs were all mixed up. At this, he laughed out loud.

Hour by hour, this place seemed more and more like home. Smith would thank him when—or if—he ever came back. But that wasn't part of the plan. Smith was the patsy, and he was the infiltrator. Once he had passed along all the secrets from Naval Intelligence, this identity would be useless, and Pedrito Miraflores would be free to become himself again.

If Smith happened to get himself killed down in Colodor in the meantime, then Pedrito's legendary ability to escape death would be enhanced even more.

Pedrito rumpled the bed, tore off the bedspread and the mattress cover, grabbed a pillow and decided to sleep on the floor. He could feel the warm glow of tequila in his stomach, could smell the residual odor of cigar smoke in the air. Yet something was missing.

He went out to the dumpster, found someone else's rotten trash, and brought it in and dumped it in the kitchen.

He curled up on a lumpy blanket on the hard floor, and smiled as he sank down into the pillow. This was more like it.

Now he felt he could face the rest of his mission.

Chapter 24

AT THE MIRAFLORES' HACIENDA, Smith stood uncertainly beside a corral. He wore the fancy leather bolero and flat-topped hat of a vaquero with silver conchas, a wide riding belt, gaucho pants, and boots to complete his outfit. He was supposed to go out riding with Bonita, but he wasn't sure he even knew how to get into a saddle.

Thirty vaqueros lounged around on the split-rail fence, taking a break from the day's chores in hopes of hearing some of Pedrito's adventures, or at least hoping to see what the wild redheaded revolutionary would do next. The other horsemen applauded his arrival, clapping him on the back and shouting encouragement.

Inside the corral, a buckskin stallion reared and plunged and squealed, circling like a hungry shark that smelled blood. A daring or foolish vaquero had managed to saddle and bridle the fuming stallion—but the reins hung loose and the hapless vaquero was even now receiving medical attention.

Smith stood ten feet from the snorting horse, on the other side of the fence, swallowing hard. The vaqueros wanted him to ride that monster—and he had trouble keeping himself upright on a bicycle!

The obese major-domo also sat on the fence, barely keeping his balance. The split rails creaked under the burden. "Go on, Pedrito. You're the only one who could ever sit in his saddle. Show us you haven't lost your touch."

"He's your own horse, after all!" another vaquero called. "A wild stallion for a wild horseman!"

"He, uh, doesn't seem to want company at the moment," Smith said. He wished he had turned around and run back to the plane with Yaquita the day before. Now he was trapped here in this ranch with people who thought he was part of the family. All the attention was nice, but the responsibilities were troublesome.

"*Aww,* that horse has just forgotten you!" the major-domo said, nudging Smith toward the corral gate. "You must remind him who is the boss."

Smith backed away from the rail, mincing his feet to avoid piles of horse manure as the vaqueros egged him on. "I think you'd better take him away. I'm a sailor, not a cowboy."

The vaqueros on the fence exploded with laughter. The major-domo slapped his knee. "That is the best joke I have ever heard, Pedrito!"

During the laughter, a new vaquero darted into the corral like a matador confronting an angry bull. He wore a floppy hat that hid his dark Turkish features. He managed to grab the dangling reins of the rearing horse, then yanked its head down. Bolo secretly slipped his palm against the horse's snorting nostrils. With a sniff, the stallion wolfed a small lump the mysterious vaquero held in his hand—and then looked suddenly cross-eyed.

The two colonels might want Smith dead, but Bolo had other plans—at least for the moment. Beaming, Bolo gestured for Smith to climb into the corral. "Come on, Pedrito—see, he is a pussycat after all."

Smith was too frightened to recognize the man. He diffidently approached the horse and reached out a trembling hand for the reins. Everyone here expected this of him, and if they grew angry, they might make Smith *walk* back to the Santa Isabel airport. He didn't have a single friend here . . . not even Yaquita.

The mysterious vaquero nudged him toward the saddle, and Smith swung himself up. He gripped the pommel desperately for balance. The stallion weaved and crossed his legs, blitzed by whatever drug Bolo had slipped him.

As the lieutenant sat up in the saddle, looking almost like he belonged there, the vaqueros cheered. "Ai! Pedrito! Ai! Pedrito! Ai! Pedrito!"

Smith lifted his hat to them, swayed backward, then held the saddle to keep his balance. "Hey, I did it!"

◆ ◆ ◆

Later, Smith rode with the lovely Bonita across an expanse of grassy, rolling plains, far from human habitation. Isolation wasn't hard to find on the five thousand square kilometers of the

Miraflores ranch. Bonita seemed to have a destination in mind as she guided them toward the steep hills thick with cloud forest.

Smith's vaquero clothes felt more natural to him now, though he still missed his Navy uniform. Fresh and smiling, Bonita wore a black riding habit and a top hat tied down with a white gauze scarf. The young woman refused to ride sidesaddle, choosing instead a voluminous split skirt that allowed her to wrap her legs around the horse's ribs.

Smith's stallion ambled erratically in the grip of the tranquilizers. Despite the easy pace, Smith rode with far too much bounce, as if standing on the deck of a ship in a severe storm.

"There's something you really need to know, Miss Bonita," Smith said earnestly. "I am pretty sure I'm not really Pedrito Miraflores Santa Garcia . . . oh, I forget the rest of the name. I might look like him, but I'm a completely different person. I've never even met the man."

Bonita let out a silvery laugh and looked at Smith with her emerald-green eyes. "Oh, you poor thing. I can see it all now, the terrible fights you've had, the close escapes, the death-defying feats. It must be battle shock! Or mental fatigue. But don't worry, Pedrito my love, I'll take care of you until your mind is all healed."

Smith tried to convince her, raising his hands so that he nearly fell from the saddle. *"I'm not Pedrito!"*

Bonita tried to calm him. "Don't say things like that—they'll send you to a psychiatrist and make you into a vegetable. Santa Isabel has some of the best lobotomy clinics in all of South America, and the doctors there are always searching for new victims. Even dogs in the street are not safe." Then she brightened. "I've got my own treatment to restore your memory." Bonita pointed ahead toward the edge of the cloud forest. "Come! I'll race you to that grove, and there you'll see what I mean."

She laid on her quirt, and her horse bounded ahead. Pedrito's stallion ran drunkenly after her, and Smith had all he could do just to hold on.

♦♦♦

They followed a thin trail into the thick, dark trees. A few lichen-covered boulders protruded from the tall grasses, but the shade inside the forest seemed very inviting. Huge banana leaves drooped like umbrellas. A colorful green toucan with a scarlet rump sat in one of the trees, watching them with impenetrable eyes as he patiently ate green berries from a bush.

"Here's the place!" Bonita said brightly. She paused, waiting for his reaction. "Don't you recognize it, Pedrito? It's where you caught and ravished me when we were young. You were just a kid, too, but very precocious! Look, there's the very log."

Smith glanced around uncomfortably. The jungle was filled with a profusion of colorful flowers and flitting butterflies. They stopped their horses near the mossy log and dismounted. "I'm sorry, Miss Bonita, but—"

Bonita pulled a large Indian blanket with triangle patterns from her saddlebag and spread it on the damp, weed-covered ground. She threw off her hat and began to unbutton her jacket. "Well, I'm not a little girl anymore, Pedrito. I'll try to make the experience a bit more memorable this time." She arched her eyebrows.

Smith stood there, staring in disbelief as she undressed. Who *was* this Pedrito, and what sort of hold did he have on so many women? Swallowing hard, he looked around huntedly, searching for some way to escape.

"Well, come *on!*" Bonita said. "Only this time you don't have to pull my hair, you naughty boy." She smoothed the blanket. "Remember, if you're not nice to me, I can always tell your father, and he'll be mad at you again."

Smith wondered, what were the chances that another man who looked just like him and who spoke both English and Spanish flawlessly was living in New York? The odds seemed incredible.

Maybe it really was all a delusion. I, Pedrito Miraflores, was mugged in Santa Isabel and lost my memory. That's all that happened. Maybe.

Smith gave up and with a sigh began to unbuckle his wide leather belt. If he had to play the part, then he would do his best.

The toucan in the tree looked down, watching curiously. Its huge black beak cracked down hard on a seed.

Bonita smiled as he finished undressing. "I see you're not a little boy anymore, either!"

Before it could be embarrassed further, the toucan squawked and flew away.

◆◆◆

Afterward, Smith and Bonita let the horses trot home. Smith continued to bounce badly, sore in numerous places from so much enthusiastic riding.

Beside him, Bonita looked at him as satisfied as a cat that had eaten all the cream. Her green eyes gleamed. "Now isn't that better than getting a lobotomy, dearest?"

"You've got a point," Smith said morosely.

"So no more of this talk that you're not the real Pedrito. If your memory ever lapses, I'll be delighted to remind you again." She adjusted her hat and took the lead with her horse. "I just can't wait until we're married."

"Why is everybody so fixated on getting married?" He shook his head.

"I read it in a story somewhere," Bonita answered matter-of-factly. "That's what women are supposed to want. Don't you know?"

Chapter 25

IN THE HACIENDA'S enormous family dining salon, white linen, crystal goblets and silver flatware decorated a table that stretched as long as a racetrack. High-backed chairs stood barely within shouting distance of each other. Cinnamon-scented candles flickered in ornate candelabra next to vases filled with fresh-cut flowers. Hummingbirds hovered around geraniums in pots that hung in the corners.

Pedrito's father and mother wore formal evening clothes. The patriarch escorted the fine lady to her seat, then took his own place at the head of the table. Smith hurried in, brushing a hand across his newly oiled hair, tugging down his formal evening jacket. "Sorry I'm late. I thought the dinner bell was some kind of alarm."

The servants chuckled politely, and one waiter led Smith to his chair next to the old family patriarch.

"I'm very pleased with your reformation these past few days, my son," the father said as Smith sat down, draping the linen napkin on his lap. "I have sent for my finest bottle of wine from the deepest cellars so that we can toast properly." He raised his empty wine glass.

Bolo appeared at Smith's elbow dressed in a servant's white jacket, cradling a dusty bottle. Smith looked curiously at the too-familiar man, but shook his head. It couldn't possibly be true. He had seen and done many things in the past few days that made his head spin . . . and much as it surprised him, he found that he had rather liked parts of it.

"Papa, our boy has turned out just as I always hoped he would," the mother said, blinking her long dark lashes at Smith. "Tell us about the amnesty arrangements. Have you confirmed all the details for our Pedrito?"

Wrestling with the wine cork, but trying to look calm and competent, Bolo became very alert, flicking his eyes from Smith to Don Pedro.

"We have the strategy," Don Pedro said. "Everyone will be at Saturday night's grand fiesta at Rancho Ramirez. Bonita's father will announce the marriage date, and that will be cause for great celebration—proof that our Pedrito intends to settle down! Then, the following Monday we'll go to Santa Isabel and petition the *presidente* directly. The man could not possibly turn us down, regardless of what our boy has done in the past. Every young man must be a little rowdy now and then, eh?"

The mother saw the brilliance of the plan. "Not with *two* leading families to offend if he said no."

"Precisely," the father said. "That is why we are so happy about this marriage to Bonita."

With iron control, Bolo did not react to the news. He finally succeeded in uncorking the bottle and went to the mother's side, pouring a half glass for her, a half glass for Don Pedro, and a brimming full glass for Smith.

To the lieutenant, all this was going by much too quickly. He looked from one parent to the other, speechless. "We're going back to Santa Isabel? What will they do to me there?"

"It's merely the formality of surrender." Don Pedro waved dismissively with a hand sporting extravagant gold and emerald rings. "They have to keep up appearances, Pedrito. After all, you have burned missions, raided villages, destroyed crops, ravished women and fomented revolution against the lawful government of Colodor. But don't worry—as I say, this is strictly a formality. I very much doubt they will execute you."

Smith reached for his water glass, grabbed the wine instead, but didn't notice until he had taken a large gulp. It was all he could do to keep from spluttering and coughing as the wine burned down his throat.

"Not so much, Pedrito!" the mother scolded mildly. "Savor the taste of the wine—this vintage is a hundred years old."

The father sipped from his own goblet. "Yes, a toast! I'm reasonably confident the Colodoran authorities will turn you loose just as soon as they've taken your fingerprints and established your identity. *No hay problema.*"

Bolo, cool and professional even with the alarming turn of events, recorked the wine bottle and set it on a serving tray. He turned about smartly and walked toward the exit door.

The mother smiled. "So you see, son, you're in good hands!"

The massive mahogany door swung shut behind Bolo, causing the cinnamon candles to flicker on the table. Once out of sight, he slipped away, his shoes making no sound on the terra-cotta floor tiles. He ducked behind a thick stand of yellow hibiscus bushes. It was time to continue with Smith's on-the-job training.

Bolo dug in his waiter's jacket and brought out a portable radio, yanking the antenna and switching on the transmit button. "Cain-Idiot-Alpha One," he said, peeping through the dark green hibiscus leaves to make sure no one could hear him. Night moths fluttered around the blossoms. "Emergency! Cain-Idiot-Alpha One, come in!"

◆◆◆

Back in the U.S. Embassy in Santa Isabel, the CIA office displayed racks of ominous guns on the walls the way some museums displayed famous paintings. A huge Central Intelligence Agency emblem dominated one part of the room, painted on black velvet and looking very classy. Beside it, the colorful flag of Colodor—with its sword-crossed banana emblem—hung across the U.S. Stars and Stripes.

A flock of servile newspaper reporters scribbled on their pads as Chief O'Halloran lectured for his news conference. He smiled with an expression that would have made any lounge lizard proud. His thin strands of hair had been neatly combed, and most of the scrapes and bruises from his recent escapade on the highway had vanished.

Hunched in an alcove, another CIA agent with a pirate patch over his eye sat by a small radio set, trying to be nondescript. None of the reporters gave him a second glance as he poked at his earphone and listened to a secret message.

"The whole program of the United States is designed to encourage peace and only peace in South America. Ecuador, Colombia, Colodor and ... and, uh, whatever those other countries are called," O'Halloran pompously told the reporters. "Any rumors to the contrary are just malicious slander."

"But sir, what about reports of American warplanes crashing in the mountains, and CIA gunmen rounding up poor musicians in a local cantina?"

"As to the American warplanes, I haven't heard any such rumors," O'Halloran offered ingeniously. "As for the band members, I think anyone who plays disco with maracas and trumpets deserves whatever they get!" He flashed a winning smile, and the news reporters applauded his wit.

The eye-patched radio man scrambled out of the alcove and tugged on his boss's sleeve. He popped the earphone out of his ear and pushed it up against his boss's. O'Halloran tried to ignore the distraction, intent on his press conference. "All this talk of CIA interference with sovereign governments such as Colodor's is utterly—"

Finally, though, O'Halloran registered what the earphone was saying. He whirled savagely to the aide, ignoring the reporters. "Pedrito! Where?"

◆◆◆

Bolo peeked through the leaves, parting the hibiscus branches. Still no one within earshot. "Saturday night at the Rancho Ramirez, thirty kilometers south of Rancho Miraflores. He'll be there—send in the cavalry."

Bolo knew that with the CIA-backed Air Force destroyed and the assault vehicles wrecked, the military arsenal was looking pretty dry. If the cavalry got destroyed, O'Halloran might end up having to resort to hunting Smith down with a stick.

In the dining room, Smith and the Miraflores family had already been served bowls of potato soup with cheese and avocado.

Bolo clicked off the transmitter with a sigh of relief and mopped his brow. Tucking the radio back in his waiter's jacket, he climbed out of the bushes, brushing away a few leaves and cobwebs. Then he returned to his formal duties. The salad course came next.

Chapter 26

ADMIRAL TURNER STOOD in his office in New York, pretending it was the bridge of a battleship. Dressed in full uniform studded with medals and ribbons, he glowered at his daughter, Joan, as he spoke in a voice that had sent many seamen trembling in terror.

But Joan was far from being an obedient crew member. She sat wearing a new outfit that had cost more than an enlisted man's weekly salary, dangling her left leg over her shapely right knee. The admiral's checkbook sat open on his desk. As her father ranted, Joan preoccupied herself by studying the polish on her fingernails.

"—the dance at the officers' club tonight," the admiral lectured. "You're not getting any younger, and you might miss your chance to get married, settle down, have babies and do all the cooking and cleaning. What's wrong with you, girl? I insist that you go to the dance with Lieutenant Smith!"

Joan rolled her eyes to the ceiling. "*That* flat tire! Why would I want to waste an evening with him?"

"If you don't go with him, then I don't write out this check, young lady." His gray hair bristled . . . but then, it always bristled.

She could tell her father wasn't kidding. "Oh, all right, anything for you, Daddy," she said sweetly. "Could you make it for an extra fifty?"

◆◆◆

At the officers' club a band played polka after polka while a few sailors attempted to dance in their dress uniforms. Crepe-paper streamers drooped from the fluorescent light fixtures. Bingo boards hung on the walls. Naval officers milled about sipping punch with their wives or girlfriends, or both. The low drone of conversation mingled with the loud music.

A row of older women, looking quite severe, sat in folding metal chairs along the wall. They had come for their weekly bingo game, and no one had told them the officers' dance would preempt them tonight. Now they had nothing else to do.

Behind a long table near the bandstand, a blue-haired lady in cat's-eye glasses ladled from a huge bowl of punch. Pedrito, in Lieutenant Tom Smith's finest dress uniform, stood awkwardly in front of the table with the beautiful Joan Turner. She was stunning in her black sequined evening dress, her strawberry-blond hair done up in a French braid. So far she had refused his every attempt at conversation. He wasn't used to women giving him so much trouble.

The blue-haired lady handed a cup of punch to Pedrito. "Please tell me what you think of it, Lieutenant Smith," she said. "Very healthy. Lots of fresh juices. Just the way you always like it."

Pedrito took a mouthful of punch and spat it out in a spray before he could compose himself and remember where he was and who he was supposed to be.

"Why, what's the matter, dear?" the blue-haired lady said, wiping punch droplets from her cat's-eye glasses.

Pedrito made an awful face, looking at the cup. "No liquor!" he said. "No rum, no tequila, nothing! Just plain fruit juice— what kind of punch is that?" He wiped his mouth with his uniform sleeve.

Joan registered surprise at her date's reaction, then she thought she understood. "It'll take a lot more than that to impress me, Smith—but I'm glad you're at least making the effort."

On the dance floor, couples had grown even sparser, exhausted from the nonstop polkas. Now, to a slower tune, the remaining dancers swayed sedately, but then the music changed to disco. Joan perked up.

"Well, I'm going to dance," she said over her shoulder as she strutted out to the dance floor. "Follow me if you like, Smith—I intend to have a good time, no matter what you do." Joan began gyrating alone to the music while Pedrito stood next to her at a loss, not knowing what to do . . . though he did enjoy watching her body move, the way it pressed against her black sequined dress.

"What's the matter, can't you dance? Didn't they teach you that in officer training?" Joan rolled her blue eyes. "My, what a surprise."

"I am a master of the dance—but that's not a tango," Pedrito said, offended. "I just can't disco!"

"Watch—and learn," Joan said. "And you'd better learn fast if you want to have a good time tonight." Her whole body went into a shiver, and she shook her hips, moving with the music. Her evening dress followed every twist and turn, flowing with her supple moves.

Pedrito Miraflores was actually a very good dancer, and since this was part of his mission, he matched her gyrations, his eyes shining as he stared at her. They moved close, rubbing together as they danced. Pedrito grabbed her around the waist and pressed her against him as they continued to move together now, growing hotter.

The row of severe old women stared in shocked disapproval, clucking at each other.

Despite herself, Joan was pleasantly surprised, as if Lieutenant Tom Smith had just turned into a different person in front of her. Pedrito was willing to play the part of the uptight, strait-laced young officer . . . but only to a point.

♦♦♦

Pedrito drove the car, lost but following Joan's directions. She enjoyed telling him where to go, and she kept glancing sideways at him, reassessing him. This wasn't the type of date she had expected at all.

"It's just up the block," she said. Ahead Pedrito spotted a neon sign that flickered with pink letters, much more high-tech than the Cantina de Espejos: *MOTEL, Vacancy.* "All right, that's the place," she said. "Good paintings on the wall, nice decor. Comfortable beds."

"Good," Pedrito said. "I like comfortable beds."

◆◆◆

Later, in the motel room, the headboard shook violently, much the way Yaquita's brass headboard always shook in her room at the cantina. A white Navy uniform lay on the worn carpet, tangled with a fancy black evening dress. Pantyhose dangled from the television antenna, and somehow one black high-heeled shoe hung from the curtain rod.

The headboard bumped against the wall in a real tango beat. "Oh, I can't wait to tell my father," Joan gasped. "He'll be so happy about this."

"*What?*" Pedrito said. The headboard stopped shaking. Why would she want to tell the admiral? Most fathers came after Pedrito with shotguns when they found out what he had done with their daughters. "What are you going to tell him?"

"Why, that I've changed my mind. We can get married within the month! This is the opportunity he's been waiting for. Just think of the big wedding he can throw us. . . . I just hope he doesn't rent that officers' club."

"Married?" Pedrito slapped his forehead. "Ai! Is that all you women can think of?"

"I read it in a story somewhere." She raised her eyebrows at him. Her blue eyes shone with languid satisfaction. "Isn't that how it's supposed to be? I'm so tired of being intelligent, independent and my own woman. A husband is all I need."

179

She snuggled up next to him, and Pedrito looked frantically around the room, wondering how he was ever going to escape from this dangerous situation.

Chapter 27

RIDING INTO THE SUNSET, just like in an old cowboy movie, Smith and Bonita trotted along. Bonita looked fine on her dapple-gray horse, dressed in a black riding habit with a white scarf tied around the top hat. Smith sat astride the once-wild buckskin stallion, who now seemed resigned to his new look-alike master.

The past several days had passed in a blur, and Smith still hadn't been able to telephone the United States. Rancho Miraflores had no phone service whatsoever.

So many people had called him "Pedrito" for so many days now, he responded to the name automatically. Even the real Pedrito's parents didn't seem to notice any difference. He hadn't seen Yaquita since the old monoplane had landed . . . which he supposed was good, considering the attentions Bonita showered on him.

Today, they had gone out together so Smith could practice shooting with the mysterious laser pistols he had found in his tan suitcase—he was curious about the exotic weapons, and blasting a few trees made him feel a bit more like wild and rowdy Pedrito Miraflores. Finished for the afternoon, they headed off for the Rancho Ramirez.

"I can't wait to see my own family when they find I've caught my man at last," Bonita sighed blissfully and batted her eyelashes. "Oh, Pedrito, we'll be so happy together."

"I hope Rancho Ramirez isn't much farther," Smith said, bouncing heavily even across the flat plains, "or I won't be in very good shape for the big reception your father has planned."

Meanwhile, on top of a nearby knoll, a squat cavalry sergeant and his trim and nervous senior officer lay on their bellies, brushing a clump of feathery grass aside so they could watch Smith and Bonita ride past.

Thirty CIA-sponsored cavalrymen and horses waited in a hollow, anxious for that night's planned ambush. One of the mounts snorted and began to munch on a tuft of grass; one of the cavalrymen snorted and began to munch on an apple.

The squat sergeant pressed bulky field glasses against his eyes, focusing and refocusing. He frowned, making his huge black mustache droop like the tentacles of an octopus.

"Is it Pedrito?" asked the trim officer, squirming for a comfortable spot on the rough ground. He shaded his own eyes, but could make out no details in the fading light.

"I can't tell, Captain Xavier, sir." The squat sergeant took down the binoculars and glared at them. "These infrared glasses from the CIA are busted. I can't see anything."

"Then go sneak down to the rancho and take a look around. Blend in." The squat man scrambled to his feet. "Come back the moment you recognize Pedrito, so we can get on with the attack," Xavier said. "I'm getting anxious here."

The sergeant scuttled down the hillside toward the fancy white outbuildings of the Rancho Ramirez.

◆◆◆

Smartly dressed vaqueros and polished black coaches stood in the courtyard in front of the large Ramirez ranch house. Torches blazed around the marble fountains. Guitar players sang from wrought-iron balconies above, raising their voices in celebration as the two new riders came through the gates.

Pulling their mounts to a halt, Smith and Bonita swung from their saddles as vaqueros rushed up to take the reins of their horses. Though servants gallantly helped Bonita down from her saddle, Smith actually needed more assistance than she did.

"Welcome, you lovebirds," Señor Ramirez said. "This way, please—you must change your clothes and freshen up. The fiesta is about to begin. Everyone is waiting! This will be a joyous occasion. We have even scheduled a championship cockfight for this evening."

Outside in the hedgerow, the black-mustached sergeant peeked between the hedge, but too many other riders moved across his field of view. He crept closer, shoving his girth into the underbrush. One gold button popped off his shirt, but he continued undaunted; if he returned unsuccessful, Captain Xavier would inflict far greater damage on him than a lost button.

The squat sergeant finally reached the windows of the hacienda's main salon. Kneeling under an overhang of red roof tiles, he pressed his face against the rippled pane to study a crowd of grandees and ladies inside. The crowd clapped in time to the movements of a male flamenco dancer who spun across the tiled floor.

The sergeant enjoyed the music until unexpectedly the lovely blond Bonita appeared, now dressed in a white ruffled evening gown. She was escorted by a befuddled-looking redhead dressed like a Spanish grandee.

The whole crowd turned their heads and waved in excitement. "Ai! Pedrito!" the crowd shouted in unison.

Outside, the sergeant clapped a hand to his mouth. After disentangling himself from the clinging hedge, he raced away to the cavalry troops waiting in the nearby hills.

◆◆◆

Smith felt like a drowning man as people surged up to him, clapping him on the back and pumping his hand. The guests jabbered on about Pedrito Miraflores' alleged exploits, and Smith couldn't believe any single man could have accomplished everything they attributed to him. *He* certainly could never have done as much—it all sounded too dangerous.

A young raven-haired girl in the crowd shouted, "Dance a *flamenco libre* for us, Uncle Pedrito!" She clapped her hands.

The crowd took up her cry. "Come on, Pedrito. Dance!"

"I'm sorry, but I can't dance *flamenco libre*," Smith said, looking from one to the other. "I don't even know what it is." He glanced at Bonita for assistance, but she smiled lovingly, full of encouragement.

The crowd whooped with laughter. "Pedrito, you *taught* us all how to dance it!"

In the shadow of the main entrance hall, Bolo slouched under a dark vaquero hat. He yanked a smoldering *cigarro* out of his mouth, then calmly removed a black bag of firecrackers hanging on a wall peg. He pulled a single firecracker out and touched his *cigarro* to the fuse. "Dancing lessons, Lieutenant Smith."

The crowd drew back, giving Smith room on the tiled dance floor, despite his insistence. "Really," he said, "I'm not fooling. I can't *flamenco libre!* Never heard of it, in fact."

Bolo's firecracker landed on the floor at his feet and exploded. Smith leaped three feet into the air. Taking their cue, the band erupted into music.

Bolo tossed one firecracker after another. As they exploded under his feet, Smith instinctively leaped again and again in a wild dance. The crowd clapped their encouragement. *"Olé! Olé!"*

◆◆◆

In the moonlit hollow above the bright hacienda, nervous Captain Xavier stood by the CIA-sponsored troops as they mounted up, ready for a rapid assault under cover of darkness.

The black-mustached sergeant puffed up, holding his rounded stomach and aching sides. "It's Pedrito," the sergeant gasped. "It's him!"

Explosions echoed from the distant rancho buildings. The horses danced with anxiety.

Captain Xavier raised his fist. "Ride in at once—he's shooting up the place! If I know Pedrito, there's a slaughter going on down there."

•••

In the salon, Smith ended the dance, shaking and drenched with sweat. The crowd shouted, "Ai! Pedrito!" over and over again.

Señor Ramirez poured wine for Smith, snaking a sinewy hand around the shoulder of his future son-in-law. "You always could make us laugh, Pedrito." He put the wine in Smith's hand, urging him to gulp it down. "I'm so glad you will be settling down with us. We missed you!" Smith's eyes watered and his throat burned from the wine, but he managed not to cough.

Bonita took his arm in a proprietary fashion. "Yes, Papa, he'll stay home and be a good husband. I'll give him good reason to. Sometimes he has memory lapses, but I think I've cured him."

Señor Ramirez clapped his hands. "May I have your attention! Everyone, please listen. We have an important announcement to make."

Bolo ran in at breakneck speed, sounding the alarm. "The CIA is coming!" he shouted. "It's a raid—run!"

Outside, as the crowd screamed in alarm, a shadowy woman crept to where the guests' horses were tied to a post in the stable yard. She ducked beside Bonita's dapple-gray, keeping out of view. "Never could trust that Pedrito. Scoundrel! Platypus! I go on a mission for a few days—long live the revolution—and he shacks up with another woman. Sidewinder! What was I thinking? How could I expect that iguana to change?"

186

With a sharp knife, Yaquita slashed the cinch on Bonita's saddle. The dapple-gray horse flinched, but she adjusted the saddle to keep it in place, intact to all outward appearances. Bonita would be in for a big surprise when she tried to mount.

That would even the score a little.

As the panicked crowd surged to escape the main hacienda building, Smith stood alone on the dance floor. Tugging his hat brim down to hide his face, Bolo swept in and grabbed Smith by the arm to propel him toward the big arched door. "Run, run for your life! They will shoot you on sight, Pedrito."

Bolo hustled him down a rear hallway toward the stable yard, while Bonita followed in her white ball gown, breathless with concern. She had managed to tie on her top hat with the white scarf.

"There, my friends!" Bolo pushed Smith out into the yard, pointing to the saddled horses. "You must go—and be quick about it!"

"Wait, I forgot my bag!" Bonita said.

Gallantly, Smith whirled about and dashed inside, finally seeing something he knew how to do. "I remember right where you put it."

From a pile of saddlebags and satchels left by the guests, he grabbed the bulging sack of firecrackers Bolo had left, rushed back out and leaped onto his formerly wild buckskin stallion. "I've got it," he said. Bolo swatted the horse, and the stallion bolted away.

Meanwhile, Bonita tried to figure out how to climb onto her horse in her voluminous white evening gown. The frilly lace was for dancing and showing off, not horseback riding. She waved toward the departing Smith. "Wait for me, dearest!"

Seeing no easier way up, she put her foot in the stirrup and struggled to lift her other leg. But with the cinch strap slashed, the saddle came off entirely, slipping around as if greased with banana peels. Bonita flopped down into a big puddle of mud.

Lying in stunned shock, Bonita blinked, looking for words of outrage. A black-sleeved hand snaked in and grabbed her top hat, snatching it away. "*Gracias*, Bonita. I can make much better use of this than you."

Yaquita ran off for her own horse, waving toward the departing rider. "Ai! Pedrito!" But Smith didn't even bother to turn around. He was having too much trouble just holding on to his saddle.

♦♦♦

Captain Xavier, the squat sergeant and thirty CIA cavalrymen galloped toward the wrought-iron main gates of the hacienda, firing their pistols into the air and screeching out a battle cry. The crowd from the fiesta milled out in the courtyard.

Bolo stood by the gate, working his way over to the whip-thin captain. He appeared so suddenly that Xavier's horse reared. The officer looked down at Bolo, who pointed across the plain after the two galloping horses.

"They went that-a-way!" Bolo said. Lieutenant Smith would certainly get a workout tonight, but Bolo felt confident the man would get away. He had the right stuff.

"Come on, men! We can still catch them!" Captain Xavier spurred off, with his troops following.

Seeing the cavalry depart without burning down Rancho Ramirez, the band decided to keep playing. The Spanish lords and ladies began to dance out in the courtyard. Someone lit off more firecrackers as the party guests continued the fiesta outside.

No need to waste a good celebration.

Chapter 28

GRIPPING THE STALLION'S MANE for dear life, Smith rode into the night as though devils were after him. As he heard thundering hoofbeats of another horse coming closer, he shouted over his shoulder, "Is that you, Bonita?"

Lit by the moonlight, another rider drew alongside him. Smith looked around, and his jaw dropped. Dark-haired Yaquita was mounted on a dun horse with heavy saddlebags behind the cantle. She wore Bonita's riding habit and top hat with the white scarf. Her radio-guitar was strapped to her back, bouncing as she rode along.

"Oh, uh, hi, Yaquita."

She turned her head to him in a rage, raised her riding crop and brought it down across his back with a vicious whack. "That'll teach you to cheat on me! And with a green-eyed *blonde* yet!"

Though Smith could hear the thunder of cavalry troops close behind, right now, Yaquita seemed the more dangerous enemy.

"Wait, Yaquita, I can explain!" Smith said. "She was my childhood sweetheart—I mean Pedrito's childhood sweetheart. . . ."

She whipped him with the riding crop again.

Smith held up a forearm in an attempt to defend himself. "I know! I knew it was a mistake. I, uh, wasn't myself."

Yaquita looked at him, far from mollified, but reading her own meaning into his words. "Does that mean you're not going to marry her after all?" Yaquita seemed more concerned about her matrimonial prospects than their impending death at the hands of the cavalry.

"No!" he spluttered. "I never wanted to marry her." And he doubted the real Pedrito had, either.

"Oh, you darling," Yaquita purred, "you are *so* attractive!"

As the stallion continued to gallop, Smith turned around and saw the snarling approach of the cavalry under the silvery moonlight, their pistols glistening. Every one of the cavalrymen was out for his blood.

Captain Xavier, riding like fury, yelled back to his troops: "Draw your sabers! Get ready to cut them into *fajitas!*"

As one, the cavalrymen drew their sabers, the metal blades ringing from their sheaths.

Yaquita and Smith thundered across the plain, side by side, dodging hummocks of grass. They neared a treacherous ravine cut by a river at the edge of the cloud forest. The horses showed no sign of slowing. Behind them the main cavalry force held glinting sabers and pistols high as they fanned out to keep their victims from turning aside. Smith saw they were trapped, and Yaquita seemed to be paying no attention to their danger.

"Charge!" Xavier yelled. The squat sergeant kicked his mount in the sides, but the nag could barely stumble ahead under its burden.

Smith looked back, then faced ahead toward the ravine, a split in the escarpment with wooded slopes on both sides. Tall eucalyptus trees covered the slopes, muffled by thick shrubs around their bases. What would Admiral Nelson have done in a case like this?

Clutching the saddle with white-knuckled hands, he saw the sack of firecrackers dangling on the pommel, and he realized it definitely wasn't Bonita's cosmetics bag. Then he snapped his fingers. In one instance, he remembered Nelson had won a victory by pouring oil on the water and setting fire to it. He could do something similar here.

Yaquita took the lead as the horses reached the ravine. Smith rode into the thick bushes, refusing to let his stallion turn aside. Riding flat out, he threw the bag of firecrackers behind a bush, and it snagged on a thorny branch. "Bull's-eye!" He laughed aloud.

The cavalry was two hundred yards away and coming fast, shooting their pistols in the air, waving their sabers like machetes. "Don't let them hide in the bushes!" Xavier bellowed. "Trap them in the ravine! We'll run them off the cliff."

Smith wheeled his stallion and fumbled in the saddlebag. "I know I put it in here." He and Bonita had just been out that afternoon for a bit of target practice. With a shout of delight, he pulled out one of the bizarre high-tech laser pistols he had found in the suitcase's secret compartment.

Yaquita pulled up just beyond him on the steep edge of the ravine. "A pistol? You can't pick them off. They're too many!" she cried. "Even the great Pedrito Miraflores could not shoot them all one at a time!"

"I'm not Pedrito," he said again, knowing it was a lost cause. She would just be worried that his amnesia or his brain damage had returned. As the two horses picked their way down the rugged slope, Smith tried to aim the laser pistol despite his cavorting mount. The nozzle-tipped barrel danced around from his target.

Smith fired the laser pistol at the bush. The grip throbbed in his hand; the weapon thrummed. A scarlet laser streak slashed into the bag of firecrackers. The black sack glowed, then firecrackers exploded just as the cavalrymen thundered into the bushes.

The squat sergeant looked up in dismay, covering his head and dropping his saber. "*Ambuscade!*" He hauled frantically on his reins. The nag screeched to a halt, nearly collapsing from the weight.

Tiny explosions went off with flashes of light, one after another, like machine-gun fire. The whole troop wheeled in terror.

"Ambush! Ambush!" the CIA soldiers cried. "Pedrito's men! They'll kill us all!"

Captain Xavier stood in his stirrups. "Come back, you cowards!" Then his horse also turned and ran, knocking him back heavily in his saddle. "Oh, hell." He grabbed the reins to keep himself mounted. "The boss isn't going to like this."

Smith and Yaquita raced down the ravine, far from the fading crackle of tiny explosions.

"Well," Xavier sighed in exasperation as he watched the fugitives race away. He used the sergeant's infrared field glasses to watch as they reached a line of trees. "The CIA didn't bribe me with very much anyway."

••••

At the office and tearoom of the official U.S. ambassador to Colodor, a jowly, sallow-faced man sat at his desk, tapping his fingers on the newest page in his day planner.

O'Halloran, across from him, clutched the radio he had just yanked out of his pocket. He half rose from his seat and stared at the jowly man. "Mr. Ambassador! Captain Xavier just called in. I think we've caught up with that goddamned Pedrito!"

"Oh, dear! I thought Pedrito was out of the country," the ambassador said, frightened. He flipped to the previous page in his day planner and scribbled hurriedly, *Did NOT meet with O'Halloran.* "Please don't involve me in spy matters. It's against protocol for me to know anything about them! Plausible deniability, you know." Then he scribbled, *Do not even know who O'Halloran IS!*

O'Halloran hunched over the radio microphone and tried to be secretive out of long force of habit. "Maintain security in your open transmissions, Agent 234.996. Now tell me, did you kill the bastard? When can I come look at his corpse?"

••••

"Oh, you mean Pedrito?" Xavier said hesitantly.

195

"You know goddamned well I mean that goddamned Pedrito!" O'Halloran snarled. The trim cavalry officer held the radio away from his ear, wincing at the storm of words.

"Uh, just checking." Xavier swallowed. "Pedrito was heading for the Rio Meta with his latest lady friend ... but ... well, I guess he kind of just ... well ... got away. We were ambushed by his men—a whole army. A firestorm of bullets—we barely escaped alive."

The radio speaker hissed sparks at him, unable to contain the CIA man's undisguised roar of fury.

"I guess I just got fired," Xavier mused, glancing at his watch. "I wonder if that Russian colonel will pay better?"

♦♦♦

In the ambassador's office and tearoom, the jowly man cowered as O'Halloran went on a tirade. "Oh, dear," the ambassador said, "If Pedrito Miraflores got away, should I burn my secret papers?" He covered his ears to keep from hearing the details of O'Halloran's interchange on the radio.

The CIA man threw the radio to the floor and stomped it into fragments with his left boot. He scowled at the tangle of broken plastic and twisted wires. Then he grabbed a requisition form from the top of the ambassador's desk and began filling out the blanks, requesting a replacement walkie-talkie, Priority One.

O'Halloran ground his teeth, glaring at his ruined radio before he looked up at the ambassador. "This is a national crisis! I need you to authorize a half-a-million-dollar price on Pedrito's head—and a new radio for me. Then we can solve this problem once and for all."

The ambassador shivered at the sheer dollar amount of the reward. "Half a million? But the Colodorans make only fifty cents a day! Why, I should think a thousand dollars would thrill one of these peons!"

O'Halloran glared at him across the desk, his horrible stare became fixed and purposeful. "I know where Hoffa's body is," the CIA man growled. "Want to join him?"

The ambassador loosened his collar, suddenly feeling very hot. "Uh, half a million isn't really so much, I guess. I mean it all just comes out of the taxpayers' pockets, right? It's not like we're spending real money." He wrung his little mousy hands. "Yes, anything to serve the national interest!" he offered more forcefully.

O'Halloran's shade of red began to lessen, and his horrible stare was suddenly averted.

"Good decision, sir." O'Halloran picked up the ambassador's telephone and contacted his radio operator back in the embassy. "Get me the Meta River Gunboat Patrol! If we can't catch him in the air, on the plains, in the city or in the jungle—then we'll get him on the water."

Chapter 29

ON THE SLUGGISH green-brown river, farther down where the ravine widened into a jungle-thickened valley, a gunboat lay against a set of rickety pilings covered with moss and tangled with waterweeds. Banana leaves and long vines drooped toward the water. Bats swooped among the hanging creepers, grasping gnats.

In the moonlight the gunboat bristled with dark search-lights and a protruding artillery cannon in the bow. On deck, off-duty sailors tossed poisoned breadcrumbs down to a flock of ducks swimming around the pilings.

Captain Morales stood inside the gunboat's bridge house, yawning as he picked up his radio handset. "Hola, Morales speaking. Sí, glad to hear from you, Señor O'Halloran. A fine night for swimming, is it not? The moon is out, and the piranha are not biting." He covered his other ear to hear better as the ducks set up a loud quacking. "Help save my country? *Half a million dollars! Por Dios!* It'll be my pleasure. Anything for Colodor."

Morales burst out the door of the bridge house, shouting, "General quarters! General quarters!"

The sailors at the deck rail threw the rest of the poisoned breadcrumbs overboard then rushed to their cabins to grab uniforms. Others boiled out of the gunboat's hatches, throwing off lines from the pilings. It had been a long time since they'd been underway on a real mission.

"The vile bandit Pedrito Miraflores is headed for the *indio* village," Morales said. "Our boat alone is in a position to stop him! Get going! Our careers rest on our success tonight."

In a cloud of oily blue smoke, the gunboat roared into motion, lumbering away into the wide and languid river.

◆◆◆

Yaquita and Smith trotted their horses through a dripping tropical forest, far down the ravine from where they had eluded the cavalry. The misty air was spicy with the smell of jungle foliage, perfume-sweet orchids and rare night-blooming plants. The two fugitives were very bedraggled, their horses lathered.

Smith looked behind them, pleased with himself at how he had eluded the cavalry. He sniffed the air. "I think we're close to the river. A good sailor always knows when there's navigable water nearby."

Yaquita gestured ahead in sudden alarm. "I see a light ahead, bonfires."

On the other side of a cleared space in the jungle stood the grass and bamboo huts of an Indian village. A huge smoky bonfire blazed in the center of the village, reflected on the rippling river behind the huts. The orange glow silhouetted a mass of male Indians who stood in a unified threatening posture, spears and blowguns ready for action. One warrior juggled his spear from hand to hand, eager to throw.

Yaquita kicked her horse to flee, wheeling it about. Smith's stallion, though, bolted straight ahead. He yanked madly at the reins, desperate to stop before he trampled the native warriors. "Whoa! Whoa!" The horse ignored his every effort. Smith winced, his mind filled with visions of Amazon shamans and shrunken heads, curare-tipped darts for instant paralysis, and other unpleasant forms of death.

The stallion charged into the cleared space by the bonfire as the painted warriors dived from his path. Smith sawed at the reins, but the horse fell over, collapsing with a crash. The natives charged as Smith rolled away from the saddle. He scrambled to his feet, ready to run into whatever shelter the thick jungle could offer.

But the natives grabbed him and boosted him up. They raised their spears in salute. "Ai! Pedrito!" they shouted with unbounded enthusiasm.

Smith nearly fainted with relief. "Sure, I'm Pedrito."

◆◆◆

In the grass hut's formal suite, Smith, Yaquita and the village chief sat cross-legged on the dirt floor. His hair was painted red with a rust-colored mud and pigment, and he seemed envious of Smith's natural red hair.

Taking a moment to freshen up, Yaquita had changed into a khaki jumpsuit. Smith now wore a white shirt and pants and tennis shoes, feeling much more comfortable. He and Yaquita were both well washed and combed. They ate so hungrily out of gourd bowls that they were in danger of splashing food all over their clean clothes.

The chief's main wife brought Smith a gourd filled with a foamy drink, and handed it to him with great ceremony. Smith took a drink, tasted alcohol, and drank again, afraid he might offend his host. "Tastes like a light beer," he said. "Is that a house specialty?"

The chief laughed. "You act as if you never drank my *chicha* before, Pedrito! Chewed manioc root fermented with saliva. My wife makes the best in the whole village." The chief's wife grinned, showing off her manioc-chewing teeth. "The prettier the woman, the better the *chicha*."

Smith's stomach twisted. "Oh . . . that's interesting."

Yaquita took the gourd from him and swigged a drink herself.

One of the chief's sons sat against the curved wall of the hut, stuck one end of a long, thin bow in his mouth, and began humming against the taut string to make an eerie, whining music.

"Pedrito," the chief said, patting him on the knee. "I know you since you so high." He raised a calloused hand two feet off the floor. "You like son to me. You safe here in our village. We chase off bad men if they come again."

Meanwhile, outside the hut, Bolo stood minimally disguised as an Indian, his skin painted, his clothes made from beaten bark fiber. He crouched next to the bamboo wall of the chief's hut, listening intently.

"We can't stay here," Yaquita said to the chief. "We're on an important mission. This isn't a vacation."

"It was supposed to be a vacation," Smith said miserably. "Now I've been AWOL for a week."

"Relax, dearest," she said. "I'm sure no one's even noticed you were gone. You have much more important work to do here. We must go upriver and over the Andes."

Eavesdropping, Bolo smiled secretly, nodding as Yaquita followed her orders. Then he tiptoed away from the hut to vanish into the jungle shadows before he could be discovered.

"Good stew, Chief." Smith slurped up another mouthful, then scraped the last drops from the bottom of the gourd bowl. "What's in it? Chicken?"

"Our very best snake," the chief said. "Bushmaster. Most poison removed, only a little left for flavor. Nothing too good for you, Pedrito."

Smith swallowed hard, looked at the empty bowl and decided not to ask for a second helping. He had only more *chicha* to wash it down.

◆◆◆

Along the bank of the tropical river, three narrow gray dugouts poked into the water. Lush foliage drooped down, green vines, dangling branches and slender leaves hiding the canoes from casual observers.

One dugout was full of baggage, including the two saddles Smith and Yaquita had removed from their exhausted horses.

Indian paddlers pushed the laden canoe into the river current, then jumped into it, swaying to keep the craft from capsizing. Other paddlers launched the middle dugout, in which sat Yaquita, her back upright, her dark eyes flashing.

Bolo, still disguised as an Indian, clutched a paddle in the stern of the nearest boat. He kept his face averted from Smith.

Two other paddlers prepared to launch the last dugout just after Smith climbed unsteadily aboard, still queasy from his meal, but the chief held them back. He gave final instructions and spoke his farewells to the redheaded lieutenant, who sat delicately balanced as if sitting on a tightrope. The canoe swayed and rocked with the slightest motion he made.

The chief swept his arm up the river, knocking low-hanging branches out of his way. "My people take you upriver, Pedrito," the chief said. He looked at Smith very meaningfully. "It is not piranha season, but watch out for crocodiles! Much danger."

"Maybe the crocodiles better watch out for Pedrito instead!" said the paddler at the bow of the nearest boat. Shrieks of laughter came from the other rowers.

The chief patted Smith on the arm. "Come back soon, Pedrito. My wife will make more *chicha* for you."

Smith turned around to keep watching the shore, but his attention fixed on the aft paddler. Behind his makeup, Bolo wore a bland expression, dressed in ill-fitting Indian clothes.

"Say, haven't I seen you someplace before?" Smith asked.

The boat pushed off from the shore, drifting out into the sluggish current. Bolo shook his head, and the canoe swayed from side to side, but somehow the Indians kept it from capsizing. He dug in his paddle, huddling into the shadows. "All Indian look-alike to outsiders," he answered softly.

"Are you sure?" Smith narrowed his eyes.

"I got plenty brother," Bolo said in a guttural accent.

Satisfied, Smith turned around and sat on the damp seat. He waved goodbye to the chief. Despite the wobbly, unstable nature of the canoe, he felt much safer out on the water, being a Navy man.

♦♦♦

Captain Morales stood on the gunboat just beside his bow cannon. Pressing the field glasses against his eyes, he swept the river ahead, patiently searching for their prey. Other Colodoran sailors stood along the deck rails, holding their rifles ready, keeping their eyes peeled and their attention turned toward the jungle-thick river banks, though they could see nothing in the night.

"Wait for it," Morales said. "Sooner or later we'll bump into them."

♦♦♦

The three dugouts glided leisurely under the silvery moonlight like long blades in the river water. Smith's and Yaquita's canoes traveled side by side. Smith supposed the situation might have appeared quite romantic; Yaquita certainly seemed to think so.

Perfectly balanced, she leaned back on her narrow seat and strummed her guitar, playing a gentle melody that whispered like honey across the water. She hummed for a few bars, and then began to sing.

He bravely looked at the firing squad.
And when the rifles spoke,
It was a call to all the proletariat
To throw off the tyrant's yoke!

"Hey, that's too sad for a night like this." Smith reached across the water to pull her dugout closer. They nearly capsized, but the Indians struggled with their paddles to keep them upright. "Give me that guitar. Let me try it."

Yaquita smiled broadly and handed the guitar across to him. "Oh, Pedrito—you have never serenaded me before."

"There's always a first time for everything."

She batted her eyelashes and leaned forward to listen. "Is it a song about me? About undying love?"

But as Smith fiddled with the strings, twisting the pegs to tune it, the guitar crackled alive with a radio voice that came from an internal speaker. "Roger-Echo-Dog Eighteen," the Cuban colonel Enrique's voice said. "Warning, warning! Patrol boat coming upriver. Revolutionary force, you must elude it. Out."

Smith stared at the instrument, hesitantly plucked a string, then stopped the vibration with his fingers. He handed the guitar back across the water to Yaquita. "I've heard of crystal balls, but never a clairvoyant guitar."

Hearing the message, Yaquita became tense, gazing astern as a shadowy shape headed upriver at high speed. "Damn!" she said. "A gunboat."

"Just like the guitar said. Oh, don't worry," Smith said, cocky. Being Pedrito was starting to go to his head. "Patrol boats are navy—and that's where *I* shine."

Yaquita took the radio-guitar from him and stowed it on the curved bottom of the dugout. She grabbed a paddle. "Maybe if we paddle fast enough, they won't overtake us."

Bolo and the natives dug in their paddles and surged upstream, quietly singing a rowing song to keep them in time.

Thinking of his hero, Admiral Nelson, Smith wished he could have at least been standing in the bow of the canoe, but he wasn't sure his balance was sufficient to the task.

♦♦♦

On the patrol boat, Captain Morales continued to scan the river with his binoculars. Sweat beaded on his brow. They should have seen something by now. O'Halloran's warning couldn't be wrong.

"The moon is going down and we're losing whatever light we had, sir," the chief officer said, standing nervously at the captain's side. "Shouldn't we tie up to the bank and continue the search at dawn?"

Morales whirled on him. "And miss half a million dollars? You must be crazy. Where's your patriotism?"

♦♦♦

The last shreds of moonlight spilled across the riverbank, but the dugouts and passengers hid in the overhanging foliage. Accompanied by the chug of a gunboat engine, a searchlight swept the water, dragging a pool of illumination from one side of the brownish river to the other.

Yaquita crouched beside her canoe and peered anxiously through the leaves. The searchlight swept by again, intent and relentless. "The patrol is going to spot us!" she said in a hoarse whisper.

The disguised Bolo huddled next to Smith, whispering insidiously to the wide-eyed Navy lieutenant. "If you just stand up so they can see who it is, they'll go away." His voice sounded eminently reasonable.

"You're joking!" Smith said, incredulous.

"No, everyone knows Pedrito Miraflores. He's a famous hero in these parts. You've seen that yourself."

"Really?"

"Absolutely! They've got to be looking for someone else. Once they know it's Pedrito, they'll just go home."

With a shrug, Smith stood up, still dressed in his fresh white clothes. The gunboat's searchlight swung and hit him.

In the bridge house, Morales held the binoculars to his eyes. *"That's him!"* he cried, grabbing the loud hailer around his neck. He put the bullhorn to his lips. "Pedrito Miraflores, make one move and you're a dead man."

Smith stood with the dazzling searchlight in his face, blinking furiously. He heard the big bow cannon swivel into position, taking aim at him and all the hidden canoes. Yaquita and the native paddlers groaned in dismay.

"But I'm not Pedrito," he said to himself, then sighed. He wondered what Nelson would have done now.

The gunboat approached, ablaze with flashing lights. Other sailors crowded the decks, carrying their weapons at the ready.

Smith decided that in a desperate situation such as this, Nelson would have led a boarding party. The gunboat crew would never expect him to run out to them. It would take them completely by surprise. He pulled off his tennis shoes, hopping on one foot in the rocking canoe as he struggled to get off the other shoe.

"No, no, no!" Yaquita said in terror, grabbing for Smith. "Remember the *crocodiles!*"

The lieutenant didn't hear her as he dived into the black water. Yaquita's hand clutched empty air, and the canoe paddlers grabbed branches to keep from tumbling face-first into the river themselves.

In the front canoe, the natives shoved their dugouts back into the current, attempting to catch the young redhead as he swam toward the patrol boat.

Hearing the splash as Smith jumped into the water, a line of crocodiles leaped off the muddy bank in a hungry avalanche up and down the river. They fought with each other to be the first to reach the fresh meat.

Bolo smiled, watching the events unfold, confident that Smith could get out of the fix. Yaquita stood in the dugout, leaning forward with a boathook, madly trying to snag Smith as he swam toward the gunboat. The other vessel was still two hundred yards away, its lights blazing into the night.

On deck, Captain Morales bellowed through his loudspeaker. "What is he doing? Men, we are under attack! Turn! Turn, hard to port! Get out of here!"

The river boiled with crocodiles gliding toward the dugouts, snapping their jaws. Yaquita looked over the side of the canoe, snarled, threw down the boathook and used an oar to bash one of the crocodiles in the snout.

Bolo grabbed the boathook and snagged Smith's belt, then pulled him to the gunwale, though Smith continued to splash and stroke. One of the paddlers yelled, gesturing toward the water. A crocodile's jaws gaped for Smith's legs, but Yaquita helped yank the lieutenant into the boat. The tooth-filled jaws snapped shut, empty. . . .

On the gunboat the chief officer shone his searchlight back at the dugouts as the gunboat veered sharply. The river was full of black and writhing reptiles. Rows of white fangs flashed.

Suddenly, he looked down and saw an enormous log thrusting up from the muddy river. With the new course, he was heading straight for it.

"*Aagh!*" he shouted in dismay.

With a mighty jolt, the patrol boat ran aground on the log, twisting the boat upward.

The bow flew up, pointing the huge cannon at the stars. The cannon discharged, knocking an unlucky bat from the air.

"I think we struck a mine," the pilot shouted.

Morales gripped the lurching deck rail with white-knuckled hands. "We're sinking!" he shouted. "Head for shore! All hands, abandon ship."

Morales jumped overboard along with the rest of his crew— right into the waiting jaws of the massed crocodiles.

One of his crewmen, struggling to keep the teeth of a crocodile from closing on him, cried out, "Sir, what do we do about these crocodiles?"

"Swim!" Morales shouted as he turned in an attempt to regain the gunboat. He grabbed the gunwale and was pulling himself from the water when a croc grabbed his shirttail.

"Wait, get this crocodile off of me!" Morales ordered the crewman.

The crocodile rolled, tearing Morales from the side of the boat, and dragged him beneath the boiling waves.

With all of the screaming and thrashing and the scent of blood in the water, the crocodiles around the dugouts quickly turned aside, looking for easier meals.

The native dugouts headed upstream. Smith, sopping wet now and taking his turn at paddling the canoe, said to Bolo behind him, "What did they go aground on? A reef? Must be treacherous waters hereabouts."

Bolo stopped paddling and raised his eyes to heaven and let out an incredulous sigh. Still, Smith had survived, and his brash and unexpected action had been successful . . . somehow.

Behind them, the crocodiles made loud splashing sounds in the water as they set to an enormous feast.

Chapter 30

BY THE TIME they reached the high Andes, Smith felt extremely saddle sore. His bony-backed burro was even worse than the wild buckskin stallion back at the Miraflores hacienda. The creature's fur bristled out like a scrubbing brush, and the alpaca blanket underneath did little to pad the thin saddle.

Smith and Yaquita made their way up a steep mountainside trail on flat, rocky pavement laid down by slaves of the Incan Empire several centuries before. Sheep and llamas had passed this way many times on their way up to the high pastures, led by Indian shepherds and their dogs.

Finally, the trail became steep enough and treacherous enough that they were forced to dismount and lead the burros; Smith was relieved to give his hindquarters a rest. He hobbled along bowlegged and sore, as he guided the first two burros wearing saddles. Behind him, Yaquita led two other burros laden with packs. She seemed bright and cheerful, as if the thin mountain air had done her good.

"Our patsy looks pretty tired," Colonel Ivan remarked from a ridge high above.

"He hasn't had much sleep," Enrique said, taking the binoculars and adjusting the focus. "He'll be more gullible then."

"*More* gullible?" Ivan laughed at the thought. "I can't believe he has survived this long. Maybe he has a bit of Pedrito in him after all."

The skyline was a background of barren peaks of bleak, wind-swept stone. Giant Andean condors rode the thermals, circling for carrion they could snatch from the mountain slopes.

The Cuban colonel scratched his voluminous beard, then clutched his wool blanket around him against the chill. The Russian didn't seem to notice the cold at all.

Through his binoculars, Enrique could see that Smith had retreated to the tail end of the procession, slumped across the last burro. Yaquita led the other three animals up front, picking up the pace.

"I feel sorry for Smith, in a way, even if he is an enemy," Ivan said. "That Yaquita would wear any man out." He mopped his brow. "I am still tired."

"I didn't know you'd had an affair with Yaquita, too!" Enrique said.

"Hasn't everybody?" Ivan answered, genuinely surprised. "She feels it's her duty to the revolution."

"Well, I certainly haven't had an affair with her!" Enrique said. "You think I'm crazy? All she ever has in mind is marriage."

• • •

The trail became steeper. Smith physically lifted a burro over a broken boulder that had crashed down the mountainside in front of them. He tugged the beast's front legs over the obstacle, then the hind legs. He shoved with his shoulder, hoping he wouldn't receive a swift kick in the head.

Yaquita and the three remaining burros waited, amused.

Before long a blizzard was blowing. White snow plastered the burros, their packs, their saddles and Smith himself. He trudged along, head down and blinking in the blinding wind. He tugged the burros' lead ropes, hoping he wouldn't stumble off the edge of a cliff.

Yaquita used the battered guitar case to shield herself from the worst of the snow.

• • •

"When our Lieutenant Smith refuses to marry her—and he will, you mark my words—she'll cut his throat from ear to ear!" Enrique said. He swiped his finger across his jugular. "Even if she does think he's her Pedrito."

Snow covered Enrique's wool blanket, and he shivered, cold and wet. The Russian colonel ignored the weather, paying attention only to the tiny procession on the mountain trail far below.

• • •

As Smith had feared, the narrow path ended abruptly at a precipice, and he barely managed to stop himself in time. Chunks of snow and rock fell down into the gorge below. He heard the cold wind whistling around him.

One of the burros stumbled half over the edge, braying in panic. Smith grabbed the lead rope, fighting the beast back onto the trail, but the burro seemed more interested in bucking and kicking than in saving itself.

Yaquita and the rest of the procession were strung out on the cliffside trail. She watched Smith's heroic efforts with a confident smile.

Before long, he had wrestled the burro back onto the path, panting and sweating from the effort. Safe again, the beast looked at him with an expression as bland as Bolo's. They continued along the perilous path, making progress.

Smith had no idea where they were going.

◆◆◆

"Oh, I'm not worried about Yaquita killing him," Ivan said, brushing snow from his shoulder boards. "She might cut off his *cojones*, but she won't kill him." He reached into his pocket to withdraw a Cuban cigar Enrique had sold him. He sniffed it with a cold-reddened nose, then lit its end, shielding the flame of his lighter from the mountain winds.

"Then why are you so worried, Comrade?" Enrique asked.

"It's Commander José I'm thinking of," the Russian continued. "Even Yaquita could take jealousy lessons from that man."

◆◆

Riding the ungrateful burro he had rescued, Smith flapped his arms, trying to keep his balance as the beast stumbled down a long rock slide, wet with snow, slick with ice and totally unstable. As the beast picked its way along, boulders shifted, stone slabs ground together, and the entire treacherous slope swayed, readjusting itself, threatening an avalanche.

Seated on her own burro, Yaquita covered her mouth to hide her laughter.

◆◆◆

"Oh, yes," Enrique said. "I forgot Commander José was in that camp. Didn't the real Pedrito utterly humiliate him during their last duel? Could be trouble for us."

"You should think ahead of such things, Comrade," Ivan said. "This is a delicate mission, requiring careful planning. Ever since their duel, José has been brewing a blood feud. He would do anything to kill Pedrito."

◆◆◆

With weak knees and a tight stomach, Smith led the first burro across a perilously swinging rope bridge that spanned a sheer-walled gorge. A small toll-booth shack on the cliff's edge appeared to have been abandoned long ago. The side ropes looked frayed and soft, the planks rotted and weak. Each heavy footstep set the bridge vibrating.

Yaquita and the other burros followed across the chasm. She had taken out her guitar and began to play a grim love song about passionate embraces and plunges to tragic deaths. Smith could not stop himself from looking down to study the mind-boggling drop to the gullet of the Andes.

♦♦♦

"I suppose there'll be a killing, then, once they reach the camp," Enrique said, indifferently. He still watched through his binoculars. "Maybe this will be the last one for Smith."

"I suppose so," Ivan said, just as indifferently. "I don't understand why Yaquita didn't just take the main paved road to the camp. It's much shorter."

The Russian sighed, then put down his field glasses. "More vodka, Enrique? I'll trade you my flask for another one of those cigars."

Chapter 31

SMALL TENTS WERE STREWN about the edge of a sparse tree-line forest of stunted pines and scraggly eucalyptus. About fifty men sat in camouflage jungle uniforms, sporting red stars on their helmets and caps. They rubbed their hands together briskly, not clothed for the high-altitude chill.

They busied themselves cleaning weapons, gambling and drinking. A skinned guinea pig roasted on a spit above a small cookfire, tended by a lanky man who looked as if he had no intention of eating the rodent meat, no matter how hungry he got. Others cooked armadillos, iguanas, and even canned Spam as a last resort.

As Yaquita and Smith approached the rebel camp with their weary burros, the men grabbed their weapons and came running. "We're under attack!"

"It's the cavalry! Mounted soldiers!" another sentry yelled.

When the four shaggy and weary burros plodded into sight, the other troops laughed at the sentries, cuffing them and sending them running into the tents.

As the redheaded lieutenant came closer, the men raised their rifles in the air, waving in wild greeting. They set up a cheer that rang from mountaintop to mountaintop. "Ai! Pedrito!"

Stormy-faced Commander José strode out of the headquarters tent, crossing his arms over his broad chest. He was an evil-looking brute with a pockmarked face and a Cuban officer's uniform. The commander pushed his way through to the front of the cheering crowd. He chopped his hand down like an axe in a signal to be quiet. "Shut up!"

Slumping on the burro's bony back, Smith felt sore and trail-worn. He saw the troops, witnessed the welcome and waved. He was just glad no one was shooting at him, for once. It was a good thing these people thought he was Pedrito.

José glared at Smith. "You are no longer in command here, Pedrito! *I* rule these men. They owe their blood allegiance to me!"

Smith was taken aback by the man's vehemence. He had no idea who this commander was, but the guy didn't seem willing to extend a warm greeting. "Uh, look—"

"No! No looks, Pedrito! These men have to attack the government garrison at Bellanova in two days, and you would just make some grandstand play out of it!"

"Attack a garrison?" Smith said. "Why would we want to do that? I can't even get a map of this damned country."

"Shut up!" José said with mounting rage. "*I* am going to lead the attack. Not *you!* Your time with these troops is finished."

Among the rebels, with a red-star cap slouched as low as possible over his exotic features, Bolo stood dressed as a sergeant. He watched José's display of bravado with confident anticipation. So far Smith had performed admirably in his unwitting role.

"But you can't just attack a government installation," Smith said in horror. "That would be . . . that would be an act of revolution! And against the law, too."

The rebel troops broke into loud guffaws as Smith looked at them, bewildered.

"Challenge him to another duel, José!" Bolo shouted. "That way you can settle who's in command once and for all."

"Yes!" someone else agreed. "It's been a week since we've seen anyone killed in a duel!"

"That's a *good* idea!" José said with an evil grin as he eyed Smith's bedraggled form. "Shall we say bayonets at dawn?"

"Couldn't we just flip a coin to settle this?" Smith muttered.

Yaquita came up and proudly slipped her arm around him. "I know you will win, my darling. The blood flows hot in you. Just pretend you are fighting for me!"

The news of the upcoming duel filled the camp with enthusiasm. They raised their rifles and caps over their heads, waving, shouting and shooting.

◆◆◆

That night Smith and Yaquita sat by a small fire, eating out of stolen Colodoran-issue mess kits. They had an alpaca wool blanket wrapped around their shoulders. Between bites, Yaquita put her mouth close to Smith's ear, talking very quietly. Her breath was warm against his cheek.

"I don't know who you really are, and you mustn't tell me—some mercenary, no doubt, who volunteered to play this double role."

"You actually believe me then?" Smith asked. "You don't think it's just memory loss or delusions?"

"I don't know," she answered. "But I know this for sure: if these men found out you're not truly Pedrito Miraflores, they would kill you for impersonating him."

"That's a switch," Smith said with a sigh. "Up until now, everyone's been trying to kill me because they think I *am* Pedrito."

On his knees, Smith unrolled a double sleeping bag under a wind-bent mesquite bush, hoping the fabric was as warm as it looked. Yaquita smoothed the fabric. "Sleep well, my darling. Everything will be settled tomorrow. You will defeat José, then we can begin our assault on the fortress of Bellanova."

In the firelight, Smith pulled off his boots. "But I don't *want* to fight José or attack a friendly country."

Yaquita fiddled with her buttons, half out of her khaki jumpsuit. In the cold, goosebumps stood out on her golden skin. She paused in her undressing, looking cross with Smith as she poked him in the chest.

"You *must* convince them you're the real Pedrito!" She went on undressing, glancing eagerly at the double sleeping bag. "He might have been a two-timing scoundrel, but he earned a lot of respect from these men. He was the hardest-drinking, hardest-riding, fastest-shooting agent anybody ever met."

"I've got to live up to *that* reputation?" Smith said, peeved. The mountain air was very cold and sharp.

"You better! I don't want you killed. We've got better things to do." Once they were together in the sleeping bag, Yaquita was very loving. She kissed him, and very shortly Smith felt warm again, very warm.

Chapter 32

AT THE EDGE of the rugged tree-line encampment, a weather-beaten old pine dangled its gnarled limbs like a gallows. The sun rose straight up in a ruddy equatorial dawn, and the rebels gathered for the duel.

Smith hadn't slept a wink, in part because of his mortal terror, in part because of Yaquita's amorous attempts to make him forget his mortal terror.

Now he stood waiting under the ominous tree, dressed in a combat jungle uniform. The gnarled pine's nearest overhanging limb hung thirty feet off the rocky ground. In the dirt around the trunk, dark patches of hardened mud showed where blood had dried in pools.

Thick liana vines trailed from the high limb of the dueling tree to the trampled ground where their ends lay in a tangle.

Smith tied one of the four burros to the nearest vine, looking around expectantly for his opponent. He glanced at the complicated Russian military chronograph on his wrist, checking the time. "You don't think José has decided to let me win by default, do you?"

Yaquita stood by the other burros, looking at him wistfully. "It would be wise of him to do so . . . but unfortunately, wisdom isn't one of Commander José's strong points."

Banging pots and pans, firing their rifles into the air, the eager commandos marched out of the camp, led by surly-faced José. Smith swallowed hard. "Nelson would say it was a good time to retreat."

Yaquita laughed and kissed him on the cheek.

Commander José came to a stop in front of Smith, glowered at him for a moment, then reached into his pocket to whip out a red-patterned bandana. He thrust the cloth toward Smith.

"What do I do with this?" Smith asked, taking a corner of the bandana. "Is it a blindfold?"

The crowd laughed extravagantly. "Ai, Pedrito! What a joke!"

"You yourself made up this style of dueling," José snapped, his pockmarked face ruddy with anger. "Don't mock it now."

Concealed by his commando disguise, Bolo strutted between Smith and José. He snatched the bandana away, looking officious. He jammed one corner in the lieutenant's mouth as Smith opened up to splutter a question, the opposite corner in José's mouth. "Each combatant holds the bandana in his teeth."

Smith gagged and tried to mumble a question, while José bit down like a pit bull terrier on a newspaper boy's shin.

"The first man to let go of the bandana loses. Beyond that," Bolo continued, "there are no other rules." He handed each of them a wicked-looking machete. "When I say 'Go!' you begin. Enjoy yourselves, gentlemen." He stepped back. "Ready, set—*go!*"

Both men surged forward, grunting muffled curses through the bandana stuffed in their mouths. José tried to strike with the machete in his right hand as he grabbed Smith's knife wrist with his left. The long blade struck sparks off the metal band of the Russian military chronograph. Smith strained, trying to get his own machete free.

The crowd was glittery-eyed with expectation. Yaquita strummed a fight song on her guitar; she had a vast repertoire of tunes about killing.

The two fighters circled on the packed ground under the gallows tree, flinty eyes locked. Smith's heart pounded with the excitement and the thin air. He felt exhilarated and alive . . . alive for a few more moments at least. This was so much different from his life as a Navy blueprint inspector.

With sweat pouring from his temples down to his chin, José grimaced with hate and strain. He pressed harder with his machete, slowly beginning to overpower Smith.

Meanwhile, the burro Smith had tethered to the liana vine watched the fight, munching dry grass. He snorted as the struggle came closer to him.

Smith's white tennis shoe stepped onto the coil of vine.

José stabbed his machete downward, though Smith maintained his grip on the commander's wrist. Still clenching the bandana in his jaws, Smith brought his knee up into his opponent's stomach. With a cough of bad breath through clenched teeth, José fell backward and hit the burro.

Spooked, the animal bolted. The liana tether jerked tight with Smith's foot caught in the coil of vine over the branch. He tried to yell as the burro ran, but the bandana in his teeth prevented him from making a satisfactory squawk.

Smith's head did a full arc upside down above José's head as the burro hauled him into the air. The commando leader also refused to release the bandana in his teeth, so Smith hauled José up with him.

The crowd laughed and cheered, shooting their guns into the air, which startled the burro even more. Smith and José went straight up until Smith's foot struck the high limb. He jerked to a stop.

The crowd stared at this feat with awe, applauding. Yaquita even stopped playing her guitar. While the two combatants hung suspended, one of the other untethered burros wandered under the tree, looking for something to eat.

Grunting and fuming, Smith and José flailed, still biting their respective corners of the bandana, still grasping each other's knife wrist. Smith's neck muscles stood out like ropes as José thrashed and dangled below him.

"Can't we talk this over, man to man?" Smith mumbled through clenched teeth. The spit-wet bandana muffled all of his words.

"I'll kill you!" José snarled, thrashing with his machete hand.

"I'm sure you must be a better commander than I, José," Smith said. "I really admire you."

José's dark eyes flared wide with surprise. "*What?*" Opening his mouth in shocked disbelief, he let go of the bandana. Before he could reach out to grab Smith, he fell tumbling. The redheaded lieutenant still hung upside down by his ankle, watching José plummet to the ground.

The commando leader struck a lone burro that had wandered under the tree, landing heavily in the thin saddle. With a bray of alarm, the beast charged off, carrying the defeated captain deep into the Andean wilderness.

•••

The crowd of rebel commandos hefted the victorious Smith on their shoulders, marching him around the perimeter of the camp.

"Ai! Pedrito!" They fired more and more gunshots. After this, Smith wondered how they could possibly have enough ammunition left for their actual military activities.

Chapter 33

THE GOVERNMENT GARRISON of Bellanova was an old Inca fort with high walls and protruding bastions. The ruined fortress was surrounded by barren, rocky ground. It had been partially rebuilt as a historical monument and tourist attraction, but then had been taken over by the Colodoran bureaucracy as an office building and military garrison. A steep gravel path led up to a barred archway, flanked by ornamental bushes. The multicolored flag of Colodor flew from the highest turret, displaying the national emblem of a banana crossed with a sword.

Bolo—this time dressed in a peon's white shirt and pants, colorful wool poncho, straw sandals and traditional felt hat—glanced stealthily over his shoulder. With furtive dashes he went from scrub bush to thorn bush along the gravel path, zigzagging his way up to the old garrison's front gate.

Holding on to the rusty bars, Bolo peered into the refurbished fortress itself. A company of uniformed Colodoran soldiers strutted about in the flagstoned courtyard, presenting arms, striding in lock step. Beyond them Bolo could see a line of camouflaged antiaircraft weapons, long barrels pointing out of bunkers in the thick stone walls whose blocks had been precisely fit by ancient Inca masons.

Bolo rapped on the barred gate with his knuckles. "*Psst! Hey!*"

A sentry popped his head out, rubbing sleep from his eyes. Bolo whispered in the man's ear. The sentry checked his notebook of approved excuses for allowing visitors to enter, then pushed the gate open wide enough for Bolo to slip inside.

♦♦♦

In the comandante's stone-walled office, crossed sabers hung on display, covering the worst lichen stains. Frilly drapes hung over the wrought-iron bars on the windows in a style much too feminine for the comandante's tastes . . . but his wife had done the redecorating in the fortress, and he could not say no to her.

He sat with his feet propped on his big desk, hands folded across his potbelly. Tilting his uniform cap on his head, the comandante puffed on an enormous American cigar. CIA chief O'Halloran sent him boxes of the cigars as part of his monthly bribe. The comandante thought they tasted vile, but at least they were free.

Bolo stood before him in his peon disguise, nervously twisting his felt hat. Fully awake now, the sentry from the gate stood watchful behind him.

"I just poor country farmer, but I want part of big reward," Bolo said. "I throw myself on your sense of fairness, comandante."

The comandante leaned forward with sudden interest. He jabbed his smoldering American cigar at Bolo. "Reward? Eh, what reward?"

"For the redheaded bandit Pedrito Miraflores. Half million U.S. dollars. I can help you catch him."

The comandante's jaw dropped and the cigar fell from his mouth into his lap. He snatched it away, slapping hot embers from his trouser legs. Then he leaped to his feet. "Did you say *half a million dollars?*"

Bolo nodded vigorously, but kept his eyes averted. "Sí, comandante. We saw it on our satellite TV in our hut. I want half of the money if I tell you exactly where Pedrito is."

"One-third!" the comandante said, emphatically. He puffed up his chest and tried to look intimidating in his government uniform. "I'll be doing all the dangerous work to capture this bloodthirsty criminal."

Bolo's shoulders sagged as he made up his mind. "As you wish, comandante. I just a poor peasant. I settle for one-third of the reward. It will be enough to buy us a new burro and some firewood." He leaned forward and whispered into the comandante's ear. "But you must take troops and leave the fortress right away. You can't miss a chance like this."

The comandante's face lit up. "We'll march out within the hour! All of my soldiers." He shouted for his secretary, immediately calling a staff meeting.

◆◆◆

Next dawn the sky in the high Andes was a colorful red. Covered by the slick leaves of tropical plants, looking out of place in the rocky scrub around the ancient Inca fortress, Pedrito's commandos scurried forward. The revolutionaries wore jungle uniforms, holding their rifles ready. Having wasted so many rounds during the previous celebration, the troops were already low on ammunition.

Smith stood in the line of commandos and spread his arms to halt the approach. Curving chunks of bark had been lashed to his arms, waist and legs, ostensibly making him look like a large tree stump. One of the high-tech laser pistols hung on each hip; a coil of line and a small grappling hook dangled from his belt, threatening to trip him with every step.

Looking at Bellanova, Smith pondered how Nelson might have taken the place. "It's comparable to an old pirate stronghold in the Caribbean, I suppose." He squinted into the brightening sunrise. Two lone sentries were visible on the fortress walls, telling each other jokes.

They had no choice but to storm the gunnels. Smith raised his arms, gave the signal for the jungle-disguised commandos to advance. The rebel troops let out a battle cry: "Long live the revolution!" Smith charged forward, running stiffly in his tree-bark disguise.

The pair of sentries on Bellanova's battlements stared in alarm at the commandos, who were tearing camouflage leaves and branches off their uniforms for greater freedom of movement. The first sentry finished the punch line of his joke about a llama farmer in the big city, and then both of them fired their rifles at the attackers.

Smith ran forward, zigzagging right and left, waving his bark-covered arms for the troops to follow. The sentries' shots pinged on either side of him. Even though he didn't really know what he was doing, he felt the thrill of adventure, just like one of his favorite chapters in *Famous Naval Battles.*

He finally reached the base of the fortress wall, holding the grappling hook and line in his hand. He tore off the bark covering his arms, twirled the hook and threw it upward. The hook sailed over the stone wall, setting its barb firmly in a very narrow crack between the tightly fitted Inca stones.

Smith tugged hard to check the rope's sturdiness, then walked straight up the wall. "Just like climbing the ratlines on a ship," he said.

He swung his leg over the top of the stone wall, stopped and gaped. As other rebels swarmed up the wall behind him, the two lone sentries fell to their knees, begging hands clasped under their chins. "Spare us, spare us!" Their rifles lay discarded beside them.

"Yes," the other one said, "we know plenty of good jokes! We could be very useful to your army."

Surprised, Smith kicked their guns aside. He stepped to where he could look down into the flagstoned courtyard. Commandos darted in and out of the wooden fortress doors, searching. From the barracks a dozen rebels had gathered up six men in underwear, who surrendered repeatedly.

One of the commandos spotted Smith on the wall above and yelled up to him, "The place is empty, Pedrito! There are no enemy soldiers."

Smith hunkered beside the blubbering sentries. "Where is everybody?"

The sentries wrung their hands. "A report came to us that Pedrito Miraflores was thirty miles downriver. The comandante chased after him with the whole command of Bellanova. He wanted the reward. Big reward."

"No word at all from them since yesterday," said the second sentry.

"I think they're lost," groaned the first, hanging his head in shame. "We didn't have any official maps."

Smith grinned down at them, finally proud of his new identity. "Well, don't you recognize me? *I'm* Pedrito Miraflores."

Chapter 34

THE SIGN ON THE CAGES in Bellanova's bird loft read GOVERNMENT PIGEONS, FOR OFFICIAL USE ONLY. A stone embrasure let sunshine into the tower room, illuminating a table used for scribbling coded messages. Confiscated terrain maps drawn before the mapmakers' union strike showed the borders, roads and terrain of Colodor.

Bolo had discreetly slipped into a Communist sergeant's uniform with a red star in his cap. He printed a message on a tiny pigeon slip, very careful with his script. *Dear Governor, Pedrito Miraflores just captured the entire province of Bellanova. Complete rout. Comandante and all government forces in full retreat. Signed—sole survivor.*

Bolo rolled the message like a cigarette paper and stuffed it into a tarnished tin cartridge. He grabbed one of the birds from the Official Use Only pigeon cages and fastened the cartridge onto its leg, then released the pigeon out the narrow open window.

"Special delivery," he said, and the pigeon flew out.

◆ ◆ ◆

At CIA headquarters in Langley, Virginia, a stream of nondescript black sedans arrived and departed. Weirdly similar men in black suits and conservative ties flowed in and out of the doors.

"Sir, we've got an urgent red tag!" an aide said, rushing down the hall into the director's office.

"Don't bother me!" the director said, annoyed as he watched his golf ball curve toward a wall studded with hidden microphones. "You made me miss my putt."

"It's urgent, sir!" the aide said. "Direct from South America by diplomatic carrier pigeon."

"Go tell it to the FBI." The director dropped another golf ball on the floor, then lined up his putt.

◆ ◆ ◆

Traffic moved by on the avenue below the J. Edgar Hoover Building. Any vehicle that decreased its speed by more than two miles per hour was photographed, its license called up on an FBI computer, and a complete security check run on the driver all the way down to his high-school grades and what pets he had owned as a kid.

The same aide rushed into the FBI headquarters and found the office of the director. "Sir! We've received word that Pedrito Miraflores is on a rampage in South America."

"Miraflores? Who's he?" said the FBI director, who looked extraordinarily like the CIA director. He sat at his desk unconcerned, reading various incriminating files over his lunch hour. He ate a sloppy tuna sandwich as he shuffled papers. "Nobody I've ever heard of, I suppose. Is his file here?"

"Miraflores is their top Commie agent, sir."

"Oh. You'd better go to the State Department, then. This is in their jurisdiction." He picked up another file, his wife's, and began to read with avid interest.

♦♦♦

At the State Department Building the same aide desperately passed his news on to another official. "—but he completely blew up the U.S. Embassy in Santa Isabel!"

"Blew it up?" the official said. "Oh, then this sounds like a job for the Defense Department. Stop bothering me about it."

♦♦♦

Outside the Pentagon, traffic crawled around and around in circles. Every side of the immense building looked essentially the same, and most of the drivers were lost.

The same aide breathlessly recounted the pigeon message to a two-star general, then to a three-star general.

"—wiped out an entire cavalry division with an ambush, wrecked the Meta River Patrol, captured a powerful military

239

fortress and brought a whole province to its knees!" He hauled out a blurry Polaroid snapshot. "Here's his photo. Look at those shifty eyes, that red hair."

"A scoundrel, if I ever saw one," the general agreed, then shooed the aide out of his office.

♦♦♦

Congressmen and Congressional aides rushed up and down the steps of the Capitol Building, followed by reporters, cameramen, demonstrators and lobbyists. A blustery Vice President looked at the Polaroid skeptically. "How can a Mexican be redheaded? And aren't they really short? Are you sure this isn't another tabloid hoax?"

"He's not a Mexican," said the aide. "Pedrito is half-German, and all trouble." To be certain that the Vice President understood the danger, the aide said, "You know, *German,* like Hitler and the Nazis—the bad guys in WW II."

"Oh, yeah!" the Vice President said. "I saw a documentary about Hitler's clones living in some country down there." With a querulous look, he asked, "Do you think this Pedrito is one of those clones?"

The aide, utterly flabbergasted, said, "That wasn't a documentary you saw, it was a movie—fictive entertainment. Called *The Boys from Brazil.* The, uh, fact is, sir, we don't know how to clone people yet. Only sheep."

"Sure we do," the Vice President said. "It worked on Elvis." Then his face burned bright red and he slapped his hand over his mouth as he realized that he'd just uttered a national secret.

"Hmmm . . ." the aide said, deadpan. "A Hitler clone. You might be onto something there! The man *is* a terror. Ask any number of fallen governments in the region."

"He has a leering smile," the Vice President said. "He sure looks dangerous—I mean, you wouldn't want to meet him in a dark alley."

"He is! He is!" In a last desperate attempt to get some help, the aide said, "Not only that, but we believe he's secretly funneling campaign contributions to your rivals. We've got to do something!"

"I agree," the Vice President growled in a fit of indignation. "We'd better go talk directly with the President himself."

•••

At the White House, the President glanced cursorily at the snapshot and the original pigeon-borne note. "Illicit campaign contributions, huh? The back-stabbers. Well, we'd better circulate his photograph and alert all South American governments and CIA stations. Issue orders to hunt down this bloodthirsty criminal and kill him on sight." The President handed the papers back to the aide with a fierce look. "I want the full treatment."

The aide stood a moment, heart thumping in anticipation. Not since the Nixon days had the CIA been authorized to give someone "the full treatment."

The President added, "And put a price of a million dollars on his head. Now skedaddle on out of the Oval Office and let me get back to my putting practice."

The President leaned over his putter, tried to concentrate, but news of Pedrito Miraflores clearly had him distraught. He swatted with his golf club, then swore. "Damn! You made me miss my shot!"

•••

Meanwhile, in New York, the real Pedrito Miraflores stayed late in Smith's Naval Intelligence office, wearing a neatly starched officer's uniform. He had nothing to do back at his apartment, and plenty of espionage to accomplish here, so he decided to put in a few hours of overtime. Colonel Enrique and Colonel Ivan were counting on him.

File cabinets hung open with papers strewn about. Piles of blueprints flanked the desk, sprawled on the drafting table. The desk lamp shone down on a missile guidance system plan. Squeezing one eye shut, Pedrito used a Minox camera to photograph the entire blueprint. Maybe the Cuban or Russian engineers could figure out the design.

Clicking footsteps approached down the hall, stopping abruptly outside his office door. Pedrito tried to sweep the plans out of sight, breaking out in a sudden sweat.

Joan Turner opened the door and barged in. "Well, Lieutenant, unreliable as usual, I see. We've got to talk about our wedding plans, and I've been waiting—" She took in the scene with widening blue eyes. Pedrito leaned over the drafting table, trying to cover the plans with his own body.

"What on earth are you doing?" Joan said, spotting the tiny Minox. "Isn't that a spy camera? I saw one in a movie once."

Pedrito stopped trying to cover up the missile system blueprint. He smiled his best charming smile and extended the small high-tech camera toward Joan. "Oh, yes," he said. "It's the latest thing. Just testing it. A Naval Intelligence special design. Your father's thinking of providing one to each of his men just to take a few family photos."

"For the wedding, I suppose?" Joan said. She crossed her arms and didn't believe him for an instant.

Pedrito lowered the spy camera and tried another tack. "You shouldn't be in here, you know. These missile files are all secret. Who knows what you might have seen. National security could have been compromised."

She looked at him suspiciously, then she became calculating, choosing her own priorities. She primped her strawberry-blond hair. "Just one question for you, Smith—you *do* intend to marry me, don't you?"

"Oh, yes!" Pedrito said hastily.

"Good. Just checking." She looked at him with a slitted predatory eye. "You'd better not lie to me." Then she walked out, pretending she hadn't seen a thing.

Chapter 35

NEWLY ENSCONCED in the comandante's office at the ancient Inca fortress, Smith looked at his new headquarters. The lacy white curtains on the barred windows did a nice job of softening Bellanova's stark stone walls.

He had changed out of his bark-stained uniform into a crisp khaki with officer's insignia and a big red star on the cap. Yaquita had found the clothes in a closet, and she said he looked very dashing in them. To Smith, it felt good to be in a formal uniform again . . . even if it was the wrong uniform.

He thumped his feet on the desk and poured himself a drink of rum; Yaquita had given him a fresh bottle, and he had grown to find it tolerable after all. In fact, it was far safer to drink the rum than the local water. Pedrito Miraflores must have done some things right. Smith held the glass up to the light that seeped through the frilly curtains, then downed the drink. His entire body shuddered, then he sighed. He wondered if the locals made rum differently here below the equator, since he had never been able to tolerate alcohol before. But then, a lot of things about Lieutenant Tom Smith had changed in the past couple of weeks. . . .

Bolo marched in wearing a sergeant's uniform. He snapped off a brisk military salute, and Smith acknowledged him without looking up, or recognizing him. "Have you seen to the antiaircraft and ground defenses, Sergeant?" Smith asked. "We can't let this fortress fall back into the proper hands . . . er, I mean into enemy hands."

"No need for those defenses, sir," Bolo said. "All governmental forces in the province have surrendered, or they're lost somewhere out in the mountain trails. No one knows where the comandante of Bellanova has gone, but quite often troops vanish without a trace, unable to find their way through Colodor's many roads and passes."

Smith poured himself another shot of rum, raised it cursorily to Bolo and gulped it down. "That's what happens when there are no official maps available. This country really needs to resolve that strike."

Bolo produced a slip of paper from the breast pocket of his uniform. "I just received orders for you personally, New Comandante, by express pigeon." Brushing the wrinkled paper flat, he set the sheet on the desk and stepped back, clicking his heels together. "Since you have resolved your differences with Commander José after the bandana duel, you are instructed to put him in charge here at Bellanova."

Smith swung his feet down to the floor and tilted his cap as he read the orders. "Leave here? Well, what am *I* supposed to do then?" His brow furrowed in puzzlement. "And who exactly do we work for, anyway?"

Bolo stared straight ahead and delivered his answer stiffly. "Sir, you are to proceed at once to our local missile site. We have its precise location here in the Andes."

"A *missile* site?" Smith perked up. "Well, I guess I do know a little bit about missiles. I've approved enough blueprints. But are you sure these orders are right?"

"Absolutely, sir," Bolo said, standing smartly at attention. "I wrote them myself!"

•••

Leaving Bellanova behind, Smith and Yaquita rode their horses down a narrow mountain road in the high Andes, followed by two pack horses. Yaquita wore Bonita's riding habit and top hat, and smiled a satisfied smile; Smith wore his jungle combat jumpsuit.

"It seems strange to me," Smith said, with a steam of cold breath drifting up from his words. Black vultures wheeled overhead, as if hoping Smith or one of the pack horses would fall off a cliff. "Who'd suspect a hidden missile site up here in the Andes?"

Yaquita nodded. "I can take you there, though it isn't on any map."

"*Nothing* around here is on a map," Smith groaned.

By high noon, Smith and Yaquita were riding through a rocky gorge, picking their way along a rugged path. During their morning coffee break, Smith and Yaquita had changed into thick sheepskin coats.

"This is such an important assignment. It shows that Colonel Enrique and Colonel Ivan must trust you," Yaquita said. "I've never been in love with a man assigned to infiltrate a missile site before."

"Who is Colonel Enrique? And Ivan?" he asked. Yaquita just laughed.

In the late afternoon Yaquita and Smith reached a lush valley sprinkled with colorful alpine meadow flowers. "This is the place," Yaquita said. They dismounted, holding the horses' reins. Smith shaded his eyes.

The grassy valley held a forest of what looked to be grain silos interspersed with a few tin-roofed buildings. Three old pickup trucks were parked next to rickety sheds; a brand-new tractor and wheat thresher sat near a barn, like props for a movie set.

"Well, look at that!" Smith said. "Wheat silos to disguise missile launching pads. Devilishly clever." He looked at his complex Russian wristwatch, then marched forward, leading his horse. He remembered his orders, though he still didn't know who the two colonels were. He hoped they were good, honest men. "Come on, we've got an appointment to keep."

A steel gate barred the entrance to the concrete silo area, providing far more security than a wheat field should ever require. Three guards dressed in white peon clothes and Cuban military caps stood holding their automatic rifles, very alert. They slung their weapons down, taking aim as the strangers approached.

Then one of the guards cracked a broad smile, elbowing his partner in the ribs as he recognized the redhead. "Ai! Pedrito!" both shouted. They hastily opened the gate for him.

Sighing with relief, Smith and Yaquita passed through, waving to the guards. Yaquita even strummed her guitar. They went deeper into the silo compound. Smith tilted his head up to gawk at the nearest concrete silo. A big sign hung over the door, *Compañia de Trigo Bocahambre. Silo no. 1. Se Prohibe Entrar.*

"Hmmm," Smith said. "The Hungry Mouth Wheat Company. Interesting cover."

"Remember to do like the real Pedrito would do, my love," Yaquita whispered to him. "Just complete the inspection and boost morale. You're their hero. I've got to go and report to my superiors here."

She spurred off, leaving him behind. Shrugging, Smith tied his horse to a coolant pipe that protruded from the side of the missile silo, then walked confidently up to the red-painted steel door. He ducked under the low entrance and stood on a metal platform. A catwalk staircase led down to a cleared machinery bay where an immense gleaming missile stood surrounded by scaffolding.

A dark-haired engineer in a white jumpsuit raced up the metal stairs from the base of the missile, waving his hands to stop Smith. "No entrance!" he shouted. "Get out!"

Smiling, Smith started down the staircase anyway, as if he belonged there. The engineer yelled, "We have an intruder! Sound the alarm!" Three technicians wearing gun belts sprinted around the bottom of the missile, drawing their weapons.

Smith came to a halt, waving cheerfully at the armed technicians as well as the main engineer. Snatching off his red-star cap to reveal his distinctive hair, he said, "Don't you know me? I'm Pedrito Miraflores!"

They stared at Smith's face, and then the technicians applauded. The engineer suddenly slapped his forehead. "Ah, the military genius who just captured Bellanova!"

Smith nodded. "That's me."

"The one who destroyed the Meta River Patrol!"

"Ai! Pedrito!" the guards and the engineer cheered.

Chapter 36

HE HAD NEVER SEEN an actual missile system before, only blueprints, and he found it fascinating.

"Just a routine inspection, ordered by Colonels Enrique and Ivan," Smith said cheerily as he climbed a staging ladder mounted to the top of the missile's guidance and payload compartment. He found an inspection door below the red nose cone and yelled down to the engineers and technicians, "Don't mind me, I just want to make sure the course settings are right."

"Glad to have it checked. Here, you will need the key." The engineer removed a chain from around his neck and tossed it up without bothering to aim. Keeping one hand on a metal rung, Smith somehow managed to snag the chain before it could fall down into the concrete flame bucket underneath the rocket nozzles. He inserted the key into the inspection access door.

The engineer shaded his eyes, looking up at Smith on the ladder. "Make sure that one's coordinates are set for Buenos Aires!"

Smith stuck his head inside the hatch, rummaging among the gyroscopes and guidance systems. He tried to remember how the systems worked exactly, but he had paid little attention to all those classified plans he had approved for Admiral Turner. Now was his chance to do something for the United States Navy, at last.

Out of sight, he used a ballpoint pen from the pocket of his sheepskin coat to do calculations on the palm of his hand. After double-checking his math, he used the tip of the pen to push the setting dials inside the missile. Latitude, Longitude, Distance— now it would go straight to Havana. If he remembered his maps right.

He gingerly climbed back down to stand with the Colodoran engineer. The technician guards had exchanged their gun belts for tool belts and went back to work in the silos under the corporate logo of the Hungry Mouth Wheat Company—a huge cartoon mouth stuffed with spiny wheat grains.

Smith casually dropped the missile key into his shirt pocket. "The settings were just about perfect," he said, brushing his hands together with satisfaction. "But maybe I better check the other silos. Just to be sure."

◆◆◆

The hand-lettered sign above the next concrete granary said *Silo No. 2.* Smith and the engineer went in.

"I'm glad of your help, Pedrito," the engineer said as Smith climbed another ladder. "You make my job much easier." Smith opened the access door, and the engineer shouted up at him, "That one's set for Rio de Janeiro. I hope the guidance system checks out."

Crowded into the small access hatch, Smith busily reset the dials. He finished calculations on his other palm and pushed the aiming dials. Right in the middle of Leningrad, he thought. Or had the Russians renamed that city St. Petersburg again?

In Silo No. 3, Smith tinkered with the next missile. "As you can see, we are prepared to dominate all of South America. This one is aimed at Caracas," the engineer called, his words echoing in the confined silo.

"Not anymore," Smith whispered as he turned the setting dials with a grim smile. "Moscow city limits."

◆◆◆

In the missile site office of the Hungry Mouth Wheat Company, Colonels Enrique and Ivan sat at a rickety table, playing dominoes. A bottle of vodka and two empty glasses stood at their elbows. Cuban cigars sat inside a Mercedes-Benz hubcap being used as an ashtray. Calendars displaying new models of farm machinery decorated the walls. A battery-powered phonograph played a scratchy LP of the "Volga Boatman."

The two colonels moved their domino tiles as they talked. "As soon as the real Pedrito gets back from New York with the plans for those U.S. anti-jamming devices, we're all set, Comrade," Ivan said.

"That will be quite a feather in our caps, won't it?" Enrique said, scratching his voluminous beard. "All of South America at our mercy. That'll be a nice change of pace."

"I hope he doesn't foul it up," Ivan said gloomily. "If this mission fails, my superiors could send me back to Russia. No nice cigars there."

"How could it fail?" Enrique said. "We're the only ones who know about the switch. No chance of a leak in counter-intelligence. We'll have to order the real Pedrito to assassinate Smith as soon as he returns."

"I can't believe Smith has managed to survive for so long," Enrique said. "Just make sure he stays put in Bellanova, where he can't cause any damage. You issued the order, didn't you?"

"Da," Ivan said. "Our Pedrito is just cooling his heels in the old fortress."

A secretary came to the office door in high heels, sheer pantyhose, and a trim business skirt she couldn't possibly have bought anywhere in Colodor. "Sirs, Pedrito Miraflores just arrived for his inspection tour of the missile base. Um, I mean, the wheat company."

The two colonels did a double take and gaped at her.

The secretary continued, oblivious. "He's quite a dashing fellow. Nice red hair, sunny disposition. The workers were all cheering him when he arrived to check all the missile settings. I want to get his autograph."

Colonel Ivan brought his fist down on the table, jiggling the empty vodka glasses and scrambling the domino tiles. "What is Bolo doing? And where's that Yaquita? She was supposed to keep him under her thumb."

The secretary hastily scuttled into the hall away from Ivan's anger. "Yes, sirs, a Miss Yaquita to see you. She's waiting right out here."

Yaquita glided in like a lioness, carrying her battered radio-guitar case. Both colonels glared at her severely, but she nonchalantly tossed her dark hair over her shoulder. Ivan quickly swept the desktop clear of bottles, glasses and dominoes so she wouldn't have anything to throw.

"You've got your nerve bringing Pedrito here!" Enrique bellowed.

"This way I can keep an eye on him," Yaquita said innocently. "You told me to keep an eye on him."

"And your thumb on him," the Russian said.

"Bolo's orders told him to come here. So we came."

The colonels blinked, then looked at each other. "That's not what we told Bolo to do. Whose side is he on, anyway?"

Yaquita put her hands on her hips. "Why shouldn't I bring Pedrito here? The men need their morale boosted, and he is their hero."

Abruptly the colonels put their heads together, whispering furiously. Finally, they nodded to each other.

Ivan took a set of plans from the desk drawer, spreading them out where Yaquita could see. "Pedrito shouldn't be here because we have an important job for him elsewhere," he said. The Russian colonel tapped one section of the drawing. "These are the plans of the CIA Communications Centrale in Colodor. It's the only thing that can mess up our missile strike."

"Pedrito has to go and blow it up," Enrique said. "It's in his contract."

Yaquita was surprised. She bent over to inspect the plans, making serious noises. "Blowing up CIA installations is always fun—but this one looks like a tough nut to crack."

"Pedrito is good at cracking tough nuts," Ivan said, then lowered his voice, "and also good at driving people nuts."

"Deliver him to the area, and then you will go wait for him at the Cathedral of Our Lady of Mercy in Sangredios," Enrique commanded. "No questions—just follow orders like a good revolutionary."

"Is it a nice cathedral to get married in?" Yaquita smiled wistfully, and both colonels nodded vigorously.

With Yaquita gone and happy, Enrique and Ivan toasted each other with a fresh glass of vodka. "I told you she had nothing but marriage on her mind," Enrique said. "For an intelligent woman, she is so gullible for all that propaganda about what women are supposed to do with their lives. Ha!"

"Well, Smith is one man she won't marry," Ivan said. "Even *he* isn't that foolish."

"Unless she wants to marry a corpse." Enrique picked up the vodka bottle, but it was empty. He opened the desk drawer to get a fresh one. "CIA Centrale is a deathtrap. He'll never make it out alive. Not even the real Pedrito could do it."

"Better send Felipe and Juan after him to make sure he actually attempts the mission," Ivan said. "After all this time, we don't want him getting smart on us."

"No chance of that." Enrique eased back in the desk chair. "Would you like another cigar?"

"Da. Would you like some more vodka?"

Chapter 37

THE FORMAL PRINTED CARD on the door to the New York apartment read *Lt. (jg) Thomas G. Smith, USN.* Not that he received many visitors anyway. Most people considered Tom Smith too dull to include in their social calendars.

Joan Turner stood in front of the sign, primping her strawberry-blond hair and using a compact mirror to touch up her lipstick. Smith had, after all, promised to marry her, and so she had a perfect right to show up any time she wanted. She had already caught him spying on his country, so what could be worse?

From inside the apartment, she heard muted shrieks of feminine laughter, a rumba beat pounding from a stereo, trumpets and loud Latin music. This wasn't what she expected to hear from mild-mannered Smith at all, but when she double-checked the address in her purse, she saw she had come to the right place.

It sounded like a party was going on. Without her.

She grabbed the knob and burst in.

The bachelor apartment she had expected to find meticulously neat and clean was now overwhelmed by chaos. A thick-cushioned divan sat askew in the center of the room. Half-empty bottles of tequila and rum stood upright on the side table; three bottles lay on the carpet, spilled over.

Pedrito sprawled on the couch half dressed and entirely drunk. Two naked women giggled next to him, also thoroughly inebriated. One draped herself over the back of the couch on her stomach, trying to dribble another drink between Pedrito's lips. Closer to the stereo, the second woman attempted to do the rumba with unsteady dance steps. She wore nothing but Tom Smith's naval officer's cap.

Despite Joan's unexpected arrival, none of them paid any attention to her. "Well!" she cried, loud and censorious, crossing her arms over her chest. She wished she had thought of something more clever or wicked to say.

Pedrito raised his head heavily and tried to focus on her. His hair was mussed, as if he had tried to comb it with a vacuum cleaner. Recognizing Joan after a moment, he waved his arm drunkenly to beckon her. "Well, if it ishn't Joan! Come on in here, you old bat, so theshe girlsh can show you how itsh *really* done! They're professhionals, you ssheee. Got them right down at the street corner—two-for-the-price-of-one sale."

Clamping her purse under her arm, Joan stormed out. She slammed the door so hard that Smith's printed address card fell onto the floor. In a raging fury she stood there, trying to think, blinking back the red haze from in front of her eyes. Then she got a decidedly brilliant idea on how she could fix that lousy bastard.

Out in the street she found the nearest telephone booth and dug in her purse for change. She attempted to put coins into the slot, but she was so furious her fingers missed, scattering quarters on the floor of the phone booth. By the time she managed to make the call, she was so coldly angry her words stabbed across the phone lines like ice picks. She enjoyed the sensation very much. . . .

In the local FBI office, a bored special agent sat at his desk, speaking with complete disinterest into the phone. He was bloated and mean, a promoted field agent, though it had been a long time since he'd been in the field. He held a pencil in his hand, scribbling on a notepad—but his notes were part of a grocery list and had nothing to do with the furious conversation the woman hurled at him from the other end of the phone.

He talked out of the side of his mouth, mumbling in a squeaky, falsetto voice. "Who'ja say yer name was?" he said, trying to sound tough. He liked to talk like a hardened criminal. "Well, lady, I ain't takin' no dope from nobody what won't give dere name . . . uh, uh-huh, yeah . . . okay." Now he wrote it down. "Joan Turner. Dat's better. Come clean now, kid. What'dja do?" He listened. "Okay, so what did yer boyfriend do? Is it a felony or a misdemeanor? Does it carry the death penalty? Does you got pictures?"

A scarecrowish-thin agent came in, looking like a dried-up convict, as the bloated agent hung up the phone. "What was that, Fats?" the thin agent said. "Don't tell me we gotta work today?"

"Aw, jus' some skirt blowin' the whistle on her boyfriend," Fats said. "Like always."

"You're not supposed to call 'em 'skirts' anymore. It ain't politically correct," the thin agent said. "You're supposed to call 'em *dames* now."

"Yeah, yeah, Lefty. I hear the bureau's issuing a guidebook for dat sort of thing." Fats made a raspberry sound. "I bet old J. Edgar is rollin' over in his grave."

Lefty reached for the pad to read the doodled words mixed in with his grocery list. "She told you someone in the Office of Naval Intelligence is a Commie spy?"

Fats peered at the pad. "How can you read this writing anyway? Where's it say that?"

"You wrote it!"

"Jesus Christ, I did!" Fats suddenly looked secretly delighted. He glanced up at his partner as he struggled to push himself away from his desk. "Lefty, dis is where you and I gets promoted!"

Chapter 38

IT TOOK HIM HOURS, but he finally reached Silo No. 13 . . . and it was just like the previous twelve.

Covering his delighted smile, Smith looked at the sign over the door as he and the Colodoran engineer exited the silo. At last he was doing real secret agent stuff. Another missile retargeted to save the Free World.

"All in a day's work," Smith said, jingling the collection of keys he carried. "Got to make sure we do it all correctly, no mistakes."

"It's so nice to have somebody trained in Russia verify my work!" The dark-haired engineer followed him like a puppy dog. "You didn't find any serious errors, did you? I'm usually very careful, but we've had the in-laws visiting, and there's the soccer-team bake sale coming up, and it's been so hectic."

"Well, six of the guidance coordinates were off by a hair," Smith said. "But I corrected them. No need to worry."

"You'll keep quiet about it?" The engineer pleaded with his eyes.

"Oh, not a word from me." Smith smiled, then snapped his fingers with a brilliant idea. "In fact, I'll even keep the missile keys so nobody can foul you up." He tucked the keys in his shirt pocket, patting them firmly.

"Oh, I'm so grateful. Thank you, Pedrito!" The engineer rushed back into his silos.

Before Smith could figure out what to do next, Yaquita approached briskly, carrying a thick wad of plans. "We're leaving," she said. "On with the next mission."

"But we just got here!" Smith said, rubbing his saddle-sore bottom and glancing at the setting sun. He didn't want to ride through the rugged Andes at night, and a soft bunk in the Wheat Company's barracks seemed more desirable than a drafty trail tent.

She took Smith by the arm, pulling him away. "Duty calls. We'll take my car this time."

"Whatever you say," he said. "Uh, long live the revolution, and all that."

◆◆◆

Yaquita's black Volkswagen tore along an Andes mountain road. Its bug-spattered headlights splashed on the black cliffs all around them. Yaquita kept the tires on the road most of the time. At every sharp corner, gravel and pebbles sprayed out into the long drop-off, vanishing from sight. Smith held his fingers over his eyes.

"You have been ordered to blow up the CIA Communications Centrale in Colodor," Yaquita said, more interested in his reaction than the treacherous road ahead.

Smith took his hands from his eyes. "Why would I want to do that?"

"The two colonels thought it was a good idea." Without slowing, she turned around and fumbled in the back seat for some papers she had stuffed there. The Volkswagen slued left and right on the narrow road, but she didn't seem to care. A terrified llama darted from the road, then leapt off the side, seeming to fly into the void like a reindeer. Smith grabbed the steering wheel to prevent them from following it off the cliff.

"Ah, here are the plans," Yaquita said, hauling them into the front seat. "The base is hidden inside a hill. Very cleverly concealed, but destroying it shouldn't be too difficult. Just drop some dynamite down the air hole." She steered with her knee, holding the plans open with one hand and pointing with her other finger. "See, look here."

Smith couldn't see, though, since he had covered his eyes again. . . .

By dawn, they had wound their way down to hilly country. The scenery was still rugged, but greener. A small town full of whitewashed adobe buildings with red tile roofs nestled in a valley, just like a postcard snapshot. Beyond the village rose a round grassy hill bristling with huge satellite tracking reflectors.

"I hope they don't pretend those satellite dishes are for agricultural purposes," Smith said, "like the Hungry Mouth Wheat Company."

"Satellite dishes?" Yaquita answered. "Those are umbrellas to protect particularly delicate crops from devastating hailstorms. Is it not obvious?"

"Whatever you say." Smith picked up the plans as Yaquita pulled the battered black Volkswagen to a halt. She let the engine sputter while they inspected the landscape.

"According to the secret plans," Yaquita said, "the air hole is right under those agricultural umbrellas on the hill. Just drop your dynamite down the shaft, and it'll blow up the whole installation—no problem. Then we can get to the cathedral of Sangredios in no time. I've already found us a priest."

"How do you know the plans are accurate?" Smith asked.

Yaquita smiled. "Some of the mapmakers on strike are really double agents. They draw up detailed blueprints of top-secret installations to earn a little spending money."

◆◆◆

The VW eased up to the entrance of a ramshackle adobe hotel. Smith climbed out, dressed in German mountaineering clothes complete with Tyrolean hat. He popped open the VW's front trunk and hauled out a canvas rucksack that smelled of mildew.

"I'll be waiting for you in the cathedral at Sangredios, my darling." Yaquita pushed her face out the window, puckering her lips for a kiss. "It's just a few kilometers farther down the road. Meet me when you're finished."

He looked around the little village, straightening the pheasant feather in his Tyrolean hat, and eyed the satellite dishes on the round hill. "I'm sure I can find the place."

"Now don't get hurt," Yaquita called with a trace of worry. "Don't harm a red hair on your pretty little head."

Smith leaned in and gave her a kiss on the cheek. "Nothing simpler."

The VW puttered away. Smith watched it go, smiling and waving, then heaved a huge sigh of relief. Blow up the place? He didn't think so. All he had to do was report in on the CIA station radio, and then he could get back home to New York and be finished with all this mess.

Chapter 39

ITS ROTORS THRUMMING in the early morning air, an unmarked helicopter circled for a landing just in front of the hill covered with satellite reflectors (or agricultural umbrellas, if the propaganda was to be believed). CIA chief O'Halloran stepped gingerly out of the craft, carrying an attaché case handcuffed to his wrist. He clapped his left hand on top of his head to keep his sparse hair from flapping in the prop wash as the helicopter departed back to another secret base somewhere in the Andes.

As he started walking nonchalantly to the round hill, the CIA chief maintained the air of a traveling salesman. A trapdoor of sod-covered earth lifted from the side of the hill, and two machine-gun muzzles rose into view. The weapons tracked O'Halloran's movements with built-in motion sensors.

The CIA man fumbled in his pocket to pull out a small box, trying to move faster than the automated machine guns. He turned a key on the gadget, and the weapons paused in their targeting, as if reconsidering. Then, with another whir, the gun muzzles dropped back down out of sight, and the trapdoor closed.

"Just like the User's Manual says," O'Halloran chortled, then turned another key in his gadget box. A large rectangular section covered with Astroturf lifted up like a garage door, revealing the main entrance to the underground installation. From there, a lighted tunnel led deep beneath the hill. O'Halloran walked in, ducking his balding head, and the hidden door closed quickly, showering the CIA man with small clods of dirt.

◆◆◆

Meanwhile, in the shabby hotel room, Smith had unpacked his rucksack and strewn the wad of plans for the hidden installation on the wobbly table. He studied the plans carefully, though he had never been good at reading blueprints, not for missile systems and not for buildings.

Dressed in the best three-piece suit he kept in his rucksack, he strolled out of the hotel like a dapper businessman. Smith walked along the cobblestone way near the satellite-dish hill as if he were an innocent pedestrian. He stopped to inspect a lump of llama dung that had clung to the heel of his shoe, surreptitiously scanning for the communication center's air shaft. Maybe he could just jump in and surrender. Then he could tell his story to the proper authorities. Admiral Turner would be so proud of him—he was a bona fide double agent!

The small trapdoor of sod moved aside, and machine-gun muzzles protruded with a whir, targeting on him.

Smith sang an old naval tune as he strode along, making sure he couldn't possibly surprise anybody.

When the machine guns were fully extended, they fired a blaze of shots. The ground around Smith erupted with bullets. After a brief moment of staring, Smith ran like mad.

He would have to reconsider this plan. Surrender wasn't going to be so easy after all.

•••

The CIA Communications Centrale was built over an old gold mine. Two centuries earlier, a Colodoran in search of ancient Incan gold had hand-dug a crazed collection of tunnels that wound over and under and around one another in an unfathomable maze. Over the years, countless Colodoran children had become lost in the maze, and their bones were scattered liberally along the corridors. In the 1960s, when the Americans came to Colodor, they had recognized at once that this was the perfect place to build a secret military base. So it was that the maze of tunnels through the sandstone twisted weirdly, as if dug by some alien insect, until they at last ended in the very deepest darkest depths—the central control room.

Here the sandstone walls gave way to banks of glittering communications machinery, liberally interspersed with vending machines and racks of automatic weapons. Moles raced along the floors, searching for the bits of Twinkies and spilled Coke on which they thrived.

Beside the aging banks of video screens and communication consoles, O'Halloran stood alert, eating a fresh banana. Hearing the sound of automatic weapons fire outside, he spun about.

"What was that shooting?" he asked, trying to figure out which TV screen showed what he wanted to know. Many of the monitors were tuned to talk shows, sitcoms and Spanish-language shopping channels.

Finally seeing the image from the hill installation's outside cameras, he pressed his face close to the screen. But the view showed only bare ground peppered with fresh bullet tracks and clouds of dust.

O'Halloran relaxed. "Probably just some damned goat."

"Or a llama," said one of the operators.

"Or a jaguar," said another.

"I heard a giraffe got loose from the local zoo yesterday. That could have done it."

"All right, all right," O'Halloran said impatiently. "We'll just chalk it up to a false alarm. Why don't you go take a coffee break in town and leave me alone here."

♦♦♦

Smith stood on the balcony of his hotel room, trying to think of another alternative. He draped his now muddy suit coat over the rail and mopped sweat from his brow. He stared at the unreachable rounded hill, where the satellite reflectors turned gradually, scanning the skies.

If that was a CIA installation, there must be *some* way to get in and tell them who he was. After impersonating Pedrito, he certainly had information his government would want. He turned to reenter his room, then stopped, so startled he almost staggered backward off the balcony. "Who are *you?*"

Two rebel Communists relaxed in his sitting room, grinning at Smith. One lounged in a chair, while another stood by the door, picking his teeth with a chicken bone. "I'm Felipe, he's Juan."

"I'm Juan, he's Felipe."

"The colonels sent us to make sure you blow up the place, Pedrito," Felipe said. "Besides, someone has to be there to tell the story of your exploits."

Juan laughed. "This should be a simple job after all your adventures! Remember the attack of the naked horsemen in the guava fields of Carabastos?"

"And who could forget the revenge of the sisters of the Nunnery of the Pink Fountains?" Felipe said with a loud chuckle. "We know you'll do the job, Pedrito, but Colonel Enrique has his reasons for sending us. Colonel Ivan isn't a very trusting sort. You know how Russians are."

Juan lowered his voice and leaned forward in his chair. "Me, I think the CIA place is full of gold or secret papers, and he wants us to snatch them." He cleared his throat. "Uh, after you blow up the installation, that is."

"So, we'll just relax here at the hotel and listen for when the CIA installation goes *boom,*" Felipe said, raising his hands to show the explosion.

Juan heaved himself out of the creaking lounge chair and spun a big revolver on his finger. "Felipe and I will be in the bar. Charging the tab to your room." He shoved the gun firmly in his belt. The two exited through the door, swaggering side by side.

271

Brushing dried mud off his suit jacket at the balcony rail, Smith frowned. He couldn't blow the whistle while those two goons were breathing down his neck. There must be some way to contact that place directly.

Smith saw an old black telephone on the side table, and his face lit up. "Of course!" He grabbed the receiver and dialed the operator. "Hello? Get me the number for the secret CIA communications installation in town."

On the other end of the line, he heard a switchboard operator with a sweet Spanish accent. "I'm sorry, sir," she said. "We've got no number for the CIA in this town."

"Then just connect me to the United States," Smith said, exasperated. "Anyplace will do."

"Sorry, sir," the operator said. "We've got no lines for that."

Hours later, Smith still stood on his balcony, still staring at the round hill. A native goat herder in a felt hat and colorful poncho shooed a group of goats under the satellite reflectors.

Smith sat down heavily on the bed, once again spreading out the diagrams of the Colodor CIA Centrale. His hero, Nelson, would study the enemy plans, learn every nuance about the opponent. He traced the layout with his fingers, and suddenly a realization came to him. "Why, the whole place is automated!"

"That's right," Bolo said, striding through the open door in a gray policeman's uniform. "And that could be their weakness."

Smith looked up in shock at Bolo, who stood just inside the door. "Excuse me? Am I under arrest?"

"Not yet," Bolo said, polishing his knuckles against his brass badge.

"Say, haven't I seen you someplace before?" Smith said. Over the weeks that he'd been in this country, he was sure he'd encountered those dark features before. "Weren't you a cabdriver once? Or a waiter?"

Bolo walked toward him, casually picking up the CIA blueprints to scrutinize them. "No. I got lots of brothers. I'm a very average-looking Colodoran."

"Oh," Smith said. "Then what *do* you want?"

Bolo turned the plans the other way around, tracing his finger along a conduit, then scribbled something in the margin. "Very good. Just checking." He handed them back to the lieutenant and turned to leave.

Smith stared after him, scratching his head. He knew he'd seen that fellow before, and had the vague notion the man was following him. He then looked back at Bolo's suggestion penciled in the margin of the plans.

It was a design for a device—an extremely complex electronic device of the kind that a Navy contractor might have dreamed up. Only a secret agent would have scrawled those notes. But a secret agent for whom?

"Aha! I should have thought of this myself," Smith crowed. "I'll just build an electronic induction cross-feed molecular cancelifier and throw it down the air hole. That'll send a neuromagnetic pulse to paralyze the automatic circuits!" Smith grinned. "Then I'll just walk right into the place and get on the radio so I can report to the U.S.!"

He nodded. The plan was set.

Chapter 40

SMITH BOUGHT A MOUND of wire and high-tech gadgets at the local electronics boutique in the small Andean farming village. He still had the espionage equipment from the secret compartment in his tan suitcase, but he needed specific items for his new idea.

Working at the courtesy table in his hotel room, Smith built a circular device the size of a basketball, its red case filled with coils and cables and a battery. He wiped sweat off his brow, set one of his laser pistols aside, then glanced again at his Russian wristwatch. Time to get moving.

Singing cheerily, he hefted the gadget, testing its weight as he double-checked the plans of the CIA Centrale. For this mission, he would have to use his best skills as both Smith and Pedrito.

♦♦♦

Inside CIA Communications Centrale, O'Halloran demanded answers. Spittle flew at the microphone as he shouted. "I need Pedrito Miraflores dead—now, or sooner! Why can't you just take care of him?" Then he realized the microphone was switched off, and he had to bellow his demands all over again.

"Any more reports on his location?" his contact in Langley, Virginia, asked over the radio, unruffled by the CIA man's anger. He had heard it all before.

"Fifteen sightings in five different countries so far," O'Halloran said, sulking. "But one thing's for certain: he's miles away from here. I'm not going to get a piece of the action."

♦♦♦

Dressed in a native felt hat and costume, Smith hid his device under his poncho. He walked stealthily toward the crown of the hill accompanied by a herd of goats he had borrowed from a local farmer. The man had seemed only too happy to loan his herd so that he could have an afternoon siesta. Smith kept his eyes open for the automatic machine guns. But the goats seemed to give him all the cover he needed. . . .

Peering through his field glasses from town, Bolo recognized Smith and the goats on the hill. He grinned his secretive smile. "It's time to add a little more chaos." He sprinted off, holding down his policeman's cap to keep it from blowing away.

The town's electrical plant was a modest building with insulators sprouting out of the roof. Inside the shack, a diesel generator stuttered and smoked, unattended. A huge busbar stood out on the corner of the building: not locked, not barred, not guarded in any way. Trusting folks, these locals—just the way Bolo liked it. He put his hand on the handle of the busbar, then watched Smith's movements. He had to choose his moment carefully.

In the distance, the disguised Smith trudged up the round hill, a simple shepherd surrounded by goats. The satellite reflectors stood like huge metal umbrellas, pivoting on their axes as they searched the sky for secret transmissions.

Beneath one of the satellite dishes, exactly as shown on the blueprints, Smith found a round air shaft four feet in diameter. He glanced around, tugging the straw hat down over his eyes. With no one watching, he removed the bright red gadget from under his poncho and tossed it down the hole. . . .

"Good, good," Bolo muttered. As the red gadget vanished into the shaft, he yanked the busbar down, shielding his eyes from the shower of sparks. Still grinning secretly, he looked up at the hill.

Now Smith wouldn't have any trouble at all getting inside.

◆◆◆

The lights went out at the radio console in the Colodor CIA Centrale. Everything was swallowed in pitch-black.

"What the hell?" O'Halloran bellowed. "We're under attack! An invasion force—every man for himself!" But then he realized he was the only man in the base, since he had sent everyone else off on a coffee break.

◆◆◆

Smith stood beside the air shaft. Inside, he could tell that all the power had gone out. The lights shining up from the air shaft had dimmed, and the antennas had all quit moving. Even the little red electronic eyes by the automatic guns had gone dim.

"Well, that was easy," he said, throwing off his hat and poncho to reveal riding boots, breeches and a wide-collar white shirt. He took a long breath, then dove headfirst into the hole.

◆◆◆

"I see you over there!" O'Halloran snarled.

The flash of his gun went off, but illuminated nothing else.

"Come on out and fight like a man!" Another shot flashed. A bullet ricocheted off a wall. One of the surveillance monitors exploded. "Hah! I got you!"

Another shot flashed, then another, until the CIA man had emptied his handgun. "Take that, you bastard!" he said, swinging hard with his fist. The sound of his knuckles slapping into the concrete wall echoed in the darkness. "And that!"

He could feel the fresh air of the air shaft above him, and O'Halloran looked up, heard the sound of something heavy sliding toward him. He tried to glimpse some sunlight shining through the hole but saw nothing.

Then, after a huge thud, the CIA man fell unconscious.

◆◆◆

The two thugs, Felipe and Juan, sat at the bar of the hotel, drinking rum and signing the tab over to Smith's room. "Did you hear all that gunfire a minute ago?" Felipe asked.

"Been quiet for a while," Juan said, gulping directly from the bottle. "Pedrito's finished all the hard work, I suppose."

"We better go collect those secret documents the colonels want," Felipe said, finishing his own shot. "Maybe we'll get a promotion."

They slid off their barstools, adjusted the guns in their belts and swaggered out.

• • •

Bolo stood at the busbar, cupping his ear, but he heard no more shots. It was time for the next step, time to keep Smith off-balance.

He turned and pushed the busbar in with a grunt.

• • •

Deep underground, all the lights flickered on and off, then went on again.

O'Halloran lay on the floor, out cold. Smith himself had fallen on top of him like a ton of bricks. Beside the CIA man, his red gadget lay broken on the floor.

Smith brushed himself off, surprised but satisfied. "Looks like my device handled all the lights," he said. "Must have been a flawless design."

He unreeled a length of wire from the red metal case and used it to tie O'Halloran's hands behind his back until yards and yards were wrapped all around the CIA man's head and body. "Double use. Good for the environment."

He dragged O'Halloran by the feet into a closet, closed the door and propped a chair up against it. "This way I won't get hurt," Smith said. "And maybe you won't hurt yourself either. I remember the problems you had with my banana truck."

Then he went exploring. He would find some way to contact the authorities and explain his situation.

The huge control board of the communications center had many switches and levers. Smith read the labels on every system, particularly the ones marked AUTOMATED DEFENSES and TOTAL DISARM. He tugged down the long lever. Good. Now he could walk out of here as soon as he had sent his message. Piece of cake.

Chapter 41

AS THEY APPROACHED the satellite-covered hillside, reeling a bit from drinking too much rum, Juan nudged his partner ahead of him. "You go first."

Felipe stopped short, swaying on his feet. "No, you go first. I've seen those automatic machine guns."

"Don't worry about them—Pedrito took care of everything." Juan gave him a less gentle shove. "What are you waiting for? Somebody to roll out the welcome mat?"

In front of them the large earth-disguised front door raised up, silently waiting for them.

"Well, look at that," Felipe said.

"See, I told you. Let's go." Together they staggered toward it.

◆◆◆

Deep underground Smith sat at a huge console, glancing up at the sign *International Communication Links.* This looked like the right place. He hoped he could make a collect call.

He scanned a series of labeled switches: *Langley, Europe, White House Emergency,* as well as a few for local pizza delivery. Smith reached for the *White House Emergency* switch and pulled the microphone toward him, clearing his throat.

◆◆◆

The President of the United States stood in the Oval Office. A large desk with numerous different-colored phones had been moved aside to make room for a putting dish.

The President spoke over his shoulder to an aide. "If I can just get my handicap raised, I'll beat Senator Twaddle. After humiliating him on the golf course, I'll have no trouble getting that appropriations bill through."

He swung for another putt at exactly the same moment one of his phones rang. The shot went wide, bouncing off an umbrella stand in the corner. He glared at the assorted phones on the desk. "Oh, which the hell one of these is ringing?"

The aide pointed to the purple phone. "I think it's that one, sir. Must be important—I don't recall ever hearing the purple phone ring."

Annoyed, the President looked at the label. "CIA, South America?" He looked up at the aide, set his putter aside and stalked toward the desk. "Why the hell is it ringing? Are we even doing anything in South America? I bet they want more funding."

"Maybe you better answer it," the aide said. "That's the best way to find out."

◆◆◆

In CIA Centrale, Smith gripped the shiny microphone, swallowing nervously. "Hello, Mr. President? You don't know me but I, uh, I voted for you in the last election." He hesitated, afraid the President would hear the lie in his voice, then rattled on. "There's a secret Commie missile base here in the Andes, in a country called Colodor. Here are the coordinates." He rattled off numbers from the map on the console.

The President's expostulation came over the speaker. "Colodor! Never heard of it."

The two thugs, Felipe and Juan, stopped in the entrance tunnel, thunderstruck as they overheard Smith. They had found their way through the weird maze of tunnels easily, drawn by the smell of stale Doritos. "What is Pedrito doing?" Juan gasped. "Why is he betraying our beloved missile base?"

Felipe slapped his forehead in dismay, but kept his voice low. "Ai! Pedrito! He is a spy, a double agent!" Drawing their weapons, they crept forward, behind the redheaded lieutenant.

Smith tried to reassure the President. "Don't worry, sir, it's all right. I changed the missiles' auto-directors to fire on the principal cities of Cuba and Russia, not on the United States. Our country is perfectly safe."

The President was furious, and the speaker jumped as he yelled, "You *idiot!* If you destroy Russia, we'll have no place to export wheat!"

Stepping up behind the chair, Juan pushed his ancient revolver against Smith's head. Felipe picked up the microphone. "I'm sorry, sir, we've got another call. Please hold." Then he cut the *White House Emergency* switch.

"Turn around slow, Pedrito!" Juan said. "And keep your hands up, you greasy traitor."

Juan stood back with the drawn revolver still pointing toward Smith. Smith looked cross-eyed at Felipe's gun muzzle just in front of his nose.

"You don't understand," Smith said.

"It don't take no understanding," Felipe said.

"We're not good at understanding things anyway," Juan snapped.

"We're delivering you right now to Colonel Enrique back at the missile base!" Felipe gloated. "Uh, I mean at the wheat farm."

"March!" Juan said.

Chapter 42

IN THE OVAL OFFICE, the President threw the purple phone onto the desk with a loud jangle; then he picked up his putter and tossed it across the room. Still not satisfied, he snatched up one of the golf balls from the carpet and hurled it through the window. The glass smashed, and the ball sailed out into the rose garden, nearly striking a tabloid reporter who was trying to eavesdrop on the President's putting practice.

The aide hurried to the window and called out apologetically, "Fore!"

The President paced about. "The CIA is going to bomb Russia and Cuba. How can they do such a thing? And who was that fool agent?" He grabbed the dark blue and silver phone from the rainbow of phones on his desk. "Air Force! I'm ordering a preemptive bombing raid on Colodor! Wipe out that missile base before they can launch. Check your own maps for the coordinates. I'll clear the strike with the government down there—they owe us a few favors anyway. Most of those South American countries do."

♦ ♦ ♦

Bolo stood on the village street not far from a mud-spattered and dented old jeep. He had chosen to disguise himself as a local cable TV repairman, so no one noticed that he stood in the same place for a long time, doing nothing.

Without a glance at him, Juan jumped behind the wheel of the jeep while Felipe pushed Smith into the back. He swung into the passenger seat, still holding his gun on their redheaded prisoner. "Head back to the secret missile base," he said to Juan. "Our friend Pedrito's got a lot of explaining to do—and I'm sure will get to do some of it under torture."

♦ ♦ ♦

At the U.S. Air Force Strategic Air Command, a colonel sat at his console, trying to remember how to react in a real emergency instead of just another training drill. He covered his uncertainty by raising his voice.

"SAC 32! Scramble, scramble! Target the secret Commie missile base in Colodor. You all know where it is—and if you don't know, make your best guess and bomb the whole countryside. *Get going!*"

A fleet of bombers streaked across the runway and then leaped into the air like silver dolphins. They roared into the sky, heading for South America.

••••

In a clothes shop near the Cathedral of Our Lady of Mercy, Yaquita preened herself in front of a mirror. This was the ninth wedding dress she had tried on, but she had to find the perfect gown no matter how long it might take. Everything had to be perfect for her special day.

She smoothed the fine white lace across her breasts, turning sideways to see how well it revealed her figure. A stack of similarly gorgeous dresses lay piled across a chest and a chair in the back of the store. Yaquita had already tried them on and set them aside for a second look. The shopkeeper stood away from the door of the dressing room. He had learned the folly of trying to suggest anything to Yaquita when she was concentrating.

She nodded appreciatively. "I think this dress might indeed be the one," she said, as she had said each time before. But she still had a few others to try on. Her redheaded young beau would be here any time now. . . .

••••

The jeep sped along a road in a gorge through the Andes, bouncing over potholes and swerving close to the cliff's edge. In the back, Smith groaned, green and carsick from Juan's driving. The thug tromped down on the accelerator.

In the missile compound office at the Hungry Mouth Wheat Company, Colonel Ivan stood up to receive a heavy attaché case from a red-faced courier. He grinned, stubbing out his big cigar. "It's finally here!"

Enrique sat back in his chair, sipping another glass of vodka. "What is it, Ivan?"

"This reimbursement just came in from Russia. For years I have been sending them receipts for my travel expenses, and finally it has arrived . . . adjusted for inflation, of course."

He popped open the lid, stared in amazement, then turned the case so Enrique could see into it. The Cuban nearly choked on his vodka.

The case was crammed with stacks of dazzling gold pieces like poker chips. Enrique held up a gold piece and gazed fondly at it. "So, Comrade, now I see why you always picked up the tab at all of those business lunches."

◆◆◆

The bombers continued on course, tearing through high wisps of cloud. Inside each jet, the pilot checked his load of explosives, armed the bombs and transmitted his readiness to the rest of the squadron.

◆◆◆

The jeep ran along Andes mountain precipices. Felipe drove now.

They had paused only briefly to let Smith be sick over the side of the vehicle, vomiting over what seemed to be a bottomless chasm. The view only made him more nauseated. Juan and Felipe had raced around the jeep, exchanging places on the treacherous mountain road like a goofy fire drill. Then they drove off again.

♦♦♦

Enrique clinked several gold pieces back into the case, watching how the coins reflected fluorescent light from the ceiling. He scratched his voluminous beard. "I suppose we've seen the end of Smith by now," he said. "Nobody ever returns alive from that CIA installation."

The Russian colonel glanced down at his watch. "We should be hearing from Felipe and Juan any time." He held up one of the coins. "I don't suppose we have to give them a bonus, do we?"

"Nyet, Comrade," said Enrique. "We will keep it—for our little farm. So we can buy the rabbits."

Just outside the secret missile compound's main office, the jeep screeched to a halt. A cloud of road dust swirled around the camp, making everyone cough. Felipe urged Smith out at gunpoint.

♦♦♦

High in the sky above, the bombers passed over the equator line—a wide line painted across the Andes Mountains in blue—and prepared to attack.

"All right, boys," the squadron leader said. "We've just been cleared to strike by the Colodoran government."

"Looks like a beautiful country, sir," said one of the other pilots. "I wonder why I've never heard of it."

"Yours is not to wonder why, Captain!" the squadron leader snapped. "Open the bomb-bay doors!"

"Bombay?" one of the pilots mused. "Are we over India?"

◆◆◆

Ivan snapped shut the gold-filled briefcase, while Enrique turned aside to scowl at a commotion in the hall. Grinning brutally, the two thugs prodded Lieutenant Tom Smith in at gunpoint.

"We found this . . . despicable iguana-lover making a radio call to the U.S.A.," Felipe said, his chest puffed with pride. "I heard him report the location of this missile base."

Juan said, "We think he's a double agent. A traitor to the revolution!"

The two colonels stared at Smith. "You tattled about the missile base? You weren't supposed to do that!" Enrique howled.

"Execute him!" Ivan said. "He has outlived his usefulness."

Smith cocked his head, listening to a faint drone of jets growing louder every second. "I don't think there's time to execute me," he said. "I hear bombers. They're already pretty close."

Chapter 43

AS THE DRONE OF BOMBERS grew louder, the two thugs, Juan and Felipe, broke their trance and jumped through the window of the office. They both raced across the landscape, weaving between wheat silos and ornamental farm machinery.

Smith stared at the ceiling of the missile base, then also turned to run.

"Halt—you running dog capitalist pig!" Colonel Ivan shouted as Smith made for the door.

"I'll get him!" Enrique said as he lunged toward the red-headed lieutenant.

Seeing no other weapon handy, Ivan threw the heavy gold-filled attaché case, which struck Enrique squarely in the head. The Cuban colonel went down like a sack of Hungry Mouth wheat. The attaché case skidded across the floor, one step ahead of Smith.

Ivan dashed after Smith, but tripped on the Cuban's body and went down, smacking his head on the corner of the desk.

Smith snatched up the attaché case. "What luck! This must be their secret plans!" He rushed out the door, nearly bent over double, trying to lug the heavy case with him.

Overhead, the falling bombs whistled, directly on target. The stealth missiles beside them whistled more quietly.

Smith ran for the jeep that Juan and Felipe had abandoned. The first bomb hit nearby, knocking him flat onto the ground.

The second bomb hit one of the wheat silos, blowing it sky high. The missile inside toppled.

Smith grabbed up the gold-filled case again and sprinted the rest of the way to the vehicle, jumping in.

◆◆◆

Shaking their heads, the two dazed colonels picked themselves up from the office floor. They scolded each other for being so clumsy, then ran out the headquarters' front door. Another explosion knocked them flat again.

"Oh, my head!" Enrique moaned.

Ivan pointed frantically at the escaping jeep and scrambled to his feet. He grabbed his partner by the elbow. "We must stop him—he's got my expense account."

They raced toward a tarpaulin-covered Land Rover hidden beside a brand-new tractor in the compound.

◆◆◆

High overhead, the bomb-bay door on the underbelly of the bomber opened. "Targeting confirmed," said the squadron commander. "You might as well drop the whole load so we can get back home. I forgot to set my VCR for tonight. Wouldn't want to miss the *X-Files*."

Stream after stream of bombs fell screaming through the air.

Another missile silo blew up. Some of the jets overshot their target and dumped bombs on the nearby mountaintops instead. The pilots didn't mind, and the explosions looked very pretty from up there in the air.

• • •

Smith flinched and tried to hide behind the windshield as he crashed through the closed gate of the secret missile compound. The jeep raced away, but Smith had no idea where he was going.

As the bombs continued to fall, another silo went up. The compound office exploded in a geyser of flames as a well-placed bomb hit its target. Colonel Enrique looked behind him in dismay, thinking of all the vodka and cigars he had left behind in his desk drawers.

Ivan, though, drove the Land Rover like a fiend through rolling black smoke. The front gate was already wrecked, thanks to Smith's escape. The Land Rover rushed through the smoke and over the broken fence.

• • •

Smith took the main mountain road at high speed, hoping he didn't run into a mule train or a herd of wild llamas on the way. He risked a glance back just in time to see the whole missile compound go up in a firestorm. The resounding explosion made his ears pop.

Smith stamped down on the accelerator. "I guess I lost them," he said, looking proudly at the attaché case he had taken from the colonels. He was getting the hang of this spy business.

Behind him, the Land Rover raced along the twisting mountain road. Colonel Ivan clutched the wheel, gritting his teeth as he concentrated on the treacherous curves. Enrique repeatedly gesticulated toward Smith's fleeing vehicle, as if the Russian could not see their quarry right ahead of them.

"We've got to catch him!" Enrique said. "Smith should have been killed back at the U.S. Embassy in Santa Isabel—he never should have lived this long, and now look at the mess he's caused."

◆◆◆

Back in the rounded hill beneath the ominous satellite dishes, a guide in a serape and straw hat wandered about the CIA Centrale control room, as if he belonged there. Under the flickering lights, he poked beneath consoles, searching for something. His expression was bland, his facial features dark and exotic.

Bolo went to the closet door and opened it. O'Halloran slouched on the floor against an old mop. The CIA man was out cold, still tied up with Smith's scavenged wire.

Bolo dragged O'Halloran out of the closet with a grunt. He tugged the straw hat down to obscure his features, then knelt to unwind the wire from the CIA man's wrists.

O'Halloran stirred and grumbled. "Who's that?" he finally groaned, groggily blinking his eyes. Then he struggled as if trying to punch someone.

Bolo danced out of O'Halloran's view and exited stealthily before the CIA man could figure out where he was or what had happened. . . .

♦♦♦

On the Andes road Smith yanked the jeep right and left. Steep volcanic mountains towered around him, black and sheer. A few peaks were graced with snow or belched steam from long-dormant thermal vents. Flames and black smoke curled up from where the bombers had dumped their explosive loads on the mountaintops instead of the secret missile base.

Smith knew he was going too fast for the curves, but he didn't see a posted speed limit, so he supposed it must be okay. On the driver's side, a gorge plunged half a mile straight down, cluttered with the rubble from ancient avalanches. He swallowed hard, then turned his attention back to the rough road, whereupon he swallowed hard again as he saw himself hurtling toward a tight new curve.

Behind him, the two colonels in the Land Rover raced from right to left. Ivan twisted the wheel violently to keep the vehicle on the road.

"Faster!" Enrique cried. "Faster!"

Smith braced himself to whip around a hairpin curve that turned around a steep spur. Beyond the curve, the precipice looked a mile deep. The jeep skidded into the hairpin, keeping only two wheels on the road.

In the jagged slopes above, a stampede of blasted rock from the accidental bombing raid tumbled down the mountain, picking up speed and dust. More boulders sloughed down with an ever-building roar. Smith looked up, saw it, and increased speed.

"An avalanche!" Enrique cried. "Watch out!"

"This has been quite a difficult day," Ivan said. "But it's just another obstacle for us to overcome in the name of the revolution. Now let's catch up with Smith."

As the colonels drove toward the tight hairpin, a cascade of displaced rocks thundered onto the road, blocking part of the lane and leaving only a treacherous strip clear next to the precipice.

Smith felt the jeep shaking, and he wrestled to keep the tires on the road as he raced away from the avalanche. More stone slid down the mountainside, and he swerved, dancing his foot on the brakes. The outside wheel of the jeep ran off the edge of the precipice, throwing gravel. Smith violently yanked the wheel to the right, and the jeep accelerated uphill where the road was a little wider, a little clearer and a little farther from the rockfall.

Behind him, the Land Rover roared into the tight hairpin in hot pursuit as the avalanche pounded around it. Sitting in the passenger seat, Enrique said in sudden horror, "When I was young an old gypsy fortuneteller warned me that I would be killed during an avalanche while I was driving along a steep Andes road beside a Russian colonel." His eyes widened. "Sweet hindquarters of a rat! Do you think this could be a coincidence?"

"I don't believe in that superstitious stuff." Ivan spun the wheel and saw the mound of rocks in the road and the endlessly deep precipice off the edge. With the trembling movement of the earth, the road cracked open.

The Land Rover shot out from behind the rocks and into the air. Like a projectile, the vehicle arced downward in a perfect parabola, plunging into open space without even touching the side of the mountain.

Still seat-belted in, Enrique cried, "*Viva la revolución!*"

"I hope Moscow never hears of this," Ivan said, thrusting his chin out in a stalwart manner as he lit a fine Cuban cigar and took a puff. "It could ruin my career."

The Land Rover crashed into the bottom of the gorge far, far below.

◆◆◆

Smith stopped his jeep on the inside slope. The avalanche had missed him and the earth had stopped shaking. He was safe.

Steam geysered from the jeep's radiator, though. Smith sat there, frowning. "Curse the luck!"

He climbed out from the driver's side, walked over to the cliff and looked down to see the smoldering wreckage of the Land Rover. He glanced down at his own torn clothes and dirty hands. "You sure can get messed up in this spy business."

He decided to go back to his hotel and get some fresh clothes. A shower would be nice, too. He wondered if Yaquita had left any of that rum in the rucksack.

Driving off, he glanced nervously over the precipice again and sighed with relief. At least now he was in the clear.

Chapter 44

ADMIRAL TURNER HATED PIGEONS. Every day they hunched on his windowsill, plastering the ledge white with their droppings, drowning out his Lawrence Welk radio station with their gurgling cooing.

Now, as he sat in the afternoon sunshine in Central Park, keeping to himself on a park bench, the verminous birds wandered around, spreading like the plague, slow-moving and oblivious. They were occasionally stepped on by passing joggers or flattened in a spray of ugly feathers by a speeding bicycle.

How could any man not be moved to laughter by such a sight?

He scowled at the other old fogies cheerfully reaching into sacks and tossing breadcrumbs to the pigeons. It looked like a scene out of an Alfred Hitchcock movie when the birds swarmed around. Didn't these retirees have anything better to do?

The admiral looked out at the small pond, watched kids playing with a small radio-controlled toy boat—and that reminded him of his glorious Navy days. He thought of exhilarating dockside brawls, drunken crews shanghaied to strange destinations, typhoons and high seas. . . .

"Ah," he muttered to himself with a wistful smile, "that's when being in the Navy really meant something."

These days, Admiral Turner was just the captain of a desk, and a damned cluttered one at that. Sitting on the park bench, he took out his crumpled brown-paper bag and spread it open on his lap. Eagerly, the pigeons came closer. . . .

The admiral glanced at his watch, wondering if enough time had passed. He knew he had to sit on the park bench to get away from his daughter, Joan. She'd been in a jealous rage for days.

She had stormed into his office, flushed, her hat askew, her strawberry-blond hair mussed. The scene with Joan was painted vividly in his mind. . . .

"Daddy, I've just been to Lieutenant Smith's apartment! He said he was going to marry me, but that . . . that snake betrayed me!" Her eyes narrowed with a sudden icy coolness that seemed much more frightening than her fury. "And he betrayed his country, too. Daddy, *Tom Smith is a spy!*"

Admiral Turner had to chuckle at that. "Smith? A spy? Don't be silly, dear—Lieutenant Smith can't even *understand* those blueprints, much less sell them to . . . to whoever our enemies are these days."

"Daddy!" Joan shrieked, and he decided it was time to back down—completely. He stood up, snatching the silver pocket flask from his bottom drawer before he went.

"All right, dear. I'll go over to his apartment right now and check it out."

Admiral Turner marched down the hallway to Smith's apartment, stiff kneed, face forward, just like a cadet on parade. When he reached the appropriate door and found it askew, he pushed it open. "Smith! I've got something to say to you!"

Instead of the clean smells of disinfectant and air fresheners, the odors that assailed him spoke more of sweat, spilled tequila and rum, and thick cigar smoke. His eyes widened and he took a deeper breath.

The prim young lieutenant certainly had changed in recent days.

Through the dim light of pulled window shades, he saw the disaster and wreckage with widening eyes. The sofa had been overturned. Empty liquor bottles lay strewn about, mixed with cigarette butts and thick tobacco ash. Pictures hung askew on the walls. A lacy bra dangled from the television's antenna; lacy panties (not part of a matching set) dangled from the volume-control knob.

"Women, booze, cigars!" Admiral Turner stood transfixed with shock in the otherwise empty apartment. "*That's* my boy! Smith, we'll make a decent human being out of you yet!"

So he had gone to sit out the afternoon on a park bench instead of returning to face Joan. He couldn't get over his wonderment. Another jogger stumbled by.

Admiral Turner reached into the brown-paper bag and rummaged around with his hand. Clucking and cooing, the hungry pigeons clustered closer, anticipating yet another soft-hearted patsy with food for them.

The admiral plucked out one of his carefully selected stones and flung it at the nearest pigeon, which squawked and flew away with ruffled feathers. He reached into the bag again, grabbed another pebble and hurled it at another target. "Bull's-eye!"

This was much more fun than using breadcrumbs.

Chapter 45

A BANDAGED O'HALLORAN sat alone at the CIA Communications Centrale console. The rest of the workers still had not come back from their coffee break.

His eye was swollen with what would certainly turn into a spectacular shiner. He gripped the microphone, speaking very respectfully with a quavering voice. "No, sir," he said. "You can tell the President I don't know who placed the call. It didn't come from this secret base. It could have been a prank, sir, or a wrong number." He drew in a deep breath. "Pedrito Miraflores? That bandit's not within a thousand miles of here, I guarantee it! But I'll keep looking."

◆◆◆

At last back in his hotel room, Smith took a long, hot shower. The pipes rattled and clanked, surrendering their water reluctantly. He emerged with a towel wrapped around himself, shaking droplets of water from his hair.

He picked up the rucksack and spilled out the contents onto his bed, then tried to stuff the stolen attaché case inside, but it was too large and too heavy.

He decided just to remove the colonels' important secret papers and save himself some room. He opened the attaché case—and stared down, bug-eyed, at the case jammed with rows of gold pieces. He clamped a hand over his mouth to keep himself from shouting about the treasure. He never knew when someone might be listening in, especially in this spy business.

Smith gazed out the balcony door, grinning. "Now I can buy my way home."

Shaking the attaché case, Smith poured a cascade of gold into his open rucksack. After the last coin dropped inside, Smith ran his fingers along the grooves of the case, making sure he hadn't missed any gold pieces.

From behind him, a voice said, "Message for you, sir."

Smith almost broke his neck snapping his head around in surprise. Bolo stood in a bellman's red uniform. Smith thought he recognized the man, but by now he knew better than to ask.

"A señorita named Yaquita telephoned to remind you that she is waiting for you at the cathedral in Sangredios. I suggest you do not disappoint the lady."

Still in shock, Smith kept a protective hand on the gold-filled rucksack.

"Yaquita? Oh, yeah, that's right. Thanks."

"Just routine service from your friendly hotel staff." Bolo turned about and went silently through the door. In the hallway he stopped and smiled his secret smile, as usual. From his belt Bolo pulled out a radio, adjusted its frequency, then pressed the transmit button. He liked to keep things interesting.

♦♦♦

In CIA Centrale a bruised O'Halloran cringed as a big metal speaker boomed above his head. The loud words made his skull ache.

Bolo's voice crackled with static; his whisper transmitted at such a high volume that the windows rattled. "This is a concerned Colodoran citizen. If you watch the Montana Hotel de Lujo in the town, you get surprise—a Pedrito surprise!"

O'Halloran's bloodshot eyes widened. "Call out all the troops!" he bellowed to the empty communications room, then sank back into his chair, holding his throbbing head.

♦♦♦

Smith came out of the hotel and walked jauntily toward his jeep, dressed again in his German mountain-climbing clothes and Tyrolean hat. None of the locals paid any attention to him, accustomed by now to strange tourists. He carried his gold-heavy backpack, trying to keep it from dragging on the ground or jingling.

Across in the alley, O'Halloran peered out, focusing a pair of opera glasses. He sucked in a quick, astonished breath. "Pedrito

305

Miraflores! He's fallen right into my hands!" A feral chicken pecked at his ankle, but the CIA man kicked it away, in no mood for fowl harassment.

O'Halloran chuckled, rubbing his hands together. The redhead drove the jeep down the street and turned left at the corner. He was taking the road to Sangredios, and the CIA man knew he could trap his quarry there for sure. On stumpy legs O'Halloran ran toward the round hill with the satellite reflectors.

Before he could get to the door, though, the whole hill blew up in a huge gout of orange flame. The shock front knocked the CIA man backward on his butt. Clods of dirt and sod thumped down in the streets like a meteor shower.

With a creaking, slow-motion groan, the metal satellite dishes collapsed through rising clouds of smoke. The hill, riddled with CIA tunnels, slumped in on itself like an ant mound.

O'Halloran sat in the dust of the street, staring at the collapsing hill. His strip of hair dangled down in front of his eyes. He knew with utter certainty that Pedrito Miraflores had caused the disaster.

He bounced to his feet and grabbed a top-secret radio out of his pocket. "Gimme the army!" he shouted. "The whole goddamned army of Colodor."

Chapter 46

A HUNCHBACKED PRIEST pulled the bell rope in the landmark cathedral in Sangredios. He reveled in the resonant clang, then tugged the rope again.

Yaquita paced back and forth before the ornately carved altar in her dazzling wedding dress. Exasperated, Yaquita clapped her hands to get the priest's attention. "Father, I demand that we get started."

"No, my daughter," he said. "We'd have to post the banns, first."

"How long will that take? I'm sure he'll be here any minute."

"The banns take three days."

"Oh, no you don't!" Yaquita crossed her arms over her chest and gave the man a glare that would have ignited coals. "You'll have to do better than that!"

"I . . . I'll take another look in the book," the priest said.

◆◆◆

Smith drove down the road, scanning the village ahead until he finally spotted the towering cathedral. "Aha! I knew I could trust my instincts."

He drove down a narrow alley into the main village square in front of the cathedral arches. Clay flowerpots overflowing with multicolored blooms stood on the wide marble steps, brightening the narrow plaza. A central fountain splashed greenish water near a few stalls where vendors hawked necklaces, handmade sweaters and ponchos, souvenir maps, bouquets of roses, and savory Inca corn fried with pork.

A train of burros went by bearing German tourists holding cameras. Every one of the tourists took a snapshot of redheaded Smith as he pulled up in his jeep—perhaps they liked his Tyrolean outfit. He waved for the cameras.

After parking in front of the marble steps, Smith admired the enormous white cathedral before him. "Just like one of the places Admiral Nelson shot up," he said. He hauled his heavy rucksack across the seat and, with a grunt, threw one strap over his shoulder. He plodded toward the cathedral, bent over from the weight of the gold coins.

Inside the church, Yaquita and the hunchbacked priest stood before the altar. The priest diligently lit candles while Yaquita continued to bargain with him. "If I steal three goats and give them to the church, would that speed up the process? You are a man of God—there must be some room for negotiation."

"Oh, dear, no," said the priest. "I'm sorry!"

Yaquita pursed her lips. "I have some money in another country. Could I write a check?"

The magnificent entrance to the cathedral was blocked by a huge, ornately carved double door with a smaller inset door that stood open in the afternoon heat. At the top of the marble stairs, Smith smelled the perfume of petunias in a big flowerpot, then turned to look back along the road he had driven.

Most of the vendors and the entire burro train of tourists were fleeing for their very lives, squealing in terror. Smith removed his Tyrolean cap and shaded his eyes, frowning. Though he had never heard of the country before, Colodor certainly seemed to be an exciting place.

Three lorry loads of armed government soldiers lurched toward the plaza at a halting speed. They drew their guns, ready for military action. Seeing new customers, a churro vendor hurriedly returned to the plaza and tried to sell his treats to the soldiers.

A smartly uniformed Colodoran general and CIA chief O'Halloran (now sporting a lovely purplish-black eye) bounced in the front seat of the lead truck beside the driver. "That's him!" O'Halloran shouted hysterically. "On the cathedral steps!"

The driver jammed the brakes in terror. O'Halloran clawed for his gun as the sudden stop thumped him forward into the dash. Other soldiers piled out and began firing at anything that moved—stray dogs, chickens, pedestrians.

Seeing the attack, Smith dived through the open portal. "Not again!" He shouted through the door, "What about due process?" A bullet twanged the doorpost.

He slammed the small door shut behind him, barring it hastily and throwing his back against it, panting. He ran down the center aisle of the cathedral. Stained-glass windows flashed color into the magnificent sanctuary. Most of the pews were empty.

Up at the altar Yaquita turned to Smith, beaming. "Oh, there you are, my darling!" She rounded on the priest and drew out a large, ancient revolver. "I've bargained long enough! Marry us!"

The priest, in total shock, stared at the blunderbuss, then cringed as if trying to hide behind his own hunchback.

Smith had lost his wits and power of speech. Calm and businesslike, Yaquita tossed her long dark hair over her shoulder. She motioned to a spot beside her and in front of the hunchbacked priest. Candles gleamed off the gold leaf that covered the carved woodwork. "Stand right there, dearest. The priest is about to begin."

◆◆◆

Outside the cathedral, O'Halloran whipped his gun out, drawing down on the arches. The Colodoran general gripped O'Halloran's wrist with both hands like a vise. "I tell you! Do not fire on a church!"

◆◆◆

Yaquita adjusted her gown. She had waited long enough for this day.

Instead, Smith ran sideways to one of the stained-glass windows, glancing out toward the town square through a riot of color. He saw uniformed soldiers piling out of the military vehicles, drawing their weapons for a massacre.

The priest began intoning words, but he stopped when Smith ran to another window, breathing heavily. Yaquita glared daggers at the priest. "Don't slow down," she growled. "He's listening to every word."

The priest gulped, then continued with his ceremony, mumbling the words in Latin, Spanish, English or any language that came to mind.

Meanwhile outside, the general still wrestled with O'Halloran, who was desperate to open fire on the cathedral.

Through the upper stained-glass window, Smith saw an old Model-T truck piled high with hay chugging along a road behind the town plaza. An Indian farmer wearing dingy white clothes drove it along at a slow speed, taking his hay to market in the central square. Smith spotted his chance for escape. He sprinted for a small side alcove, with a curving stairway that led up to a balcony and a higher window.

"Come back here!" Yaquita yelled, her hands clenched. "What are you doing?" She stalked toward him in her wedding dress. "This is no way to start a marriage!"

Smith got both straps of his backpack over his shoulders, and its weight made him hunch over just like the priest. "Look outside!" he stammered. "I see an escape vehicle."

"Escape? You're just like all other men!" Yaquita shouted. "Trying to run out on me!"

•••

The Colodoran general finally managed to secure O'Halloran's gun, snatching it from the CIA man's hand. Pointing the pistol at O'Halloran, the general backed away from the military vehicle. The other uniformed soldiers stood around, not knowing what to do or whom they should shoot. There were no longer any pedestrians in sight.

The general gestured toward the cathedral, his face florid and sweating.

"We cannot enter that sacred place," he said. "We must wait till he comes out! It may be that Pedrito will demand sanctuary, but until then we lay siege to the church."

O'Halloran stood behind the windshield of the vehicle, apoplectic at the general's stupidity. "You dumb bastard!" he shouted. With a sweep of his hand, O'Halloran snatched his gun back from the general, who gasped at his now empty hands.

In a savage motion the CIA man slid behind the steering wheel of the truck and engaged the gears. "I'll get him myself!" He tromped down on the accelerator, heading directly for the marble steps of the church.

As the lorry surged forward, O'Halloran yelled back after the general, "Colodor will never be more than a third-world country if you can't solve a simple little personnel problem."

Chapter 47

OBLIVIOUS TO THE MILITARY assault outside, Yaquita's rage towered in the cathedral. "I knew it! You can't toss me aside like a helpless flower, after you've had your way with me, Pedrito . . . or whoever you are!"

Smith tried to talk, backing away toward a small alcove, a stairway and escape—escape from Yaquita as well as from O'Halloran's attack. He just wanted to get out of this crazy country.

At the altar, the hunchbacked priest tried to look very small and unobtrusive as he continued mumbling the marriage ceremony. He didn't know what else to do.

Outside, the roar of the oncoming military truck grew louder, wheels clattering on the marble steps as it knocked the big flowerpots aside. The engine backfired, echoing like gunshots, then O'Halloran fired real shots.

Yaquita fumed, wondering how best to get back at Smith. With a sudden idea, she rushed to a stone slab on the floor and grabbed a heavy iron ring set in its center. Heaving and straining so hard that seams popped on her wedding dress, Yaquita lifted up the trapdoor to reveal the entrance to a crypt. With her white wedding dress billowing around her, Yaquita dropped into the dank tomb.

She knew exactly what to do now.

The hunchbacked priest looked up as O'Halloran's truck crashed through the immense front doors of the cathedral, splintering wood and knocking candles aside. Its engine roaring full bore, O'Halloran drove headlong into the sanctuary.

Smith, his gold-filled backpack sagging on his shoulders, climbed the belfry rope, swinging back and forth, increasing his arc and preparing to dive out the balcony.

On the floor below, O'Halloran jumped from the driver's seat and pointed his gun at Smith. Bullets ricocheted off the domes overhead, the confessionals, the holy water basins. The hunchbacked priest stumped forward and scolded O'Halloran for all the damage he had done in the house of God.

Smith continued to swing like Admiral Nelson in the rigging of a man-o'-war, watching the hay truck through the window and choosing his time carefully. Finally, he released his grip and sailed out through the open arched window.

The Model-T truck chugged just alongside the church. With a yelp, Smith landed feet-first in the piled hay and vanished from view, swallowed up in the dry bales. The Indian farmer drove complacently, chewing on a piece of straw, as if red-haired men leaped from cathedrals into his hay truck every day.

◆◆◆

O'Halloran's lorry wheezed in the church, cluttered with the remains of the splintered door and fallen beams. The CIA man stood next to the vehicle, frowning at his now empty pistol. "Pedrito got away. He got away!"

Peasants from the square swarmed into the church, carrying clubs and shaking their fists. The churro vendor set up his stand near the altar. The Colodoran general stood beside him. "Sacrilege in a church! *Tsk, tsk, tsk.* Now you'll be cursed by God, Señor O'Halloran. You'll never know what torment fate may have in store for you."

◆◆◆

Beneath the floor of the ancient cathedral, bones and skulls cluttered the crypt chambers. Tomb plaques hung on the walls, engraved with names now obscured by thick growths of mold.

By candlelight, Yaquita sat on a stool at a card table set up in the crypt. She hunched forward to a shiny radio and pulled headphones down over her wedding veil.

"Roger-Echo-Dog Eighteen to Havana, direct," she said into the microphone, her voice trembling with fury. A bitter, cruel smile grew on her face. "Emergency message to report. Pedrito Miraflores is an enemy agent! He is a double agent!" After giving particulars, Yaquita sat back among the skulls and bones, hoping she never saw anyone who looked like Pedrito again.

On the other hand, she thought, that bandaged CIA chief looked somewhat attractive. He had seemed so powerful when he crashed into the cathedral after his quarry. At least O'Halloran had ambition, and connections. Besides, with his black eye and his injuries, the man would no doubt need some tender care.

Yaquita smiled. Perhaps she could catch him before he left the country.

◆◆◆

Near Havana, in the Cuban operations room deep inside Morro Castle, Maria, the radio operator, busily wrote down a decoded message. Sweat glistened on her forehead as she scribbled, her hard eyes wide in disbelief. She yanked off her headset as she turned to rush away. She brought the message to another set of Russian and Cuban colonels, who had taken over the operation from their predecessors, Ivan and Enrique.

The Russian colonel read the message. "By the night light in Lenin's tomb!" he said. "This explains why our missile site was blown up! We have a double agent in our midst!"

The Cuban colonel grabbed the message out of the Russian's hand and began to read. "By all the saints whose names I can't remember!"

Both raced to the center of the room. Paper flew in the commotion; aides dashed out of the way as the two colonels crossed to different radios, hammering at the operators in Spanish and Russian.

"Radio Moscow!" bellowed the Russian. "Comrade Pedrito Miraflores is a traitor!"

"Cuban Navy—get out an all-points on Pedrito Miraflores!" shouted the other colonel. "Kill him on sight!"

Chapter 48

BACK IN THE UNITED STATES, things were no calmer for the real Pedrito. He had bundled up all his microfilm and stolen documents and marched away from the office. He drove to his rendezvous, anxious to be out of this country and back to his own interesting life.

Unseen behind him, a green, unmarked sedan eased to a stop alongside the road. Three people sat crammed in the front seat, the bloated Fats stuffed behind the wheel, Lefty crushed against the passenger door, both of them pleased to have Joan Turner crowded in the center and pressed against them.

Joan, though, was more intent on the object of her vengeance than on her discomfort. "That's him," she said bitterly.

Pedrito Miraflores, in a starched naval uniform and formal white-topped cap, parked his car and strode briskly up the steps of a Connecticut roadside restaurant. Buzzing pink neon letters proclaimed EAT!

"Dat long surveillance paid off, Lefty," said Fats in his overblown convict accent. He chewed on a matchstick.

"He goin' to make de drop," said Lefty, imitating his partner's mode of speech.

Like two gangsters, the bloated and scarecrowish federal agents elbowed their way through the crowded diner, knocking customers aside while trying to remain unobtrusive. "Oh, boy!" Fats said. "We're going to get promoted if we catch dis sucker, Lefty."

They were grim-faced and discourteous as they made a bee-line across the dining room toward a pair of tall coffee urns where they could survey the crowd.

A jukebox played country-and-western songs about broken-down trucks and hound dogs that died before their time. Back in the kitchen a potbellied short-order cook added extra dollops of grease to his culinary creations, then set them to steam under the heat lamps.

When the two agents reached the coffee machines, they turned around, ready for action. Lefty carried a standard-issue 35-mm camera, intent as a hawk. "Dere he is, Boss." He took pictures.

Unaware of the surveillance, Pedrito took a seat by the huge colonial glass window. He looked deeper into the diner, scanning the booths and counter, as if waiting for someone.

"Where's his contact?" Fats asked.

A rugged-looking woman in a hat, veil and flowered-print dress sat alone at a table about a third of the way into the restaurant. She batted her eyelashes at Pedrito, who looked away.

"Dere she is!" said Lefty. "It's dat ugly dame."

Pedrito nonchalantly sauntered toward the rugged-looking woman. "Yer right! Dat must be her," Fats exclaimed, spitting out his matchstick.

Leaving his partner behind, he slid through the crowd, getting into position. A waitress bustled by him, popping her gum. Momentarily fearing that it was the sound of a gun, the agent grabbed for his weapon. Once he recognized the source of the sound, he fumbled the gun back into his shoulder holster.

Pedrito stood by the woman's table, reaching into his uniform pocket. He extended something in his right hand, while she surreptitiously placed an envelope into his left.

In front of the coffee urns, Lefty snapped a picture of the event.

Fats' handcuffs clamped onto Pedrito's wrists just as the woman made the trade. "Gotcha, you Commie bastard!"

Without an instant's hesitation, Pedrito shouted, "Emergency Plan Q!"

Gripping a microfilm capsule in her hairy-knuckled hand, the ugly woman bolted toward the coffee urns where the scarecrowish Lefty stood clicking pictures.

Pedrito, hands cuffed and still gripping the payoff envelope, grabbed Fats' wrists and swung him counterclockwise. The enormous agent sailed around, his feet knocking the nearest table flying. At the height of his momentum, Pedrito released his grip. The bloated agent flew at the huge glass window, squalling like a baby. He crashed through, skidding across the gravel parking lot like an albatross making a crash landing.

The customers screamed in panic. Some of them applauded.

At the coffee urns, the rugged woman grabbed Lefty by the

wrists and spun him in a similar fashion. The FBI agent's feet came off the ground.

His camera dropped from his hands and broke open, exposing his roll of film. "Hey!" he cried. "Dose are my vacation pitchers!"

She slammed the rail-thin agent broadside into the coffee urns, then rushed off as the urns fell on top of Lefty, spilling hot coffee and brown grounds.

Pedrito, still confined in the cuffs, used his hands to secure his white Navy cap in place. He rushed toward the shattered window and dove through the hole in the smashed glass, all the while retaining his grip on the envelope.

Fats lay stunned under the window, trying to get up on hands and knees. Broken glass lay all around him. Pedrito landed on top of him like an airplane crash, knocking him flat again.

Rolling off the agent, Pedrito tore through the bloated man's pockets until he found the handcuff keys, then ran across the parking lot.

Inside the diner, the rugged-looking woman dashed into the men's washroom, wobbling awkwardly on high heels. Her floral-print dress flew around her as she shoved the door shut. A truck driver standing at the urinal looked at her in surprise. "Wrong room, lady."

"Shut up," she growled in a deep male voice.

The woman yanked off her out-of-style hat, tore away the veil and wig and pulled off a plastic mask. Colonel Enrique's reedy aide from Morro Castle tossed the disguise into the trash can and began ripping open the floral-print dress, unstuffing rags from a large bra. The truck driver watched so intently that

Enrique's aide turned his back to the man. "Can you unzip me, please?"

The truck driver fumbled with the dress zipper, and then the aide shoved him toward the washroom door. "Thanks—now get the hell out of here!" After the truck driver had fled, the aide shucked out of the frumpy dress to reveal a Cuban military uniform.

The door behind him opened. Lefty marched in, covered with steaming brown coffee grounds, his clothes drenched with hot liquid. He held out a heavy Colt revolver. "Dat's damned unladylike behavior!" he growled, more than half crazed. "Heads up!" He raised the Colt and blew the brains out of the Cuban aide, who fell dead backward into the urinal. "Or off—as da case may be," Lefty said.

◆ ◆ ◆

Pedrito tore open the door of the green FBI car, clamping the envelope in his jaws. "Hi, Joan," he leaned over and mumbled through his clenched teeth. As she squealed and flashed her claws at him, he grabbed her arm.

Pedrito yanked her out so hard that she hit the pavement and bounced twice on her butt.

Joan sat in the parking lot screaming at him. "You can't get away, Smith!" she shouted. "Traitor! I'll tell Daddy!"

Pedrito used the bloated FBI agent's keys to start the car, then raced off, gripping the wheel with his cuffed hands. Pedrito fishtailed out of the diner parking lot and squealed down the road.

Fats picked himself up from beneath the window, wheezing to catch his breath. His face purpled with anger as he stormed toward where Joan Turner sat looking very undignified on the pavement. "Hey, dem was my wheels! You let 'im get away!"

An enormous car pulled slowly up to the diner, a big silver Cadillac that had been bought new many years before, washed often and driven little. An elderly citizen hunched like a gnome over the steering wheel, driving with such extraordinary care that he posed a safety hazard to all normal drivers.

Fats popped open the Cadillac's door and hauled the driver out. He shoved the old man back, holding up his hand like a traffic cop.

"Sorry, sir. FBI business!"

Lefty ambled out of the restaurant, looking smug as he blew smoke from the barrel of his Colt and reholstered the gun, proudly holding up the confiscated microfilm canister. "Dat lady spy won't be giving us no more troubles."

Fats honked the horn at him. "Come on, Lefty! I got us a new set of wheels!" Lefty hustled across the parking lot and leaped into the passenger-side door.

"Get Smith!" Joan shouted, still sitting awkwardly on the pavement.

The big Cadillac rushed off in pursuit with a scream of tires. The gnomish old man came over to Joan, extending a hand to help her up. She slapped it away.

◆◆◆

Pedrito tore down the highway in the green FBI sedan as he tried to work the key in the handcuffs. Frustrated, he spat the envelope out, and it showered the front of him with loose bills. He ignored the payoff money for the moment.

"Time to reassess a few things," he said. "Women got me in trouble."

He glanced up into the rearview mirror. The pursuing Cadillac came on madly, with the two furious agents in the front seat. With a twist of his fingers, one handcuff finally sprang open. Pedrito worked on the other, but the loose money was in his way. He angrily swept the bills aside, and they fluttered like startled pigeons around the dashboard in front of him.

"Liquor got me in trouble, too," he said. He looked back again. The Cadillac was closing, its engine roaring like a large piece of farm equipment. Lefty leaned out, trying to draw a bead with his Colt revolver.

Pedrito worked on the other handcuff with the tiny key as he drove. He kept missing the keyhole, and the chain from the loose cuff dangled down, clacking against the steering wheel. Money blew onto his face.

The Cadillac closed the gap, pulling up right behind the green FBI car and attempting to pass.

"You might say that dissipation has been the undoing of me," Pedrito groaned as the handcuff key went in at last. He got the cuff off, poised his arm to fling it out the window, then saw the pursuing Cadillac pull alongside. Lefty aimed his Colt at Pedrito and grinned as he prepared to pull the trigger.

Pedrito hurled the handcuffs, and they shattered the windshield of the big Cadillac. The driver veered. The gunshot went wide. Fats wrestled for control, but the big car slued, skidded sideways and rolled into the ditch.

Pedrito looked forward, driving like mad, but his face was very serious.

"Oh, women!" He shook his head ruefully. "Oh, liquor. When I get out of the U.S. and back to a nice, pleasant tropical climate, one Pedrito Miraflores has got to reform!"

Chapter 49

AN OLD FREIGHTER lay at anchor in a harbor on the west coast of Colodor, silhouetted in the moonlight. Waves lapped against its rusty hull. Rats squeaked in the hold and a guard snored on the deck.

Banana plantations filled the coastal lowlands of the country, while mangrove trees and shrimp ranches covered the edges of the wide jungle river that emptied into the Pacific. In the harbor, fishing boats and canoes clustered along the docks beside seafood shanties on the wharf.

Panting and weary from his long, hard day of near-death and near-marriage, Smith clomped up the gangplank of the freighter and went to see the captain directly. The snoring guard didn't stir at all.

"Captain," Smith said, banging on the door of the cluttered bridge house, "I understand you're going up along the coast and through the Panama Canal to Jacksonville, Florida."

The captain scratched his sweaty beard stubble. "This ain't no cruise liner."

"That doesn't matter so long as I can get out of South America and back to the United States." Smith still wore his German mountaineering clothes, but by now they were rumpled, stained and speckled with leftover flecks of hay. "I can, of course, pay my way." He held his heavy rucksack by one strap.

On an unbalanced table in the captain's office, a half-full tequila bottle held down a stack of scattered charts. The brass porthole was so corroded it looked green in the lamplight. "Where's your passport?" asked the captain.

"I kind of lost it," Smith said with an innocent shrug. "My baggage was mixed up when I landed in Santa Isabel. I won a free vacation, you see."

"So why don't you go to an American Embassy? They're always eager to help." The captain wrinkled his brow.

"The embassy blew up," he said. "But if you can land me somewhere quietly in the U.S., I'll pay you very well."

The captain raised his eyebrows. "Five thousand dollars, or get off my ship. That's my terms—take them or leave them."

"Okay," Smith said. "I'll pay in gold, if that's all right."

Startled, the captain rose and made a mockingly servile bow. "In that case, I'll show you to your room, sir!"

The shabby cabin was single-bunked, dim and smelled of old fish. "Not luxury accommodations by any means," Smith said as the captain closed the door behind him. "But right about now, a few hours of peace and quiet is worth any price. And at least nobody's shooting at me."

Smith reached into his rucksack and fished out his paperback of *Famous Naval Battles*. With a long, heavy sigh he stretched out on the bunk and kicked off his shoes. "Now maybe I can finish this book at last."

◆◆◆

Back in the bridge house, the scruffy-looking captain sat at his desk. He juggled eight gold pieces in his hand, studying how the light glinted along their faces, along their edges; he slid them into his pocket.

With a smile, he snapped open a drawer in his console and pulled out a sheaf of papers held together with a bent brass brad. He turned to the fourth one from the top. "Ah, there it is," he said, then yanked it out of the stack. "I knew I'd heard that red hair mentioned someplace." He scanned the words again. No doubt about it.

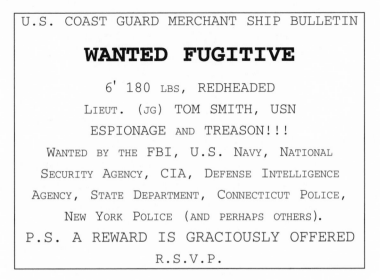

```
U.S. COAST GUARD MERCHANT SHIP BULLETIN
```

WANTED FUGITIVE

6' 180 LBS, REDHEADED

LIEUT. (JG) TOM SMITH, USN

ESPIONAGE AND TREASON!!!

WANTED BY THE FBI, U.S. NAVY, NATIONAL

SECURITY AGENCY, CIA, DEFENSE INTELLIGENCE

AGENCY, STATE DEPARTMENT, CONNECTICUT POLICE,

NEW YORK POLICE (AND PERHAPS OTHERS).

P.S. A REWARD IS GRACIOUSLY OFFERED

R.S.V.P.

♦ ♦ ♦

As the freighter left the port and headed northward toward Central America, the captain powered up the radio, tuning to the correct frequency.

"Key West Coast Guard, come in! Is the reward still good for Lieutenant Tom Smith, the fugitive?" He paused to listen. "Aha! How about doubling that?" he frowned. "Well, can I talk to your supervisor then, please?"

Much later, as the freighter plowed through choppy water approaching the Panama Canal, the captain leaned back in his chair and smiled. He glanced down at his chart, moving the tequila bottle to uncover his position. "All right, I'll deliver him right into your hands."

Chapter 50

AT NIGHT, ABOUT TWO MILES off Key West, Florida, Smith stood at the deck rail. The freighter had chugged its way through the Panama Canal, across the Gulf of Mexico into the Caribbean and up to the southern tip of Florida. He could see the coast nearby lit up like a swarm of fireflies. Disney World, here I come, he thought. He decided not to risk saying goodbye to the scruffy-looking captain. It was time for Smith to swim.

He pulled down his goggles, adjusted his wet-suit seals, checked the weights on his belt. The gold-filled rucksack, waterproofed and flanked with slabs of cork, hung on his back. He was getting good at this spy business.

Smith climbed onto the rail, prepared to go over. Maybe he would get reassigned once he was back at Navy headquarters. He hoped Admiral Turner still remembered who he was.

Taking a deep breath and securing his mask and snorkel tube, he dived from the low deck of the battered freighter. Behind him, he couldn't see the streams of green-yellow phosphorus that trickled from a surreptitious cartridge on his wet suit, following him as he moved through the water. . . .

The freighter captain sat at the radio, looking out the window. He saw Smith jump overboard, heard the loud splash. The redhead never suspected how his suit had been marked.

"He took the bait," the captain said into the microphone. "Watch for him—he's on his way."

♦♦♦

On the dock a group of military brass and civilian law enforcement waited nervously in the Coast Guard radio room. A young sailor manned the radio, feeling the expectant eyes on his back. "Exactly what was your position when he dived?" the radio man asked, reading the prepared message one of the Navy officers had written for him.

"Do I still get my reward if I tell you?" the freighter captain's voice answered through a crackle of static.

A Coast Guard captain knocked the radio man to one side and grabbed the mike himself. "You'll get it, you'll get it! Just tell us where we can find that traitor, Smith. Your nation's security depends on it."

Army and Navy high-ranking brass waited beside this week's director of the FBI, a dapper man with sunken cheeks and a gray mustache. The Coast Guard captain glared at the microphone, fuming and impatient. Everyone stared at the speaker in the ceiling, tense as cats.

"One-point-six miles south of Key West," the freighter captain's voice said. "He'll be easy to spot. Look for the phosphorus tracer."

Collectively, the gathered brass let out a sigh of relief.

◆◆◆

A snorkel tube protruded from the surface of the water, moving swiftly along. Behind it floated the cork-lined backpack, making a larger wake. Smith swam toward shore, breathing regularly, pumping his flippers.

Soon he would be at Key West, back in the United States again, back home. He wondered if anyone would plan some sort of party for him. It would be nice to see Joan again. . . .

◆◆◆

A helicopter hovered over the water, facing out toward the sea. The side of the helicopter bore an enormous shield of the Federal Bureau of Investigation and the words Director of the FBI (Special Parking Privileges Allowed).

The helicopter pilot snugged earphones over his head. "Looks like he'll reach the landing stage in another minute, Mr. Director, sir." The pilot pointed down at the swirling yellow-green line Smith unknowingly trailed behind him.

The FBI director scowled, brushing down his neat gray mustache. "I want to make this pinch myself. Think of all the publicity I'll get! Good publicity for once! I'll be a national hero." The director leaned over to look out the helicopter's side bubble window. "I'll make millions on product endorsements."

A barricade of bales and boxes surrounded a large cleared space on the dock area below, where Smith was expected to land. A railed stair led down to a landing stage on the calm, dark water. Everything appeared innocently empty.

However, behind the barricade crouched a company of Marines with leveled rifles and two dozen FBI agents—including the two banged-up and bandaged agents, Fats and Lefty, who had botched the capture of the spy at the roadhouse diner in Connecticut. Now they wanted a second chance. Nobody bothered to ask how Tom Smith could have gotten all the way down to South America in only a few hours.

Behind them, where they could watch without risking their skins, huddled the top brass. Even farther out of sight beyond the well-protected top brass, stood a cadre of television and newspaper reporters, cameras ready for a big story.

"I hope those other bastards down there don't think they're going to get any credit. Goddamned publicity hogs," the FBI director snarled, scowling at the docks below. "The FBI runs this country, and don't you forget it!" He shaded his eyes in the helicopter cockpit, scanning the water below and looking for Smith.

"Do you see the bastard yet?"

Smith popped up out of the water, removed his snorkel from his mouth, and paddled as he stared straight ahead, toward shore. Above the sloshing sounds of the waves at his ears, he could hear the sound of a chopper's motor, but the helicopter was not in view. Everything seemed clear. He stroked harder. Of course, he should have nothing to fear once he was in his own country.

Panting from exertion, Smith reached the landing stage at the water's level. He clutched the edge to catch his breath, then, dripping, he hauled himself onto the wooden platform. He looked at the plank stairway that led to the dock above, where a barricade of bales and boxes blocked his view. The night seemed very quiet and peaceful.

Flopping in his swim flippers across the dock platform, Smith made his way to the sloping stairs, still wearing his goggles, still hauling his sopping rucksack filled with gold coins.

The two bandaged FBI agents huddled with a federal executive in back of the barricade. The executive held a walkie-talkie, whispering viciously to Fats, shooting a glance up toward the distant helicopter. "The director wants you to go out there alone and identify Smith, personally. We can't afford to have any screw-ups on television."

The bloated Fats quailed. "But he'll recognize me. He just punched me out this afternoon."

The federal executive shoved him forward viciously. "He won't know you. That bandage covers half your face."

Fats stumbled along behind the kneeling, rifle-holding Marines, worming his way forward until he could scramble over the barricade. From below, Smith climbed the last few stairs, his clumsy flippers slapping on the wet boards. He paused a moment to stuff the snorkel into his belt, then waddled out onto the flat dock. An FBI agent belched. Smith looked around cautiously. "Hello? Is anyone here?"

He peered through his goggles as he scanned the too-quiet area in front of him. With a sigh, he reached to fumble in his wet-suit key pouch.

The line of Marines and sailors behind the barricade instantly raised up a few inches higher. They slid their rifles out, ready for a firefight.

Fats emerged from behind the barricade, nervous. "Ah, here's somebody." Smith extended a gold coin to Fats and pulled the goggles up off his face. "My man, could you give me some change so I can phone for a taxi?"

Fats' eyes were riveted on the gold coin. "Russian gold! He's been paid off," he shouted. He looked up at Smith's face. "Identification positive—it's Smith!"

Fats fumbled around his own girth to reach for his back belt holster. "Surrender now and you won't be hurt, you miserable traitor."

Marines and sailors popped up along the barricade, rifles leveled. Smith stared and took a step forward, hands outstretched. "Wait a minute, there must be some mistake. This is my own country—"

Fats finally managed to get his .357 Magnum out and poked it toward Smith hysterically, more to fend him off than to shoot him.

With a loud roar, the FBI chopper swooped down to the dock and landed ten feet away, its pontoon skids just touching the planks. Reacting quickly, using the skills he had reluctantly practiced in the past couple of weeks, Smith grabbed Fats' gun wrist with one hand and with the other arm seized him around the wide body. He hustled the bloated agent sideways toward the helicopter, using him as a hostage. He switched the gun to his own hand as they moved.

"Don't kill me! Don't kill me!" Fats wailed.

Smith covered himself with the agent's large body as he stepped onto the pontoon with one drooping flipper. He wrapped his gun arm around a strut, pointing the Magnum upward.

"Take off!" Smith shouted to the helicopter pilot.

The federal executive scrambled to the top of the dock barricade as all the soldiers leveled their weapons to blast the helicopter out of the sky. The executive screamed frantically, "Don't shoot! You'll hit the director of the FBI!"

Smith and Fats both teetered on the helicopter's pontoon. The dapper FBI director gawked down at them through the passenger-side window. Smith pointed the gun straight at his head, and the director flinched back into the cabin in terror.

The director's aide leaned out the open door, aiming his own gun down at Smith. "This'll teach you to betray your own country!"

The director grabbed the aide's wrist. "Don't shoot! He's got me covered! Besides, look at all the TV cameras—the bureau can't stand the publicity."

Smith held the pontoon and bared his teeth as he cocked the .357 Magnum, jabbing it meaningfully at the director. The director ducked hastily back in, to whatever shelter the cockpit might offer. "He means it!" he yelled to the pilot. "Take off! Do as he says."

Down on the dock, the federal executive and a Navy admiral stood on the barricade, hands on their hips. The Marines and sailors milled around in confusion. They had been spoiling for a more rigorous fight.

Back at a safe distance, the invited TV cameras and press photographers were getting it all, capturing every minute and broadcasting live. The federal executive looked at the TV cameras, thought of the publicity, and tore at his hair.

The bureau chopper lifted into the air and sped out to sea, carrying Smith and Fats precariously balanced outside.

Chapter 51

AS THE HELICOPTER RACED above the ocean, Smith looked at Fats drooped over the pontoon. "Why, I think he fainted!" He tried to steady the bloated man, making sure he wouldn't get hurt.

But Fats suddenly convulsed and fought against him in terror, slapping at Smith so violently that he slipped and fell off the pontoon. Smith tried to catch him, but Fats plummeted into the sea far below. "I hope he can swim," Smith said with a frown. "I think they teach that at Quantico." Then he stood upright on the pontoon and worked his way to the cockpit door with tiny steps in his big-flippered feet.

"Throw out your guns!" he shouted.

"Don't provoke him!" the FBI director said, cringing back into his seat. "You don't know all the terrible things this man has done!"

"I just saw him throw our agent overboard in cold blood," the aide said. The aide and the director promptly tossed their guns out the window. The weapons tumbled in long arcs to splash into the blue Caribbean.

Smith wrestled the cabin door open and climbed in, his wet suit dripping. He held the bloated agent's .357 Magnum before him. The director and aide quailed, while the nervous pilot tried to make himself look indispensable.

Smith was wet and cold and tired and angry. He had hoped to sleep peacefully in his own bed tonight, and now dawn was just starting to break over the Caribbean. He made the other men move aside so he could squeeze into the cockpit. He slid the door shut behind him, muffling the chopper noise.

Keeping his eye on the two cowering FBI men, Smith spoke to the pilot. "Since my own country keeps trying to kill me, you may as well fly me to the nearest point in Cuba. What have I got to lose?"

"But this is an FBI chopper!" The pilot stared at Smith in terror. "With these markings they'd shoot us down on sight!"

Smith said, "I wouldn't blame them, after the way the FBI is acting today."

The dapper director mellowed his voice to wheel and deal. "Let's be reasonable, Smith. I can provide you with a false identity, just like we do for all major criminals. We can let you live in high style someplace you won't be recognized—entirely at government expense."

"My hero, Nelson, would never make a deal like that," Smith said indignantly. "No honor in it."

"Nelson?" the director said, baffled. "You mean Baby-Face Nelson? We didn't make a deal with him. We just shot him. But that was a long time ago. With today's FBI, you have a better opportunity than he did. What do you say, Smith?"

"I say you guys are crazy," Smith said. "First the CIA and now the FBI. Come on, just take me to Cuba, where I'll be safe!"

"Wait a minute," the FBI aide said. "I've just thought of a way for him to get to Cuba without us getting shot out of the sky." He covertly winked at the director. "There's a small island just on the edge of Cuban waters. It's called Pirate Key—disputed territory, totally uninhabited. We can fly over, circle slowly, and if Smith will just parachute—"

"What?" Smith said. "If we're going to go all the way there, why don't you just land and let me off?"

"That would be illegal without a landing permit." The aide casually reached into the rear of the cockpit cabin. "Here, let me get your emergency chest-pack parachute."

Behind the passenger seats, boxes of smoke flares and tear gas had been stowed. The aide's arm clawed around, knocking over boxes of flares, getting hold of the parachute as he talked. "Besides, it wouldn't be wise to land the FBI director anywhere near Cuba. He's their number one most wanted man."

The aide brought the emergency parachute out from behind the seat and extended it toward Smith. "Now, if you'll just put this on, we'll drop you off. Everybody's happy."

"And I get to play Robinson Crusoe," Smith said sourly.

"There's Pirate Key, right down there," the pilot said, pointing to a low patch of land about a mile ahead of them. Daybreak spilled over the waters. "Very close to Cuba. You can hunt for pearls in the oyster bays on your leisurely swim over. I promise, you'll be happy."

Smith looked out the front windscreen at a yellow-sand island with a low hill in its center, surrounded by emerald water. "Doesn't look like too bad a place." He pursed his lips as he studied the beaches, the trees, the small hill.

The aide elbowed the director and jerked his thumb toward the rear seats. The director snaked his hand back and grabbed a tubular flare and hid it under his coat.

"It looks a long way down, though," Smith said. "I'm a sailor, not a paratrooper. I've never done this before. Are you sure I can make the jump in these diving flippers?"

Smith put the chest pack on, wrestling the straps around his gold-filled rucksack. "I'll do it," Smith said, "since I don't want to get you guys in trouble—no need for the pilot to land." He managed to keep the FBI men covered with his Magnum, though the aide helped him fuss over his heavy rucksack.

"And we promise not to tell anybody on our side where you went," the aide said soothingly. "We'll say the FBI director here threw you out of the chopper. He'll look like a hero, and the rest of us can just forget about this little incident."

"Word of honor?" Smith asked innocently.

"On my honor as an FBI man."

The aide's hands tugged the last strap in place, giving the lieutenant a pat on the shoulder. Smith diverted the gun by giving the last strap a tug. "All right. I don't want anybody to get hurt."

The aide saw his opening and reacted with lightning speed, knocking the Magnum out of Smith's hand. The weapon clattered on the floor of the cockpit.

"Now!" he screamed.

Snarling, the director brought the tube flare out from under his coat. "I'll kill you, Smith!" He fumbled with the flare's firing tab.

"No, no!" the aide said, urgently trying to grab the flare from the director.

"I believe you're pointing the wrong end, sir," Smith said.

With a squealing *whoosh*, the flare blasted like a comet into the pile of boxes behind the seats. A cloud of smoke hit Smith.

"You guys are nuts!" he said, but his words were drowned out by the pop of exploding flares. Smith grabbed the cockpit door, swung it open to the fresh sea air and dived out, his swim flippers flopping in the air.

As he turned somersaults, Smith grabbed at the rip cord, missing repeatedly. When he finally yanked the cord, his chest pack spilled out. The parachute opened with a jerk.

Reorienting himself, Smith watched the helicopter flying like a drunken, blazing bumblebee as it receded northward. Huge clouds of black smoke poured from the cockpit and trailed after. Smith shook his head in amazement, glad to be away from the insanity.

Pirate Key was about five hundred feet below him, but he had drifted off course, some distance off shore.

Smith dunked into the water with a splash, and the parachute settled over his head like a fishnet. Falling into the sea didn't really matter to him, since he still hadn't changed out of his wet suit.

♦♦♦

"Mayday!" the director said, coughing and choking. His voice sounded like the yelp of a dog. "Mayday! Mayday! Mayday!"

"Sir," the aide said, "you need to use the radio."

◆◆◆

Back in Florida, the high-level brass gathered around a table, incredibly serious, jaws clenched, as if each one chewed on a particularly tough lump of gristle. A Coast Guard captain and a Navy admiral sat in the center of the group.

"We should send out a flight to oversee the safe return of the FBI director," the captain said.

"To hell with that boob," the admiral said. "We're after Smith! He's a traitor to the U.S. Navy, and I won't stand for that."

He jabbed a ballpoint at the chart and circled a tiny dot, a small key close to the north coast of Cuba. Using the pen like a stiletto, he stabbed it. "Smith's gone down on Pirate Key. He must have some sort of secret rendezvous set up. But we can catch him if we move fast enough. Send out a missile frigate at once, flank speed to saturate bomb the whole island!"

The ballpoint stabbed again, and this time the point went clear through the paper.

Chapter 52

WHEN HE FINALLY REACHED the shore of Pirate Key, Smith crawled along on his hands and knees. He still wore his sopping backpack, but he had cut away the parachute harness. Sloshing up along the beach, he got to dry sand and collapsed face-first. Small beach crabs scuttled out of the way. His swim goggles hung on a rubber strap around his neck, but the wet-suit hood still covered his red hair.

Smith spat sand from his mouth. "Safe at last!"

The muzzle of a rifle appeared with a sudden stab just in front of his face. He went cross-eyed, looking down the barrel hole. Finally, he raised his eyes to see a black Cuban soldier standing over him, more curious than hostile. A second guard with a complexion as smooth as a lemon stood nearby. Both carried outdated, but deadly, firearms.

Smith pried himself slowly off the beach, leaving a wrinkled intaglio pressed into the sand. "This place is supposed to be uninhabited," he said with a sigh. "Just shows you can't trust a single thing the FBI tells you." He climbed to his feet, shaking his swim flippers as he looked at the black guard. He had gotten beyond fed up with all the problems dumped on him ever since his prize vacation had started. "So, who are you, anyway?"

"Who are you?" the lemon-faced guard said.

Gambling on his infamy, he said, "I'll show you who I am." With great assurance, Smith pulled back his wet-suit hood to display his famous red hair. "I am the great Pedrito Miraflores! Everyone has heard of my exploits."

The two guards looked at each other and blinked. They both leveled their rifles and circled around behind him, weapons pointed at his back.

"Wasn't that the right thing to say?" Smith asked. "I can be Lieutenant Tom Smith instead, if you like."

"March!" the black guard said, nudging him with the rifle toward a rugged coral outcropping. Smith could make out a masked vertical door set into the dark rock.

They escorted him through the doorway and along dank, sloping tunnels into the bowels of the small island, along wide passageways with overhead fluorescent lights and floors of solid concrete. This underground outpost looks much finer than that dumpy CIA place in Colodor, Smith mused. His flippers made wet slapping noises on the cement floor.

Down a side passageway, Smith spotted the radio room. A Cuban operator sat at a sea-foam-green metal desk, surrounded by communication equipment. The operator glanced at the new prisoner without much interest, lowered his head back to the radio equipment, and snapped his gaze up in a double take. Smith waved at him, hoping to find a friend.

The guards prodded Smith deeper into the secret compound. He glanced to the left and stared down a passage that ended in a barracks room. Ten Cuban soldiers lolled about, shooting dice, tossing playing cards into a garbage can, throwing knives at a dartboard. This was the most populous uninhabited island Smith had ever imagined.

A sergeant near the barracks door looked up with no interest. He suddenly raised a finger, pointing aghast at Smith.

"Nice welcome I'm receiving," Smith muttered.

The two guards urged him toward a barred steel door at the end of the underground passage. The lemon-faced soldier stopped Smith while the black guard raised the bar and pushed the heavy door half open.

"Come on out here, you!" the guard shouted into the room.

Lieutenant Tom Smith's identical twin stepped from the half-opened door, dressed in the tatters of a naval officer's white uniform. The rank braid on the cuffs was torn, half the buttons were gone. His shirt was filthy, the collar awry, the black tie twisted to the side and over one shoulder. Somewhere along the line, he had lost the cap. His hair was rumpled.

Smith stood there with his mouth open. "What . . . what have you done to my uniform? My career? My rank?"

The real Pedrito Miraflores looked at Smith and pointed an accusing finger as well. "You! You did this to me! You've ruined my reputation. How am I ever going to get work as a revolutionary leader again?"

Smith and Pedrito faced each other, glaring.

The two guards looked from one to the other, confused. "The first one arrived at dawn," the black guard said.

"And now we've got two," the lemon-faced soldier said, pointing his rifle from Smith to Pedrito and then back at Smith. "Must be one of those double agents I've heard about."

"Yes, but which is which?" the first guard said. "We don't want to execute the wrong one."

Chapter 53

"OKAY, I'LL MAKE IT EASY for you. *I'm* Pedrito Miraflores!" Smith took the lead. He tilted his head under the fluorescent lights of the secret base, cocking an eyebrow and showing off his red hair.

"Hey, *I'm* Pedrito Miraflores!" Pedrito said, outraged.

The black guard looked from one redhead to the other. "We got orders to send only one Pedrito Miraflores to Havana to be shot as a traitor as soon as the gunboat arrives. We can't send two!"

"Okay, then *he's* the real Pedrito," Pedrito said, pointing.

Smith blinked. "*Hah!* Only the real Pedrito would think so fast to turn the tables on a situation."

Both guards scratched their heads. Pedrito scowled, and his shoulders slumped. "All right, you'd better call your comandante," he said in a flat voice. "We wouldn't want such an important decision on your heads."

347

"Good idea!" The black guard sighed with relief and turned to walk briskly away. As he brushed past, Smith seized the guard's rifle barrel and thrust it up toward the ceiling. The guard yelped, the rifle fired and the bullet ricocheted from the concrete ceiling.

In the same instant, Pedrito grabbed the lemon-faced soldier around the neck and wrestled the man in front of him, relieving him of his weapon.

Recovering from the firing of his rifle, the black guard snapped about and leveled his weapon. Pedrito threw the lemon-faced soldier at him, and the black guard instinctively fired. The rifle shot struck the soldier full in the chest and knocked him back against the wall.

"Hey! That was self-defense!" the black guard cried.

Smith, meanwhile, snatched the rifle from the fallen lemon-faced soldier and shot the black guard, who stumbled twice, then fell on top of his dead partner.

His face flushed, Pedrito bent down to snatch up the black guard's rifle, chambering another round as he snarled at Smith. "I can't believe it! What did you do to get me condemned by my own side? Sentenced to death in Cuba! That wasn't supposed to happen."

Shadows bobbed along the corridor as other soldiers ran to investigate the gunfire. Smith chambered a round in his own rifle and fired down the corridor. The approaching soldiers yelped and dove for cover in side alcoves.

Smith spoke angrily at Pedrito. "What did I do? Excuse me, but what did *you* do to the U.S. Navy? I had a reputation to uphold!"

Pedrito made a gagging sound. "Your reputation! I'm well acquainted with your miserable reputation, thank you!"

A scrawny arm whipped around the corner and rolled a grenade, which bounced down the cement floor toward them. Pedrito darted forward to grab the grenade like a fumbled football. "Damn you, Smith, you loused me up!"

More interested in arguing with his look-alike than in paying serious attention to their attackers, he hurled the grenade underhand back around the corner where it had come. "I had a good, fine plan for stealing U.S. secrets."

He motioned for Smith to hunker down into shelter. The two of them crouched back in the corridor, covered their ears and squeezed their eyes shut.

An orange belch of flame burst from the side corridor. Soldiers shrieked, and mangled bodies flew from one side of the corridor to the other.

The two redheads let go of their ears, and Smith shouted, "Yeah, well, I was a fine, upstanding naval officer. You wrecked my whole career! What do you have to say about that?"

Pedrito shrugged. "Wasn't much of a career."

With Smith leading the way and stumbling in his wet-suit flippers, they ran along the corridor in search of an escape route. When he came upon the first cross-corridor, Smith dropped on one knee and fired the rifle to the left. "Face it, Pedrito—you bungled the whole thing!"

Pedrito dropped on one knee, aiming down the corridor in the other direction. "Don't blame me for your incompetence, Smith!"

In the radio room the Cuban operator frantically worked his equipment. He glanced in terror in the direction from which the furious sounds of battle erupted. "Havana, Havana! Rush up that frigate you were sending for Pedrito Miraflores! He's shooting the place to bits! We've got a war going on here."

◆◆◆

Pedrito rushed to an ammunition bunker with a huge red sign on the door, EXPLOSIVES. He yanked the bunker open and grabbed sticks of dynamite, which he shoveled at Smith.

"You could never handle this lifestyle, Smith. I bet you brought the troubles down on yourself with women—" Pedrito grumbled, "probably the same women I'd already learned my lesson with."

Smith frantically tied the sticks of dynamite together. "Me? You're the womanizer! They fell all over me because of your reputation. Yaquita, Bonita—they were only interested in getting married."

"Don't forget Joan Turner," Pedrito snorted. He fired three shots at a group of approaching guards. "Same story there. It's like they're all brainwashed." He shook his head in disgust.

Smith lit a long fuse stuck into the dynamite. "You're the one who doesn't know how to handle yourself, Pedrito. I bet you brought it on yourself with drink!" he snapped back. "Be honest: you boozed it up and wrecked my nice apartment in New York. Didn't you?"

"It wasn't a very nice apartment to start with."

Pedrito ducked a hail of bullets from inside the corridor, then fired his rifle again. "Besides, I don't drink anymore!" he snarled. "I gave it up."

"From what I hear, you're a sot!" Together, they sprinted up the passageway.

"Your bartender wouldn't give me anything but milk." Pedrito spat. "Vile-tasting stuff. Comes from cows!"

Smith hurled the package of dynamite with the burning fuse. Ahead, a mob of sentries barged into the ammunition bunker through the splintering outside door. They opened fire without even looking for targets.

Kneeling, Smith and Pedrito shot repeatedly, aiming carefully. The sentries went down in a tumble. Smith and Pedrito rose and dashed for the outside door. "My bartender is a good judge of character. He probably took one look at you and could tell you weren't to be trusted, Pedrito."

"Are you calling me a liar?" Pedrito said.

They charged through the bunker's outside door and dove for cover behind a nearby sand dune. The dynamite fuse burned down.

"Yes, I'm calling you a liar!" Smith sneered, buckling his flippers tighter around his ankles in case he had to run again. He glanced at the Russian chronograph on his wrist. "Get down!"

The whole bunker exploded in a towering pillar of flame and debris that rolled up into the clear Caribbean sky.

The sand dune offered little protection from the blast. Pedrito and Smith covered their heads. Debris pattered and thunked all around them, chunks of fused sand, smoking plywood and smoldering Spanish fashion magazines.

Pedrito balled his fists. "Then I'll have to challenge you to a duel, Smith!"

A huge slab of concrete fell next to them like a bomb, spraying sand. "You're too yellow to fight me, Pedrito," Smith said with scathing contempt.

They hauled themselves to their feet and stood face to face. Pedrito's cheeks turned purple with rage. "I'll kill you, Smith!"

"Big talk!" Smith said. "You couldn't even swat a fly!"

"I won't swat him—I'll shoot him. Pistols!" Pedrito said.

"Suits me!" Smith agreed. "Dueling pistols!"

Pedrito hesitated, then frowned. "Well, we haven't got any dueling pistols. But you can't get out of it like that—we'll use rifles instead!"

Smith swung down his gold-heavy backpack. "Wait, I've got these fancy laser pistols—"

"You've got my laser pistols?"

"They were in the false bottom of my suitcase. I mean, your suitcase. Say, whatever happened to my own suitcase?"

"Forget the suitcase—you won't need it after I kill you. And forget the laser pistols, too," Pedrito said. "Not messy enough. I want to watch you bleed."

Smith slung his rifle. "All right, rifles it is." Grim and businesslike, he gestured toward the hill in the center of the island. "There's a level place on top of the key. We'll duel there, where you can't duck into any holes."

Pedrito held his rifle at his side, and Smith gave him a push toward the indicated spot, but the other redhead walked directly beside him. "Don't try to get behind me," Pedrito said. "You'd shoot me in the back!"

"Look who's talking! The back-shooter of all time! You can trust me—I work for the U.S. Navy."

"Oh, is that why you blew up the CIA installation in Colodor?"

"Stop giving me reasons to shoot you, Pedrito."

They marched grimly toward the rise, where one of them would die. Smith's wet-suit flippers made him look like a duck.

Chapter 54

FROM THE RISE in the center of Pirate Key, stunted palms and clumps of pampas grass blocked all but a strip of the surrounding turquoise sea. Scattered clouds scudded across the morning sky. Smith and Pedrito marched across a level stretch toward a large sinkhole in the center of the hill.

Pedrito pointed with his rifle at the hole. "There's our landmark. We'll each go fifty feet on either side and then we'll turn and fire when I give the word." Pedrito laid his rifle against his shoulder.

Smith looked at Pedrito. "Hah! What's your word worth?"

Pedrito froze with a retort on his lips as he looked past Smith toward the open sea. He gasped, and his arm slung out to knock Smith into the sinkhole.

"Get down!"

Smith scrambled to his hands and knees in a rage, spitting sand. He hauled back his fist to strike. "Foul play!" he said. "I knew I couldn't trust you—I could tell by your shifty eyes and your criminal features."

As a whistling scream arced overhead, Pedrito dove next to him, knocking Smith flat on his face. Violent explosions erupted near the sinkhole, a flare of greenish light followed by a shower of sand.

Coughing and sputtering, both redheads peered cautiously over the edge of the sinkhole. A Cuban missile boat cruised in the water like a prehistoric shark. The missile boat fired another round from its bow gun, and a second shell exploded near the sinkhole, inundating them both with wet sand.

Pedrito knocked dirt from his clothes and hair, very peeved. He slapped Smith in the shoulder. "See the trouble you got me into, Smith? Now my own side is shooting at me!"

Smith opened his mouth to retort, but a new sound filled the air.

"Lieutenant Tom Smith, we know you're on the island!" a voice said from a bullhorn. "Show yourself! Surrender and face the music! You're a traitor to your country."

In tandem, the look-alikes scrambled across the blasted sinkhole and peered cautiously over the opposite edge. On the side of Pirate Key, a U.S. Navy missile frigate bristling with deck guns skimmed across the waves toward the island. The Stars and Stripes flapped from its signal bridge yard. A blast belched from one of the bow guns as the ship fired a missile.

Pedrito and Smith covered their heads. "And that's my side shooting at me!" Smith wailed. "Now look what you've done."

Another flash of green light, another violent explosion, and more sand showered into the hole. The U.S. missile frigate fired again and again from one side, while the Cuban ship fired from the other. More explosions followed.

"They got us surrounded," Pedrito said. "Thanks to you!"

"No, thanks to you, Pedrito!"

"You should have planned this better, Smith. You're a disgrace."

"It was your plan! I just thought I was getting a prize vacation to Colodor."

"Some vacation!"

◆◆◆

The signal bridge of the Cuban frigate had no roof against the pounding Caribbean sun. The captain pressed a pair of field glasses to his eyes as he listened to the distant explosions. "I never could understand those capitalist dogs," the captain snarled at his gunnery officer. "Why is that Yankee frigate shooting at their own spy?"

"Maybe it's a new example of East-West detente," the gunnery officer said.

"Well, our orders are to kill their double-agent Pedrito Miraflores," the captain said. "Keep firing on Pirate Key. We'll send in a crew with brooms and dustpans to bring back his body."

◆◆◆

A U.S. four-stripe captain and his own gunnery officer stood on the bridge of the missile frigate, looking through binoculars toward the low island. White, acrid smoke from the pounding bow guns drifted back across the men, making them cough and choke.

"Why are the Cubans shooting at him, too?" the gunnery officer asked.

"Trying to destroy the evidence of their spy?"

"Damn the evidence—just kill that bastard Smith!" The captain gasped from the artillery smoke. "We've got to wipe him out before the Cubans do. It's a matter of national pride."

"Yes, sir," the lieutenant said. "We'll get him with repeated fire."

The captain set his jaw. "Shift to full automatic fire control and saturate the place!"

Missile launchers on the forward deck of the U.S. frigate adjusted their aim to blast Pirate Key. Rockets streamed out.

♦♦♦

Smith rummaged in his backpack, brushing sand away. Happily, he pulled out a bottle of rum and sat with his back against the side of the sinkhole.

Pedrito squatted beside him, shoulder to shoulder.

"Both ships have increased their fire," Pedrito said.

Smith pulled the cork from the rum bottle. A blizzard of sand from a nearby explosion rained from the sky, and he covered the open bottle. "Might as well die happy." Smith took a long swig. Rockets whistled overhead.

Pedrito looked at him, incredulous. "You and rum? I thought you didn't drink, Smith. Too strait-laced."

"Have some?" Smith offered the bottle.

Pedrito shook his head in disgust. "No more for me. Never again." They both flinched from another rain of dirt and debris. "I've reformed! Completely!"

"So have I!" said Smith. He gulped another long swig.

Pedrito turned around and inched up toward the top of the hole. "I want to take a look at the U.S. frigate."

Smith swatted him back. "Get down! That U.S. craft has an automatic heat control firing system. I know—I approved the blueprints myself. If they sense a steady heat source—like your hot head—they'll home in right on it!"

"Is that a crack about my red hair?" Pedrito said.

"You mean our hair," Smith said. "No, it's a fact. If we show ourselves, we're doomed."

"Well, you're the naval expert," Pedrito said. "So think of something!"

Smith jolted with a sudden thought. "Wait a minute." He dug in his rucksack and came up with one of the high-tech laser pistols.

Pedrito was incredulous. "What, you want to duel to death after all?"

"Nope. This is going to save us." Smith smiled with supreme confidence.

"How are you going to sink a frigate with a pistol?" Pedrito held his aching head in his hands.

Smith carved a notch in the sand of the crater lip and lay down, aiming the laser pistol through the notch. He squinted with one eye and aimed at the Cuban frigate's bow plates. "Just watch me."

He adjusted the sensitivity dial on the laser, then pressed the trigger. With a loud sizzle, a pencil-thin beam of light stabbed out of the muzzle, striking the bow of the Cuban ship. Smith cradled the pistol to hold the beam steady.

A large area of the steel plate on the Cuban frigate went cherry red, heating up to violet blue and smoking. The sailors on the frigate ran to the deck rails, looking over the side and shouting.

Smith smiled and continued firing. . . .

The automatic targeting systems of the U.S. missile launchers suddenly shifted upward to fire at a higher angle. The heat-seekers locked in, and a shower of missiles spat out.

A huge gout of water geysered just beyond the Cuban captain on his signal bridge. "That Yankee is firing at us," he said in astonishment. He and his gunnery officer stared at each other for a fraction of a second, then the captain shouted new orders. "Shoot back! Forget the island—just blast those capitalist dogs out of the water. This is war!"

The Cuban gunnery officer leaped to his own missile launchers, changed the aim point, then fired with everything he had. A salvo of missiles sailed up from the Cuban ship in an arc over Pirate Key.

Farther along, another salvo of rockets sailed from the U.S. frigate toward the Cuban ship, trailing white smoke over the island. At the peak of their trajectory, they turned downward, sensors activated, hurtling toward the red-hot spot on the Cuban bow plates.

The Cuban ship exploded into flame and fragments.

A moment later the U.S. frigate did the same.

Pedrito stuck his head up above the edge of the sinkhole. He stared in astonishment at the smoking wreckage of both ships. The island fell silent, with only the sound of the wind, the waves and a few sea gulls overhead.

Smith calmly tucked the laser pistol back in his wet rucksack on top of his waterlogged paperback of *Famous Naval Battles.* "I just moved Nelson into the twentieth century," he said.

Chapter 55

FORLORN, SMITH AND PEDRITO trudged along a flat, sandy beach on the bomb-battered Pirate Key. The bright sunshine, lapping waves, fresh air—and above all the peaceful silence, now that the two attacking warships had been sunk— made the small island into a Caribbean paradise. Both redheads negligently carried a rifle by the breech at hip level.

Ahead, they spotted a rubber inflatable boat drawn halfway up onto the beach. "Maybe we could take that raft and escape," Pedrito suggested.

"Even if we got out of here, there's no place to hide," Smith said. "We've got to face it, the U.S. is against us."

"Yeah," Pedrito said, "and Cuba and Russia are against us."

"And we're certainly not welcome back in Colodor . . . in fact, probably not anywhere in South America."

Pedrito stopped as inspiration struck him. "Hey, we can always start a revolution somewhere else. I'm good at that."

"That's brilliant. Let's do it together—what do we have to lose?"

Pedrito gestured toward the inflatable raft with his rifle. "We better get out of here, then. Time's wasting."

"You get the first shift rowing," Smith said as they trotted down the beach.

Suddenly, Bolo stood up out of the inflatable raft like a jack-in-the-box. He wore a trench coat with the collar turned up and a fedora slouched over his face. His hands at his sides were empty. "Hello, my friends," he said with a bland smile. "I've been waiting for you. Congratulations on your survival, both of you."

Pedrito halted in surprise. "Bolo!" He peered closely, suspicious. "Say, are you the one who radioed me to come to this spy assembly station in the first place? That sounds like something you'd do."

"That guy sure looks familiar," Smith said.

Bolo shrugged and beckoned for them to join him in the raft. "Come along, we've got some business to discuss. A proposition." He stepped out of the inflatable boat and prepared to launch it without saying another word. Smith and Pedrito looked at each other with raised eyebrows, then climbed into the raft.

◆◆◆

At dusk on the calm ocean, an unmarked submarine lay in the water like a beached whale. As the inflatable raft carrying Bolo, Pedrito and Smith approached, no one moved about on deck. The submarine's conning tower and forward deck shimmered copper in the last rays of the setting sun.

After he lashed the inflatable raft to the sub, Bolo clambered aboard and moved to a large hatchway in the forward deck. He lifted the heavy metal hatch and stood waiting for the two redheads. "Come on, sirs. This is what you've been waiting for all along."

Smith and Pedrito, still carrying their rifles, went down the hatch into the submarine. Smith moved awkwardly in his wetsuit flippers, and Pedrito gave him a hand. Bolo followed last, closing the hatch from below. Then he pressed a signal button on the wall. With a low growl of engines, the sub moved forward slowly, submerging. It had a long way to go to its final destination.

Up on the surface, as the submarine dove, the rubber raft raced forward for a moment, as if it were being dragged by an enormous fish. Then it dove underwater. Moments later, as the raft popped like a balloon from the tremendous stress, a ball of air rose out of the ocean with a sound like an enormous belch.

Smith and Pedrito walked side by side in a narrow passageway. Bolo directed them to a closed stateroom door, which opened mysteriously ahead of them. "After you," said Smith.

"No, you," Pedrito smiled politely. "Always let the man in flippers take the first steps. It's a spy tradition."

"Oh, okay," Smith said and entered a lavish submarine wardroom.

On the other side of the wardroom, a man stood behind a table and turned to face them. He wore a general's uniform, but no cap. He had a yellow moonface, dark almond eyes and ridiculous dangling Fu Manchu mustaches. He spread his arms wide in an enthusiastic greeting, displaying immaculately long finger-nails.

"Ai! Pedritos!" he said with a glad cry. "Welcome to the Chinese Secret Service! We're happy to have you here."

•••

As he discussed his plans and his country's offer, the Chinese general sat on one side of the rectangular table. Across from him Smith and Pedrito took seats beside each other but not too close.

At the head of the table, Bolo folded his hands in front of him, very pleased and confident. He had changed clothes into the uniform of a colonel of the Chinese Army with a wide array of medals on his chest . . . but who could tell if it was just another disguise?

Bolo said, "Yes, I pretended to cooperate with Colonels Enrique and Ivan, but all along we were just testing you both. On-the-job training, you might say, to see if you have the right stuff to work for us."

The Chinese general was very jovial and relaxed, tugging on his drooping mustaches. "You see," he said, waving one long-nailed hand, "we have secret influence all around the world that can't be traced to us. We'll straighten out this silly misunder-standing with both your governments, and you can both go home as heroes—and double agents."

"Triple agents, actually," Bolo said.

Smith and Pedrito just sat there, unable to believe what the Chinese general was offering.

"What do you get out of this?" Smith asked.

The general chuckled, very pleased with himself. "My government will have spies in both places. We can even switch you around, if you like! Oh, we're so wily when we want to be."

"Isn't that a cliché?" Smith asked. Pedrito and Smith snapped their heads around to lock gazes as it all became clear. They had heard the hackneyed old stereotype many times before. "Damned clever, these Chinese!" they said to each other.

With a shrug, they reached out to shake the general's hand. "We accept!"

Bolo sat at the end of the table, smiling his secret smile.

About the Authors

L. RON HUBBARD

BORN IN A RUGGED and adventurous Montana, L. Ron Hubbard lived a life of truly legendary proportions. Before the age of ten, he had already broken his first bronco and earned that rare status of blood brother to the Blackfeet Indians. By age eighteen, he had logged more than a quarter of a million miles, twice crossing the Pacific—before the advent of commercial aviation—to a then still mysterious Asia. Returning to the United States in 1928, he entered the George Washington University where, drawing from far-flung experience, he began to shape some of this century's most enduring tales.

By the mid-1930s the name L. Ron Hubbard had graced the pages of some two hundred classic publications of the day, including *Argosy, Top-Notch* and *Thrilling Adventures.* Among his more than fifteen million words of pre-1950 fiction were tales spanning all primary genres: action, suspense, mystery, westerns, and even the occasional romance. Enlisted to "humanize" a machine-dominated science fiction, the name L. Ron Hubbard next became synonymous with such utterly classic titles as *Final Blackout* and *To the Stars*—rightfully described as among the most defining works in the whole of the genre. No less memorable were his fantasies of the era, including the perennially applauded *Fear,* described as a pillar of all modern horror.

After the founding of DIANETICS® and SCIENTOLOGY® (the fruition of research actually financed through those fifteen million words of fiction), Ron returned to the world of popular fiction with two monumental blockbusters: the internationally best-selling *Battlefield Earth* and the ten-volume MISSION EARTH® series—each volume likewise topping international bestseller lists in what amounted to an unprecedented publishing event.

In 1983, and in what has been described as the culmination of a lifetime commitment to fellow authors, L. Ron Hubbard directed his estate to found the WRITERS OF THE FUTURE® Contest. Dedicated to the discovery and encouragement of new talent within the realms of speculative fiction, the contest has since proven both an integral part of the greater L. Ron Hubbard literary legacy and the most successful competition of its kind. Accordingly, contest judges have comprised the most celebrated names of the genre, including Frederik Pohl, Orson Scott Card and Frank Herbert. To date, the contest has helped place some two hundred novels from new authors on worldwide shelves, very much including the works of Kevin J. Anderson.

KEVIN J. ANDERSON

BORN IN 1962, and raised in the small town of Oregon, Wisconsin, Kevin J. Anderson truly represents a rising star of speculative fiction. Entering the WRITERS OF THE FUTURE Contest for eleven consecutive quarters, he eventually broke into professional ranks with *Resurrection* before the age of twenty-five. Within the last four years, twenty-three of his subsequent novels have appeared on national bestseller lists, including *Lifeline* (co-authored with Doug Beason) and his *Star Wars* "Jedi Academy" trilogy—all three *New York Times* bestsellers and top-selling science fiction titles of 1994. Kevin J. Anderson is further the author of three novels based on the *X-Files* television series—all likewise international bestsellers. Kevin J. Anderson has also established a very unique writing relationship with his wife, Rebecca Moesta. Together they have authored no less than fourteen volumes of the "Young Jedi Knights" series.

By way of research for his novelization of L. Ron Hubbard's *Ai! Pedrito!* Kevin J. Anderson traveled extensively through the Andean mountains of Ecuador, tropical rain forests and Amazonian tributaries. He is currently at work on three prequels to Frank Herbert's *Dune* series—to be authored in conjunction with the late author's son, Brian Herbert.